SPIDER SHEPHERD: SAS

(Volume 2)

By Stephen Leather

D1344936

Stephen Leather is one of the UK's most successful thriller writers, an eBook and Sunday Times bestseller and author of the critically acclaimed Dan "Spider" Shepherd series and the Jack Nightingale supernatural detective novels. You can find out more from his website www.stephenleather.com and you can follow him on Twitter at twitter.com/stephenleather. The six short stories in this collection have previously appeared as self-published short stories. They cover Shepherd's time in the Middle East and Afghanistan with the SAS and recount how he narrowly escaped with his life. The stories also introduce Lex Harper who appears in the Spider Shepherd novels.

Personal Protection

The Rope

Planning Pack

Friendly Fire

Dead Drop

Kill Zone

PERSONAL PROTECTION

CYPRUS

November, 1997

The change in the engine note as the Hercules began to descend woke Dan 'Spider' Shepherd from a fitful sleep. He glanced around him. As usual Jock McIntyre and Geordie Mitchell were still sleeping. Both of them had the uncanny ability to sleep anywhere at any time, no matter what noise and distractions - even gunfire - there might be, yet on a whispered word of command, both would be instantly awake and alert. James 'Jimbo' Shortt's lanky frame was also prone among the jumble of equipment stacked and lashed to the Hercules unforgiving steel floor and walls, but his eyes were wide open, staring at the ribbed metal roof.

Shepherd yawned and stretched, then peered out of the tiny window to his left. As the Hercules banked around, he caught a glimpse of the radomes of the listening station high on the flanks of Troodos Mountain. Beneath him, the dark shadow of the Hercules was etched across the brilliant white salt flats north of Akrotiri, the heat rising from them in shimmering waves. The aircraft rumbled in and touched down with a thud that shook Jock and Geordie awake.

'Ladies and gentlemen, welcome to Cyprus,' Jimbo said. 'Thank you for flying Crabs Airlines, please remain in your seats until the aircraft has come to a complete stop outside the terminal and the pilot has switched off the seatbelt signs.'

'You'd have made a lovely stewardess,' Geordie said, 'if you weren't so butt ugly.'

The Hercules juddered to a halt and as the tailgate was lowered, Shepherd hoisted his bergen onto his shoulders and led the others down the ramp on to the concrete hardstanding of the UK Sovereign Base Area. It was a fiercely hot day but after the tropical heat of Sierra Leone the lack of humidity in the air was as refreshing as a cooling breeze.

'Not much of a welcoming party,' he said as he looked around. A lone figure, dressed in shorts and a T-shirt was striding towards them. He was craggy faced and greying at the temples and though his legs and upper body were hard muscled, the thickening around his waist suggested that he was now spending more time driving a desk than on training and ops.

'Anyone know him?' Shepherd muttered as the man approached.

'No,' Jock said, 'but you can tell he's been around a bit, one of the old and bold.'

'How do you know?'

'Just look at his right hand.' Shepherd followed his gaze and saw that the man's fingers were curled over.

'All the old guys get like that,' Jock said. He held up his own hand. 'In fact it's started to happen to me too - it comes from holding a rifle for years.'

'Morning guys,' the man said as he walked up to them. 'I'm Rusty. I don't think I know any of you, do I?'

'You're not Rusty Nail?' asked Jock.

'The very same,' said Rusty, narrowing his eyes. 'Do you know me?'

'Not personally, but I know you by reputation,' Jock said. 'You've worked on a couple of team jobs with a mate of mine: Spud.'

Rusty broke into a smile. 'Bloody hell, that's a blast from the past. Any friend of Spud's is a friend of mine.'

Shepherd nodded. Jake 'Spud' Edwards had been one of his trainers back at the SAS Stirling Lines camp in Hereford and was a bit of a legend in the Regiment. The others introduced themselves. 'So are you just passing through like us, Rusty?' Shepherd said.

'No, I'm based here.'

'I didn't even know we had a presence in Cyprus,' Shepherd said.

Rusty nodded. 'It's not an operational section, purely administrative.'

Shepherd glanced around, squinting against the bright sunlight. Beyond the usual sprawl of hangers, concrete buildings and Portakabins that characterised every overseas base, he could see pine clad mountains in the distance to the north, and the sails of windsurfers and yachts speckling the Mediterranean beyond the sandstone cliffs and beaches flanking the peninsula that surrounded the base on three sides. 'Looks like a pretty cushy posting,' he said.

'You can have it, if you want it, and welcome to it,' said Rusty sourly.

'So what happens here?'

'Workwise? Not a lot. The Regiment has a permanent cell here, but it's only two guys - grey-beards like me seeing out the last few years of service before being pensioned off. There are a few Scalies to run the signals equipment and deal with messages to and from the Head Shed in the UK.' Scalies was short for Scaleybacks, in reference to the radio equipment the signallers carried on their backs like turtle shells.

'So if it's that quiet, why is the Regiment here at all?' Jimbo said.

'Partly because historically we've used the Base Military hospital here as a stopover to repair guys ill or injured on operations in Africa and the Middle East before sending them on to the UK, but that's about it.'

'And the other reason?'

'Because of those.' Rusty pointed towards the radomes on Mount Troodos, just visible through the heat haze. 'Being here gives the Regiment prime access to the intelligence generated through the listening station up there. It's run by GCHQ on behalf of us and the Yanks. Just about every terrorist organisation in the Middle East maintains an office on Cyprus. It's a convenient centrally located meeting place where they can launder their money and arrange the purchase of weapons, and it's also useful as a jumping off point to gain access to Europe through Greece. So both the UK and the US maintain a good sized security presence on the island, but life here is nowhere near as interesting as that makes it sound, at least as far as we're concerned. Most of the time we're just watching the grass grow and the dust blow. It's bloody frustrating. I'm out in a few months and I need to be back in the UK working on my contacts, getting onto The Circuit so I've a job lined up for when I hit civvy street, not twiddling my thumbs and counting down the days to my retirement in a dead end job on a sunbaked rock in the middle of the Med.'

'Why did they send you here then?' asked Shepherd. 'Punishment detail?'

Rusty smiled. 'You'd think so, wouldn't you, but it's mainly because I speak fluent Arabic and, having worked all over the Middle East - Oman, Jordan, the UAE and a couple of places we don't talk about - I know the culture too. I guess they thought that if you're going to carry out surveillance on Arab terrorists, it probably helps if you can understand what they're saying to each other.'

'So that just leaves the question of what we're doing here,' Shepherd said. 'Because none of us speaks a word of Arabic.'

Rusty spread his hands wide. 'On that one, your guess is as good as mine. While you're waiting to find out, you can work on your suntan or go windsurfing and wake-boarding down at the Lemming Beach Club at Happy Valley, or even clubbing at Ayia Napa if that appeals. When I first came here, back in the day, before I'd even joined the regiment, Ayia Napa was just a sleepy little village, with the most perfect beach you've ever seen a couple of miles down a one-track dirt road. Nissi Beach was a horseshoe-shaped cove with a little rocky island just off-shore that you could walk through the shallows to reach. The water was crystal clear and as warm as a hot bath. That's all still true, but back then there was a small camp-site and a grass-roofed beach-hut where you could buy a beer or an ice cream, and that was it. Now Nissi Beach is wall to wall with high rise hotels, and Ayia Napa is all amusement parks, bars and vomit-strewn streets full of stag and hen nights, clubbers and pissed up squaddies.'

Jock shook his head. 'Bloody hell, Rusty, you must be even older than you look. Ayia Napa's been like that as long as I've been passing through here.'

'Sounds perfect,' Jimbo said, 'I might take a look tonight.'

'I won't,' Shepherd said, 'I can see enough pissed-up teenagers in Hereford without going looking for them here as well.'

The SAS compound was in a corner of the base, wired off from the RAF section. There was the usual concrete admin building, still with its Cold War protection of berms and concrete blast walls, and offices the size of broom cupboards and a slightly larger briefing room. Surrounding it was a huddle of tents and Portakabins. 'That's yours,' Rusty said, pointing to a converted shipping container screened from the sun by an awning and with a clanking, rusted air conditioning unit precariously attached to the outside.

'All the comforts of home,' said Geordie.

'The canteen's there.' Rusty gestured towards a huge khaki tent on the far side of the office block, 'or if you fancy something edible, there are food shops and cafes in Episkopi at the western end of the base area.'

'And bars?' Jimbo said, trying not to sound too eager.

'I use the Beach Club at Happy Valley. There's a spare Landy you can borrow to get down there.'

Rusty left them to unpack their gear. 'So what's Rusty's story?' Shepherd asked Jock.

'He's a bit of a legend,' said Jock. 'He's one of the few to have worked undercover in Belfast. His Irish accent is pretty much perfect, Spud says. He was into some pretty heavy stuff over there in the early eighties.'

'Shoot to kill?' asked Shepherd.

'That's the story according to Spud,' said Jock.

'Let's give him a few beers and see if he'll tell us some war stories,' said Jimbo.

'I doubt that'll happen,' said Shepherd. 'He didn't seem the sort to go running off at the mouth.'

Shepherd and the others stashed their kit in the shipping container and within half an hour they were stretched out on sun loungers on the sand in front of the Beach Club.

'I've said it before,' Geordie said, 'and I'll say it again: this is the life.'

'Remind me, why are we here?' said Jimbo.

'Because our masters, in their infinite wisdom, have sent us here. Who are we mere mortals to question it?' As usual, Jock's low, growling voice and impenetrable Glaswegian accent made even the most anodyne statement sound like a declaration of war. 'People pay good money to come here on holiday and we're here for nothing, courtesy of HMG. So stop your whingeing and enjoy it.'

'I'm not whingeing, I'm just wondering how long we'll get to enjoy it before we're re-tasked.'

'The longer the better as far as I'm concerned,' Shepherd said. 'After a couple of months in Sierra Leone, rescuing diamonds from the mercenaries for HMG - and getting bugger all thanks for it - we're due a bit of downtime. With a bit of luck they might even forget we're here. If we stay long enough, we'll not only get a sun tan, we might even get a bit of skiing in the mountains as well. Now pass the Ambre Solaire and get the beers in.'

'I hate to tell you this, but it's your round,' Jock said.

Shepherd sighed and shook his head. 'You've tried that scam on once too often, you tight-arsed, tartan-wearing, bagpipe blowing, Irn Bru supping, deep fried Mars Bar guzzling git. It's your round and don't give me the old "I've forgotten my wallet" line either because I can see it in your pocket'.

'That's not his wallet, Spider, he's just pleased to see you,' Geordie said with a laugh. 'Anyway, when you two drama queens have finished arguing about who's paying for it, mine's a pint.'

Jock departed for the bar, still grumbling. Shepherd lay back and closed his eyes, enjoying the warmth of the sun on his body. He was just starting to unwind when a shadow fell across his face. 'About time too, Shepherd said. 'I've got a thirst you could flaming photograph.'

'So glad you're pleased to see me.' They were not Jock's gravel-throated tones, and the accent was English upper-crust, not Glaswegian. 'After what you said to me last time we met, I wasn't sure what kind of welcome I'd receive.'

Shepherd shaded his eyes, squinting into the sun. A tall man was standing over him, his face shaded by a Panama hat. He wore an immaculately cleaned and pressed cream linen suit and a white cotton shirt and, despite the heat, he was also wearing a tie.

Shepherd scowled at him. 'And you're no more welcome now than you were then,' he said. 'What do you want?'

Jonathan Parker's professed occupation of Third World importer and exporter was a cover for his work as an MI6 officer. Shepherd and his team had first encountered Parker in Sierra Leone when they'd rescued a botched operation that Parker was supervising and there was no love lost between them.

There was a mouthful of expletives from Jock as he came out of the bar and caught sight of Parker. Geordie and Jimbo looked equally unhappy at seeing the MI6 officer. Parker ignored their surly looks as he brushed the sand from a sun lounger with his handkerchief and the perched himself on the edge of it. 'I've a little job for you,' he said, having glanced around to make sure they could not be overheard.

'We've got jobs,' said Jock. 'We're in the SAS, or have you forgotten that?'

'No need to be tetchy,' said Parker. 'Wouldn't you rather be doing something soldierly than lying on a beach?'

'The only lying going on is when you open your mouth,' said Geordie.

'Guys, come on now,' said Parker. 'There's no need for this. I've got a job that needs doing and you're the perfect candidates for the task at hand.'

'Send someone else,' Shepherd said. 'We've only been here about twenty minutes after two months on ops in Sierra Leone. We're due some R and R and then a spell on stand-by before we go back on ops.' There was a rumble of agreement from the others.

'Sorry chaps,' Parker said imperturbably. 'No rest for the wicked and all that. There's a rather delicate situation in a certain Middle Eastern country and we need your expertise. There is no one else available with your range of skills, and don't worry, it's already been cleared with the MoD and Hereford.'

'So have some of your pet mercenaries gone rogue on you again?' asked Shepherd.

Parker flicked a speck of dust from his lapel, as if brushing away the comment. 'No, nothing like that, this is purely a training task.' He paused. 'Now I don't want to spoil your fun, but it is a matter of some urgency. Shall we say 1600 hours in the briefing room back at the base?'

'If it's just a training task, why the urgency?' Shepherd said, but Parker was already walking away up the beach.

The four SAS men were in a mutinous mood as they filed into the briefing room just before four o'clock. Rusty was already there and Parker swept in a moment later, followed by five signallers, between them carrying a piece of electronic equipment the size of a three-drawer filing cabinet.

Parker glanced around the room, then cleared his throat. 'Right then, you are to deploy on a top secret bodyguard training task in a Middle Eastern country. After neglecting the Middle East in the dash to join the EU, HMG is concerned to maintain what little influence we still have in the region and the state in question is a crucial part of that.' He paused, and made eye contact with them one at a time. 'Background: there are two cousins from the ruling family locked in a power struggle. The Ruler is a modernist aligned to the West. He has two wives, one an American Muslim, a college graduate and a licensed pilot. The second wife is the daughter of another Middle Eastern ruler. She was brought up as a strict Muslim but is trying to modernise her outlook with the help of wife Number One.'

Jimbo laughed out loud. 'Any man who wants two wives needs his head examined,' he said. 'Twice the nagging.'

Parker ignored the interruption. 'The ruler is an interesting character, a trained F16 pilot who also flies his own Airbus, and needless to say the country's huge oil reserves mean that he's one of the richest men in the world. So far, all pretty straightforward. However, the ruler's religiously conservative cousin is determined to get back what he believes, probably rightfully, is his throne.'

'Why rightfully?' asked Shepherd.

Parker grimaced. 'We deposed his father in a bloodless Palace coup several years ago - he was threatening the security of our oil supplies and even flirting with the Russians - so we sent him into exile in London and he lived out his days in a Park Lane hotel before dying a few years ago. His son insists that if we had not deposed his father and forced him into exile, he would now be the legitimate ruler of the country, so he has set out to depose his cousin and reclaim his throne.'

'Sounds like he has a point,' said Jimbo. 'Who are we to decide who runs a country? Our politicians do a shit job running the UK, they've no business telling other countries what to do.'

Shepherd threw Jimbo a warning look. 'Is the cousin a serious threat?' he asked Parker.

'He's been missing from his usual haunts for several weeks now and sigint and humint suggest that he's recruited a group of Chechen mercenaries. It looks as if he is getting backing, money, arms and men from somewhere, though we're not sure where as yet.'

'Now why does that not surprise me?' said Jimbo.

Parker ignored the interruption but his lips tightened. 'We picked up electronic intelligence on the plot, and so we've decided to dispatch you to train a hand-picked cadre of the ruler's troops as an elite bodyguard group,' he said. 'And of course we want you to keep the ruler alive until the BG group you've trained is operationally ready and the coup plot has been dealt with.'

'Why us?' Jock growled.

'Because you're the best available team and you're already on the spot,' said Parker. 'You're here and you now your stuff. The proverbial bird in the hand.'

'Now that I could work with,' said Geordie. 'A bird in the hand is just what I need right now.'

Parker gestured towards the signallers' equipment. 'I've brought along something that should help, state of the art electronic gadgetry to support your team in-country.'

Parker nodded to one of the signallers, a ginger-haired guy in his late twenties whose Adam's apple wobbled when he cleared his throat. 'It's an electronic comms and suppression system,' said the signaller in a West Country accent that hinted of cider and sheep-filled fields. 'It can detect bugs and intercept them and also put a blanket transmission blackout on an area. It will also suppress signals to detonate IEDs and other types of bomb. The system operates largely automatically and is part of a network run from GCHQ in Cheltenham.'

'What's it weigh?' Shepherd asked.

The signaller frowned, not understanding the point of the question. 'Just under one hundred pounds,' he said.

'Then the system's fine,' Shepherd said, 'and we can make good use of it, but if that's all it weighs and it operates semi-automatically, why do we need a five-man team of Scalies to run it?' He saw a couple of them bridle at the use of the semi-derogatory nickname the SAS used for signallers but he was in no mood to be sparing feelings.

'Because,' Parker said, with exaggerated patience, 'you need them available 24-7 and working the same hours that you do.'

'Exactly. And we'll only need one man for that. We work hard and he can do the same. Having too many guys lying around with nothing to do is just a recipe for problems in-country. He glanced across at the signallers. 'So which one of you Scalies is the most experienced?' he asked.

'That would be me,' said the one who had spoken before. 'Mike Smith. They call me Beebop'.

'And if I tell you that we will be working all the hours God sends and maybe a few more on top, Beebop, would that put you off?'

Beebop grinned. 'No, it'll keep the boredom at bay.'

'Good, you'll do then,' said Shepherd. He looked at Parker. 'You can send the rest packing. Beebop's all we need. ' Parker nodded at the remaining signallers and gestured at the door with his chin. Shepherd waited until the other four had filed out of the room before continuing. 'Okay, so a five-man team then: me Jock, Geordie, Jimbo and Beebop.'

'And I'll be there from time to time to liaise with the Sheikh on behalf of HMG,' Parker said.

Jimbo's hackles were up straightaway. 'I'm guessing you'll be doing your liaising from the comfort of a five-star hotel in the capital, not in a tent in the middle of the desert with us,' he said.

'I'd sooner he was in a hotel anyway,' Shepherd said, heading off Jock, whose short fuse was legendary. 'That way he won't be getting under our feet. Right, let's get on with the planning. Usual rules: if you don't speak up at the planning stage, you don't get to complain about anything afterwards.'

'Just before you start,' Rusty said. 'I may be talking out of turn here but, correct me if I'm wrong, none of you guys speak Arabic, do you?'

'No, we'll be using translators,' said Shepherd.

'Well, like I told you before, I speak fluent Arabic and I've worked extensively in the Middle East. Make me part of the team and I can run the admin for you.'

Shepherd grinned. 'At this rate, we're going to be up to battalion strength before we even get out there.'

'But it makes sense to take Rusty,' Jock said. 'He's up to speed on admin, right?'

Rusty nodded. 'I know what I'm doing,' he said,

'It'll make the training a whole lot easier with an admin guy who can anticipate our needs,' said Jock. 'If the ammo is on the firing point before we arrive we can get straight into the training. If the vehicles are filled up and serviceable when we need them, that saves hours if not days out in the desert. And don't forget the daily grind of making sure we're properly fed and watered allows us to get on with the job in hand.'

'I'm your man for that,' agreed Rusty. 'Plus you won't find a better Arabic speaker.'

As Shepherd still hesitated, Rusty added, 'Plus if I'm on the ground in the Middle East, I'll be in a much better position to latch on to some work for when I leave the regiment.' He grinned. 'You'd be doing me a big favour.'

'What about the admin here?' asked Shepherd.

'My oppo can cover it,' said Rusty. 'There's not enough work for one, let alone two of us here anyway.'

'Fair enough,' Shepherd said. 'All agreed?' He looked around the circle of faces. Jimbo, Jock and Geordie all nodded. 'Then you're in, Rusty. Welcome aboard. You can start by giving us the Intel brief.'

'Brilliant, thanks,' said Rusty. 'There's little to add to what Mr Parker has already told you. We're monitoring the ruler's cousin and his group and they have been flagged as top priority, but there's not much sigint, electronic chatter or any other sign of immediate concern.'

'Okay,' Shepherd said, 'Let's get the kit sorted. Weaponry?'

'Just one point on that,' Rusty said, 'unlike bodyguards in Western countries, it's normal for BG's in the Middle East to carry their weapons openly, so there's no need for the usual worries about concealment. You can have whatever you want.'

'Thanks,' Shepherd said, 'you're proving your worth already. So, what do you reckon Jock?'

The Scotsman thought about it for a moment. 'I think we'd be best with the Heckler and Koch MP5K,' he said eventually. 'There's nothing better for close quarter work. And for shorts we'll use the Browning 9mm pistol. They use the same ammunition and I'm assuming there'll be no shortage here?' He looked over at Rusty and Rusty nodded. 'Anyone disagree?' asked Jock. There were no objections; everyone could see the sense of his suggestions.

'Now, let's talk training,' said Shepherd. 'Geordie?'

'I'm assuming that most of the guys we'll be training won't be university educated,' Geordie said. He glanced at Rusty for confirmation.

'They'll probably be illiterate,' said Rusty. 'But that doesn't mean they're unintelligent and their powers of recall may surprise you. Because they don't write anything down, their memories are generally pretty good. They'll speak very little English, though.'

'Okay, so we're best sticking to an uncomplicated syllabus,' Geordie said, 'with much of the normal intellectual content removed. We can take out the complicated large convoy drills and keep it simple, with just the three vehicle drills. We don't need to do any visiting Heads of State planning now; we can do that later when the internal security situation has stabilized, and we can cut out the counter-bombardment and anti-sniper training completely.'

They spent the next two days planning the training, assembling the equipment and stores they would need and loading them on to an RAF Hercules. On the evening of the second day they took off and flew due south over the waters of the Mediterranean before turning east to cross the desolate, desert wastes of Saudi Arabia. They followed the old pre-jet age route of pipelines and pumping stations before entering the target country covertly, flying at low level without navigation lights. In the distance they could see the glare from the capital's glass and steel skyscrapers piercing the night, lit up like an Arab Las Vegas. But as they flew on into the ink black night, the vast emptiness of the desert was broken only by the occasional tiny flicker of a Bedu camp fire.

The Hercules landed at an air strip deep in the desert and they unloaded their stores and equipment under the curious gaze of the men they would soon be training. Rusty took charge of the stores and having seen them stowed to his satisfaction he began sorting out the camp routine, planning training sessions and meals around the regular Muslim calls to prayer.

The training base was a tented camp with rudimentary facilities and, like all desert locations, it was burning hot by day, and bitterly cold as soon as night fell. The SAS men shared two tents while the Arabs slept in a large communal marquee. There were a couple of showers, one for the Brits and the other for the Arabs, which were topped up daily by a municipal water bowser that trundled in across the desert each morning. The same vehicle also supplied the water for all of the other camp requirements.

The Sheikh arrived early the next morning in a convoy of vehicles that raised a dust trail that could be seen from miles away. Armoured vehicles and troop trucks travelled at the head and tail of the convoy, with three armoured Mercedes limousines with blacked out windows in the centre.

Geordie laughed out loud at the convoy. 'All we're missing are marching bands and fireworks. Is there no Arabic word for covert?'

'He's a Sheik,' said Rusty. 'That's how he travels.'

'How do I address him, Rusty?' Shepherd said as they watched the convoy rumbling towards them.

'When you first greet him you should call him "Ya Sheikh min al Shayookh" which means "Oh Sheikh of the Sheikhs". The Ya always precedes the greeting and makes it more respectful. After that you should call him "Ya Sheikh" unless you're talking to him later on a private, one to one basis, then you should call him "Ya Seedee" which means "Oh Sir" But he's Western educated, just calling him "Sir" will probably be just fine.'

The convoy swept into the compound and after a pause to allow some of the dust cloud to dissipate, the sheikh emerged from his Mercedes, followed by his retinue. He wore traditional dress - a thobe in dazzling white cotton decorated with gold thread, and a light sandy brown bisht also with elaborate gold trimming - and his skin colour and features were unmistakably Arab, but when he spoke, his accent was pure Eton and Oxbridge. 'Gentlemen, I bid you welcome,' he said, 'you are honoured guests in my country.'

'Ya Sheikh min al Shayookh,' Shepherd said, hoping he was pronouncing it right, 'we are proud to be of service to you.'

He introduced himself and his team and the sheikh then led them into a marquee, spread with a huge Persian carpet. The sheikh's servant served mint tea and then withdrew leaving them to talk. 'I walk a tightrope in my country,' the sheikh said. 'I try to do enough to keep happy those who, like me, want to see our country modernise and play the part in the world that our wealth and our destiny requires. But it also has to be slow enough to take with us as many as possible of the more traditional and conservative elements of our society.' He sipped his tea. 'It is necessarily a slow process but we are winning, though there are those such as my cousin who would seek to set the country on a different path.' He sipped his tea again. 'I assume that, once trained by you, the bodyguard teams will work in very close proximity to myself?'

Shepherd nodded. 'Yes, Ya Sheikh,' he said.

'And how would you select those men?' asked the sheikh.

'We would normally use a process based on the physical fitness regime of the SAS to select the most suitable candidates,' said Shepherd. 'Fitness and skill with weapons. They would be our main criteria.' Jock, Geordie and Rusty nodded in agreement.

'I'm sure that will often be the correct approach, but not in this case,' the sheikh said. 'These bodyguards will be working cheek by jowl with me, will they not? And they will be armed with a round in the breech, so they could kill me in a heartbeat.' He waited for Shepherd's agreement before continuing. 'So the men you will train as my bodyguards, will be selected not on the basis of their physical fitness but purely on their loyalty to me. The men outside are all Bedu, of my own tribe. Their loyalty to me is absolute and unquestioning. These are the men you will train.'

Shepherd could see that it was an order, not a request. But he knew that the sheikh was talking sense. Loyalty was the prime concern. He nodded in agreement. 'I'm sure that's the most sensible option,' he said. 'Sacrificing expertise for absolute loyalty makes perfect sense, but rest assured, Ya Sheikh, that after we have trained them they will all have the skills they need to protect you.'

The sheikh smiled. 'That is good to hear,' he said. 'Can you tell me exactly what will you be teaching them?'

'Body protection and some explosive recognition, but the main effort will be devoted to teaching them a simplified version of a Presidential Escort group,' said Shepherd. 'A PEG as we call it. I'm afraid acronyms are an occupational hazard in the forces.'

'Don't worry,' the sheikh said. 'I trained at Sandhurst myself, and I'm quite used to them, but please explain how a PEG operates.'

'Well, a PEG consists of three Presidential Escort Sections,' explained Shepherd. 'Each section is four cars and crews with any associated support. Car One, with a driver and four crew, travels in advance of you to check the routes and search the venues that you will be visiting. Car Two, with a driver and another four crew, travels immediately in front of your vehicle to protect you in case of ambush or attack. Car Three, with a driver and four more crew travels immediately behind your vehicle, ready to respond in the event of an ambush or attack. And the Team Leader travels with you in your vehicle and will protect you with his body in the event of an attack. The three sections work one day on duty, one day stand-by and one day rest.'

The sheikh nodded, satisfied. He asked a few more questions and then began preparing to leave, but Shepherd had one further request to make. 'Forgive me, Ya Sheikh, but we would also want you to wear a PLB - a personal location beacon - at all times so that, in the unlikely event of you ever being kidnapped or going missing, your bodyguard team will be able to locate you using their communications system.' He saw the sheikh hesitate and reached into his pocket to pull out a tiny PLB, not much bigger than a penny. 'As you see, it is very small and discreet,' he glanced at the sheikh's hand, 'and could be fitted, for example, inside the gold signet ring you wear on your little finger. If you're ever required to activate it, just a sharp tap on a solid object will start it transmitting.'

The sheikh frowned for a second or two but then he nodded. 'Very well, if you feel it is essential, give it to me and I shall have it done.'

The sheikh and his convoy set off back to the capital a few minutes later in another cloud of dust. As soon as he had left, Shepherd and the team started work. The Bedu tribesmen were indeed all illiterate, but far from stupid. They had no problems memorising instructions and were quick learners.

Training began at five-thirty each morning, shortly after the Bedu had finished their dawn prayers. Throughout the day the men broke off to pray together, facing Mecca. They broke off training at midday and sunset to eat. The cooking facilities consisted of two Pakistani cooks using brushwood fires to cook Bedu food in large aluminium vats. The SAS men joined the trainees, eating together from enormous aluminium platters about six feet in diameter. The ate with their right hands, either rice with vegetables or goat, and naan bread.

The weapons training involved a lot of range work and the first session was a vivid demonstration of how much there was to do. When the first batch of trainees were issued with their weapons they immediately began firing them into the air.

Shepherd yelled at them to cease firing. 'You know what we say?' Shepherd said, when he'd brought the firing to a stop. 'When people start firing upwards, it's time to get indoors because every round is going to obey the laws of gravity and come down again. If it hits you, it'll kill you just as dead as if it had been aimed at you in the first place. It's also a waste of ammunition, so that was your first and your last burst of celebration gunfire - understood?'

Rusty translated and the men looked at the ground guiltily.

There was more wild firing over on the range, with rounds spraying all over the hillside behind the targets. This time Shepherd let them fire away because there was no danger of them hurting anyone. Once they had emptied their weapons, Shepherd gave them the lecture they needed. 'That was terrible,' he said. 'You can see that from the fact that most of the targets are untouched.' He waited for Rusty to translate before continuing. 'You will almost certainly be operating these weapons at close quarters in what will often be crowded areas, because where the sheikh goes a crowd will gather. So the aim is to kill the terrorist, not the innocent bystanders and that means aimed shots, double-taps, not bursts.' Rusty translated again.

Once the ground rules had been established, the Bedu proved quick and able pupils. Jock, Geordie and Jimbo had built a Close Quarter Battle area, dug out of the face of a sand dune and divided into sections with baulks of timber, in which they trained the bodyguards relentlessly, firing off thousands of rounds until every man could put a double tap into a target in the blinking of an eye. Jock had given up the lead role when it became clear that none of the translators could understand his Glaswegian accent, and instead Geordie led the sessions.

The bodyguards also had to learn explosive recognition and body protection drills, and vehicle convoy drills. That took a great deal of patience and time to perfect because there were no tarmac roads anywhere near the training camp and the Bedu trainees were not the best drivers in the world.

As soon as the first Presidential Escort Section was trained up, Shepherd took them up to the capital for on-site familiarisation training. Rusty went with him, since the bulk of his admin work was finished and with the systems he'd put in place the camp practically ran itself. They had developed an excellent working relationship and Shepherd found Rusty's local knowledge and his extensive understanding of Arab culture a great help.

After a few weeks the other two sections were also fully trained and arrived in the capital to begin their work with the sheikh. There had been no sign of the rumoured threat from the sheikh's cousin, but Shepherd was relieved that his team was back together. After observing their trainees in action for a further couple of weeks, they were ready to complete the formal handover to the Bedu team leaders, and then return to the UK, unless the Head Shed chose to send them somewhere else.

They were unwinding with a beer after the day's practice drills when Jonathan Parker appeared. Jock gave a snort of disgust when he caught sight of him. 'How is it that every time I'm relaxing with a beer in my hand, you seem to appear?' growled the Scotsman.

'Sheer good luck, old chap,' Parker said, with a mirthless smile. He was carrying a battered leather briefcase.

'Good luck for who?' was the baleful reply, but Parker ignored him. He sat down at their table, opened the briefcase and took out a typewritten document. The heading 'TOP SECRET - UK EYES ONLY', was the highest possible security classification. 'We have an intel update,' Parker said. 'Sigint suggests that the sheikh's cousin is now supported by a band of Chechens and they have succeeded in infiltrating the country through one of its porous desert borders. They are now believed to be in hiding.'

'You mean you've lost them,' said Jimbo. 'I tell you, you secret squirrel boys would be lucky to find your arses using both hands.'

Parker ignored Jimbo and passed the sheet of paper over to Shepherd. 'They pose an immediate, serious threat to the safety of the sheikh. You will need to take a closer role in his protection until the situation is resolved.'

'I'm not sure that's necessary,' said Shepherd. 'We've trained the sheikh's PES for exactly this kind of eventuality. They're well-armed, well-motivated, and well-trained, and they're well on top of the situation. I'd back them against a Chechen rabble any day. We should be returning to the UK, not staying to nursemaid them when they don't need it.' There was a rumble of agreement from the others.

'Be that as it may, you will be required to remain here for the time being,' said Parker. He took the sheet back from Shepherd and put it in the briefcase. 'The safety and security of the sheikh is of vital importance to HMG's interests and influence in the region. I shall be remaining here as well.'

'That's all we need,' Jock growled.

'And I will keep you updated on any additional intel we receive,' Parker said, as if Jock hadn't spoken. Parker stood up and walked away. Shepherd swore. It was clearly a fait accompli and they had no choice in the matter.

A couple of days later Shepherd received a summons to the sheikh's palace. He was ushered into a marble-pillared receiving room and a few minutes later the sheikh appeared, alone. They sat together on a large overstuffed sofa. 'I've been contacted by my cousin, who wants to meet me to talk over our problems,' said the sheikh. 'He wants me to meet him alone at a remote location in the desert where we will be safe from prying eyes and can maintain secrecy from the various tribal factions.' He held up his hand as Shepherd began to protest. 'A reconciliation or at least an arrangement with my cousin would bring great benefits to my country,' he said. 'It would unify our nation and also neutralise the greatest potential source of threat to my rule. So it is a prize worth risking much for.'

Shepherd shook his head. 'You will be putting your life at risk, Ya Seedee. Out on your own, in the desert? It's asking for trouble.'

'My cousin has guaranteed my safety on his honour,' said the sheikh.

Shepherd wanted to tell the sheikh that a man's word counted for nothing when imaginable wealth and power were at stake, but he held his tongue, not wanting to appear disrespectful.

'If I reject his offer, my own honour will be impugned, so I am morally obliged to meet him and have agreed to do so,' the sheikh continued. 'We are to meet alone without any advisers or bodyguards.'

'Ya Seedee, with respect, this breaches every rule of bodyguard training that we have instilled in your men. If they are not with you, they cannot protect you.'

'Nonetheless that is my wish.' The sheikh's tone was that of a man whose word was law and Shepherd knew there was nothing he could do to change his mind.

Shepherd returned to base and briefed Parker and his SAS team. 'We can't allow him to do this,' said Shepherd. 'But I don't see how we can stop him.'

'He can be stubborn,' said Parker.

'Can't you explain how stupid he's being?' asked Shepherd.

'He's an absolute ruler,' said Parker. 'Western educated, but he's not going to let me tell him what to do.'

'But you can tell him how dangerous it'll be.'

'He knows that already, I'm sure. But he thinks he can trust his cousin, obviously.'

'Then you need to tell him that he can't trust him. Come on Jonathan, the cousin wants to meet the sheikh alone in the desert. How is that going to end well?'

'It seems to me that our option is to follow him covertly,' said the MI6 man.

'So you'll be coming with us, will you?' asked Jimbo, his voice loaded with sarcasm.

Parker swallowed. 'Actually yes, I will.'

Jock scowled. 'Do me a favour, You'll be more of a hindrance than a help; we've no room for passengers or dead weight.'

'I'm afraid I'm going to have to insist,' said Parker. 'I was given the responsibility of ensuring the safety of the sheikh, and my neck is on the line if anything goes wrong.'

'All right,' Shepherd said, after a lengthy pause. 'But if anything kicks off, do as you're told and keep out of the way. This isn't a job for amateurs. Right, we need vehicles. Jimbo, what can we get our hands on before sunset tonight?'

Jimbo uncoiled his lanky frame. 'There's nothing armoured, the best we can do at this notice is a couple of 4 x 4s - Toyota Landcruisers.'

'Then they'll have to do,' .Shepherd said. 'But because of the risk of IEDs, we need to reinforce the floors with sandbags.'

'Sandbags?' said Parker.

'It's pretty rudimentary protection but it's better than nothing,' said Shepherd. 'Jimbo and Geordie, you get that sorted, and Jock, you take care of the weapons. I doubt that the Chechens won't have any armour, but a couple of GPMGs will take out their vehicles if it all goes tits up.'

At sunset that night, they took up positions from where they could observe the two main entrances to the sheikh's palace. Shepherd, Rusty and Parker were in the lead vehicle, and Jock, Geordie and Jimbo in the other. Just after midnight, with the capital's streets deserted, Shepherd saw a nondescript black car drive out of the rear gates of the palace. The way the guards on duty snapped to attention told him that the driver was the sheikh. Shepherd passed the word to Jock's group over the net and they began to track the sheikh as he drove across the city towards the desert.

They followed him without difficulty until he left the tarmac road and set off across the desert on a graded track. Away from civilisation, they were forced to switch off their vehicle lights and resort to using night vision goggles. That slowed them down and the sheikh's car began to pull away from them. Shepherd saw the lights of the sheikh's car disappear from view as it breasted a rise and dropped down the other side. He accelerated, driving on the limits of visibility through the NVGs, and as he crested the ridge he saw the black car stationary in the distance ahead of them. It was surrounded by a group of armed men who were dragging the sheikh out of the car.

There was no point in any further attempts at concealment and Shepherd switched on the lights, floored the accelerator and banged on the horn. In the seat beside him, Rusty slipped off the safety catch on his sub-machinegun. Shepherd cradled his own MP5 on his lap, ready to jump out firing as soon as he brought the vehicle to a halt. As they closed on the sheikh's car there was a blinding flash, a roar like a thunder-clap and the Landcruiser was blown high into the air. All three men inside were knocked semi-conscious as it crashed back down with a sickening impact.

As Shepherd shook his head, trying to clear his blurred vision and silence the ringing in his ears, small arms fire raked the ground around them. There was a screech of tyres as Geordie drove the back-up car between the damaged vehicle and the Chechens, drawing their fire. It pulled up and Jock, Geordie and Jimbo piled out, firing at the muzzle flashes from the Chechens' weapons. Shepherd twisted around in his seat. Parker lay dazed and semi-conscious on the back seat of the wrecked vehicle. There was more gunfire and Shepherd and Rusty stumbled out and began picking out targets. The firefight was short and bloody, the Chechen ambushers were no match for the SAS in accuracy or rate of fire.

The firing ceased and Geordie and Jimbo moved across the desert to the ambushers' position, weapons at the ready. The group of Chechens were no longer a threat to anyone, each one stone dead, their bodies riddled with rounds.

Through the ringing in his ears, Shepherd heard Jock's voice. 'You all right, Spider?'

'We're okay, but what about the sheikh?' answered Spider. As they scanned the desert around them through their NVGs they realised that there was no sign of the sheikh or his captors.

After a futile search of the area, the team assessed their options. Jimbo, gung ho, was all for launching an immediate pursuit, but the older, wiser heads prevailed. 'Think about it Jimbo,' Shepherd said. 'We've only one vehicle left, we don't have enough fuel or water to be driving much deeper into the desert, we don't know what might be waiting for us and if we hit another IED, we're unlikely to be as lucky a second time. It's galling I know, but the best option is to head back to the capital, gather what intel we can and plan our next move from there.'

Geordie nodded in agreement. 'That makes sense.'

'The one bit of good news in this is that if the sheikh's cousin had wanted to kill him outright, he'd already be dead,' said Shepherd. 'The fact that his body isn't here shows the cousin wants him alive, either to extract concessions from him directly or to use as a bargaining chip in negotiations with us. Either way, he's alive and we need to keep him that way.'

They squeezed themselves into the remaining vehicle and drove back to the capital in silence, each man lost in his own thoughts. Parker was still in shock from the firefight, his normally immaculate clothes torn and stained. There was a livid bruise across the side of his face. When they got back to camp he spoke only to agree to get GCHQ focussed on listening for any communications between the sheikh's cousin and his surviving Chechens. For the moment, Shepherd and the rest of the team could do nothing more than listen in to the various wavelengths on their comms system. There was no useful chatter to be heard, but as evening approached the sheikh's PLB began to transmit. They gathered around a monitor as the signal from the PLB began moving towards their HQ. Thinking the sheikh was on his way back, they suspended operations. Three hours later, as the signal showed that the PLB was entering the city, they went to intercept the sheikh and escort him back to his palace only to discover it wasn't the sheikh but a

Bedu tribesman bearing a small box. Inside it was the sheikh's severed little finger, complete with the signet ring containing the PLB.

Rusty interrogated the Bedu but after a couple of minutes it was clear what had happened. Rusty gave a weary shrug of his shoulders. 'He's innocent,' he said. 'Just a tribesman the bad guys flagged down and paid a few dollars to deliver the box.'

'It's a proof of life from the sheikh's cousin,' Shepherd said. 'It's a sign that they want to negotiate. If they hadn't, they would have sent us his head instead.'

Shepherd and the rest of his team sat down with Parker to discuss their options. Parker seemed more concerned about the possibility of the British Government losing influence in the region. 'We cannot have the cousin taking control of the country,' said the MI6 man flatly.

'I'm more concerned about getting the sheikh back alive,' said Shepherd. 'You need to fake interest in opening negotiations while we find a way to separate the sheikh from his captors.'

'If we're going to do that,' Jimbo said. 'It would probably help if we knew where he was.'

Geordie whistled in mock admiration. 'Your flair for stating the bleeding obvious never ceases to amaze me, Jimbo.'

They back-tracked the route of the PLB and eventually pinpointed an isolated oasis in the middle of the Great Sand Sea Desert, fringing Ar Rub' al Khali - the Empty Quarter. They studied maps and satellite imagery of the area and then assessed their options. 'There's only one road into the oasis' Shepherd said. 'It's not going to be easy. There's a real risk of IEDs and any approach will obviously be monitored by the Chechens. If they see us coming there's every chance that the sheikh will be killed out of hand. Suggestions?' He looked over at Rusty.

'The only way to approach the oasis is going to have to be across the Great Sand Sea,' Rusty said. 'It's an area of sand dunes the size of Wales and pretty much impassable unless you know what you're doing.'

'Which you do, of course,' said Shepherd.

Rusty grinned. 'If we are going to do it,' Rusty said, 'we're going to have to find some vehicles that can cope with the terrain.'

Jimbo nodded. 'And the place to start looking for those would be the garages at the palace. The sheikh seemed to have enough exotic vehicles in there to make an entire premiership football team green with envy. The presidential guards' vehicles are also kept there.'

The sheikh's garage was the size of a supermarket with more than fifty vehicles and a team of overalled mechanics. There were five Bentleys, a gold Rolls Royce, and several supercars that Shepherd had only ever seen on TV. There were a dozen Range Rovers in various colours, several with attachments on the back for hawks to perch on while the sheikh was out hunting. Most of the sports cars were red – Shepherd lost count of the number of Ferraris and Porches.

'Bloody hell,' said Geordie, his hands on his hips as he surveyed the ranks of gleaming cars. 'How does he decide what to drive?'

'He has a similar problem deciding which of his wives to test-drive,' said Rusty.

'Can we take the Ferraris?' asked Geordie. 'Pretty please?'

'We need desert vehicles,' said Jimbo. At the far end of the massive garage was a line of military vehicles, including three 'Pink Panther' Land Rovers. The Land Rovers, painted a pinkish hue to blend into the desert sand, were a favourite among SAS reconnaissance team and were usually fitted with machine guns and larger fuel tanks. 'I'd go with these,' said Jimbo.

'Personally, I'd prefer the Dodge Power Wagon,' said Rusty, pointing at two bright red SUVs. 'The Pinkie started out as a good idea but it quickly got bogged down in the usual morass of MoD planning and general incompetence. It was given an operational requirement range of one thousand miles and consequently had to carry a couple of hundred gallons of fuel. So it ended up as an overweight, underpowered, useless piece of kit that could not deliver its crew or weapons where they were required.'

Shepherd looked at Jimbo. Jimbo shrugged but didn't argue.

'The Dodge was originally developed as a military stores carrier during the Second World War, but it's been continually upgraded ever since for civilian roles,' said Rusty. 'It's been used throughout the Middle East by the oil companies to travel deep into the remotest regions searching for oil. It has an excellent power to weight ratio and in the right hands is capable of travelling anywhere.'

'But the Pinkies are painted to blend in with the background colour of the desert,' Jimbo said. 'The Dodges are bright red. They'll be seen from miles away.'

'They're painted red so they're visible from the air,' Rusty said, 'and can be found easily in an emergency. But once we've splashed some pink paint on them, they'll blend.'

'We'll not be travelling in daylight when we're approaching the target,' Shepherd said. He patted Jimbo on the shoulder. 'Rusty has the local knowledge of local, we have to trust his judgement, so the Dodges it is.'

Jimbo nodded. 'No sweat.'

Shepherd winked at him. 'Now, Comms: we'll be maintaining radio silence unless there's a crisis, so we'll take Motorola body sets with sets in each vehicle. Scaly Beebop will organize frequencies that won't be compromised by the IED suppression system we'll be using. Weaponry: Jock, can you sort that out and we'll see to the rest of the kit? They've no armoured vehicles or artillery, but they may have mortars and GPMGs.' Jock nodded.

'I'll take charge of water supplies,' Rusty said. 'I'm going to nip down to the local souq and pick up a few chuggles.'

'Chuggles?' said Jimbo, frowning.

'They're carriers for cooling drinking water,' Rusty said. 'They're made from hessian sacking with a metal pouring spout.'

'Do me a favour, that's sacking, isn't it?' said Jimbo. 'You can't carry water in a sack.'

'As a matter of fact, you can. They're made by Indian craftsmen and can be bought cheaply in any souq in the Middle East. They're made from closely woven hessian and when filled with water, the hessian expands to become waterproof enough to carry water without losing too much of it. You tie them to the sides of your vehicle and as the airstream blows over the hessian, it cools down your drinking water. They're brilliant - far more efficient than modern water coolers.'

Jimbo's expression remained sceptical, but Rusty was already on his way out of the door. The rest of the team spent several hours kitting out the vehicles with weaponry, equipment, fuel and a little food. 'Eating is not going to be a priority on this job,' Geordie said, tossing a few packs of assault rations into one of the Dodges, 'so these will do the job.'

They also fitted a camera system on the back of the other vehicle, consisting of a telescopic carbon fibre pole which could be raised up to 150 feet using hydraulic pressure. The pole was strong but so thin it was almost impossible to see at any distance over a couple of hundred yards. At the top of the mast there were a range of small high-resolution cameras, including infra-red and thermal imaging as well as colour cameras for daytime use. 'We'll be able to use the cameras to view ahead of our route through the sand dunes,' Shepherd said. 'It'll cut down the number of recces we have to do.'

At the final briefing that evening, Rusty talked them through the techniques for driving over dunes of soft sand. 'Sand dunes are shaped by the wind,' he explained. 'On the windward side they're convex and can be several hundred metres in height. On the lee side they're usually concave. The skill to driving in the dunes is to accelerate up the windward side until you're almost at the top, but then you must take your foot off the throttle and use the impetus of the vehicle to just clear the crest. Then you can coast down the lee side using the remaining impetus of the vehicle and gravity to keep up your momentum. If you're going too fast, you risk the vehicle plunging down the lee side and turning turtle with potentially serious consequences for the crew. If you are going too slowly you will be constantly getting bogged down in the sand. That means a lot of digging and the use of sand channels - perforated aluminium sections in a sort of flattened-out U-shape. In areas where the sand is soft we might have to offload the vehicle and carry the stores to where the vehicle has been moved to. Trust me, that's bloody tiring and uncomfortable in those extreme temperatures. So whoever's doing the driving has to know what's doing.'

Shepherd grinned. 'Well after that build-up, you'll have to put your money where your mouth is and drive the lead vehicle yourself,' he said. 'I'll take the second vehicle unless anyone else thinks they can do a better job.'

'One other thing,' Rusty said. 'You often find hard gravel plains among the dunes. They may only be going in the general direction of your route but you can drive at high speed across them. So you may have to do drive three sides of a square to keep on your general heading but it will still be quicker than travelling the direct route across the sand.'

'I'll remember that,' said Shepherd.

They set out at dawn the following morning, laden with weaponry, fuel and ammunition and with Rusty's chuggles lashed to the outside of the vehicles. Despite Jimbo's scepticism, Rusty's faith in them proved correct. Despite their porous skins they lost remarkably little of their contents during the day and the water was always pleasantly cool to drink.

Parker, who had still not fully recovered from the IED blast, stayed behind with Beebop to co-ordinate any support they might need. 'When we give you the word,' Shepherd said, 'we'll need your magic electronic filing cabinet to put a temporary black-out over the area, blocking any transmissions, particularly IED detonation signals. Can do?'

Parker glanced at Beebop who was operating the equipment, then nodded. 'No problem,' said the MI6 officer.

'You not coming with us this time, Jonathan?' Jock said, his expression a picture of innocence. 'Had your fill of desert trips with us after the last one?'

'Let him be, Jock,' Shepherd said. 'We need someone back at the base.'

They maintained radio silence as they drove all day through the searing heat of the Great Sand Sea. They followed a course well to the west of the sole road to the oasis and made slow progress through the shifting sands. That night they camped in a depression in the desert inhabited by semi-wild camels. 'There are never any totally wild camels,' Rusty said. 'The Bedu just turn their camels loose to find their own grazing and then recover them when they need them.' Now firmly established as their desert expert, he then began telling them about some of the desert fauna while they ate their rations. 'Have any of you heard of camel spiders?' he said. 'They're as big as dinner plates and covered in hair just like the hair on a camel. They're reputed to inject their victims with an anaesthetic and then eat their flesh. Incredibly creepy.'

'Can you get us one?' asked Geordie. 'Spider here likes nothing better than to chew on an arachnid.'

Rusty grinned at Spider. 'Is he serious?'

'I did it once, for a bet. During jungle training.'

'What did it taste like?'

'Like a spider. What do you think?'

'I was hoping like chicken.'

Shepherd laughed and shook his head. 'No, definitely not chicken. The trick is to burn the hairs off with a flame. That stops it sticking in your throat.'

They bedded down for the night. The following day they resumed their long, slow haul through the dunes, eventually arriving in the area of the oasis towards sunset. They raised the camera pole to survey the area. On the high resolution screens they could see thousands of date palms planted in orderly rows and interspersed with small gardens of exotic fruits and vegetables. There were even gardens of exotic blooms flourishing in the shade of the trees and a shaded pool of water, but they also spotted several patrols of heavily armed men.

'We're in the middle of the desert, miles from the nearest watercourse,' Geordie said. 'Where the hell does the water come from for all this?'

'Out of falajas,' Rusty said. 'They're circular-section, stone and mud watercourses running underneath the sand.'

'Like water mains?' Jimbo said.

'Yeah, but bigger, they're more like sewer pipes. They were built by either the Assyrians or the Persians in the dim mists of time, long before the birth of Christ. They were designed to bring water from the mountains, where it's plentiful, into the desert. It meant the Bedu tribes could survive in the most arid areas and set up agricultural communities. They were built to tolerances of a drop of one yard over a thousand yards, allowing a gentle flow of water all year round.'

After dark, using the thermal imaging camera, they began to realise how difficult a task they had set themselves. Cutting through the foliage they could see the body heat of a man slumped against a date palm in the middle of the oasis, the ropes securing him showing up in the thermal imaging as thin black lines across his body. He was closely guarded by two men with AK 47s and other weaponry.

'They might kill him at once if they detect a threat or hear an attack,' Shepherd whispered. They withdrew to consider their options but Shepherd could not see a solution to the problem until a thought suddenly struck him. 'Those falajas you were talking about, Rusty,' he said. 'Is there any way to access them?'

Rusty nodded. 'Sure, there are stone slabs every few hundred yards, like modern drain covers. They allow access to shafts leading down into the falajas, so that the Bedu can get water or get into to the tunnels to remove blockages and repair damage from roof falls.'

Shepherd grinned. 'Then that could be our way in. Let's take a look.'

Rusty and Shepherd set off to recce the falaj a couple of miles from the oasis. After searching for a few minutes, they saw a flat stone slab, its rectangular shape making it stand out against the sand and gravel of the desert floor. They slid it aside and found themselves looking down into a narrow vertical shaft, some twenty feet in deep, with a series of rough hand- and foot-holds carved out of the shaft walls. At the bottom, Shepherd could see the glint of running water.

They replaced the slab, hurried back to where the rest of the team were waiting and quickly formulated a plan. 'I'll infiltrate using the falaj,' Shepherd said, 'but if we all try to go in that way and are detected we'll be caught like rats in a trap. One grenade or burst of fire will take us all out. So you guys lie up on the edge of the oasis and wait until you hear me open fire. I'll take out the two guards on the sheikh, and then try to hold off the rest of the Chechens long enough for you to arrive and finish the job.'

Shepherd set off at once so that he would be in position by dawn. He climbed down into the bottom of the water-course, finding the water surprisingly cold as it flowed around his feet. It was pitch black inside the falaj but he knew that he only had to follow the direction of the water flow to emerge by the pool in the oasis. The tunnel varied in diameter between two and four feet and as he crawled along it, his MP5K slung across his chest, his shoulders brushed against the rough stones of the walls. There was an occasional partial blockage where part of the falaj wall had given way, but he was able to clear enough of a passage to squeeze past.

After crawling for over an hour he became aware of a faint glow of pre- dawn light ahead of him and realised he was nearing the end of the falaj. He peered out and saw that he was by the pool in the middle of the date palms. He quickly orientated himself before moving slowly through the trees.

Eventually he reached the edge of a small clearing. He peered through the screen of vegetation. He could see the sheikh still tied to the tree on the far side, with his two guards close by. Shepherd released the safety catch on his MP5K, stepped out of cover and put two shots into the Chechen guards. Almost immediately he heard Jimbo, Jock, Rusty and Geordie open fire.

Shepherd barely glanced at the sheikh before taking up his stance with his back to him, shielding him from any threat. Two more Chechens burst into the clearing, firing as they ran. Shepherd put a double tap into the first man as he broke cover. Every instinct and all his SAS training would normally have seen Shepherd diving and rolling after the first shots, throwing off the second gunman's aim before taking him out with another double tap from a prone position on the ground. But to do so would have left the sheikh exposed, so Shepherd stood his ground and calmly put another double tap into the other Chechen. He heard the crack of MP5Ks getting closer as his team mopped up the last of the Chechen fighters.

A figure moved through the vegetation at the edge of the clearing. Shepherd swung his weapon to cover the threat but then lowered the barrel as Jock moved into the open, followed by the rest of the team. Geordie, the patrol medic, sprinted across the clearing and flung his medical pack onto the ground next to the sheikh. He was about to start treating his injured hand when he caught a glimpse of something visible at the neck of the sheikh's robe. He gently eased it open a fraction and saw that a crude, home-made bomb vest had been fastened around the sheikh's chest.

'Spider, you need to come and take a look at this,' he said, his voice icily calm.

Spider and Rusty jogged over and immediately realised the seriousness of their situation.

'You're going to have to stay absolutely still,' Shepherd told the sheikh.

The sheikh nodded and forced a smile. 'I had already come to that conclusion myself,' he said.

'I've had experience with demolition work,' said Rusty.

'Specifically bombs like this?'

'More blowing up bridges, but the principle is the same.'

'We could take him back to the base and deal with it there,' said Jimbo.

Shepherd shook his head. 'I don't think we want to go shaking it around.'

'There could be a time on it,' said Rusty. 'Or some sort of distance trigger.'

'They said it would go off if I ran away,' said the sheikh quietly.

Shepherd nodded. 'Okay, Rusty and I will deal with this. You guys get to a safe distance.'

'Sod that,' said Geordie. 'All for one and one for all.'

'I'm serious, Geordie. If anything does go wrong, we don't want everyone hurt.' He smiled at the sheikh. 'I'm sure it'll be fine, really. I'm just covering all the bases.'

The sheikh nodded but he didn't say anything.

Geordie, Jock and Jimbo walked to the far side of the clearing and took cover.

Rusty was already scrutinising the crude vest. 'We can't remove it without cutting a wire.'

Shepherd nodded. 'So all we have to do is deactivate the detonator and the vest will be safe. But which wire controls the detonator?'

Four wires led from the vest. Rusty eliminated two of them but that still left them with a life or death choice. 'Which one?' Shepherd said, feeling a bead of sweat trickling down his brow.

'Your guess is as good as mine,' said Rusty.

'I'd rather not depend on a guess,' said Shepherd.

'Let me check the circuit again,' said Rusty. He stared at the circuit and eventually settled on one wire. 'This one.'

Shepherd nodded and took out his penknife. He flicked out a blade. 'You're sure?'

'Sure as I can be.'

Shepherd took a deep breath and winced as he cut the wire, bracing himself for the flash of light and the searing pain that would be the last sensation he'd ever know if Rusty was wrong. He breathed out as he realised that all was good. 'It's safe,' he said to the sheikh.

'Thank Rusty,' said Shepherd.

'No need to thank me,' said Rusty. 'I was using the old "eeny meeny miny moe" technique.'

'Please tell me you're joking,' said Shepherd, but Rusty only laughed.

Geordie ran forward, examined the sheikh and quickly diagnosed that he had lost a lot of blood due to the traumatic amputation of his finger and was also severely dehydrated. Shepherd radioed Parker to ask for a casevac. The helicopter had been on standby at an airbase in the capital ever since they had set off into the Great Sand Sea, and it arrived in a whirlwind of dust and noise within an hour.

Although the Chechen terrorists had all been eliminated, there was no sign of the sheikh's cousin among the bodies and after the casevac was completed, Shepherd and the team fanned out and began carrying out a systematic search of the oasis. They eventually found the man cowering in a mud-walled farmer's hut, covered in dirt and in a state of shock. They cuffed their prisoner's wrists with plastic ties and force-marched him back to the vehicles.

A few days later the team, by now ensconced in one of the capital's finest hotels, were summoned with Parker in tow to see the sheikh, in his hospital suite. He was well on the way to recovery, with only his missing little finger as a permanent reminder of his ordeal.

As soon as they appeared, he began thanking them. 'You have saved my life and my country,' he said, 'and I am forever in your debt. In the Arab tradition it is "alla sharifnee" which translates as "on my honour". And from this day onwards, if any of you ever have a problem of any sort, it is my duty to provide help to solve it. All you have to do is ask. However first of all I have a further favour to ask of you. I would like you all to stay on in my country as my military advisers. What ever Her Majesty's Government is paying you at the moment I will double, tax-free, and all your transport, accommodation and living expenses will be covered.'

There was a stunned silence for a moment. 'Ya sheikh,' Shepherd said at last. 'Your offer is most generous and very tempting, but we are still committed to our army service for our country, with many more years yet to serve.' He glanced at the others for confirmation. Geordie and Jock were nodding in agreement but Jimbo looked as if he was considering the sheikh's offer, then he too began to nod. 'So I regret that the four of us must reluctantly decline your offer,' said Shepherd. He paused. 'However, Rusty's position is different. He is not only a fluent Arabic speaker, with a deep knowledge of your culture, he is also due to retire from the Regiment in a few months anyway. If he's willing, I'm sure ways could be found to deal with the technicalities and bring forward his retirement date.'

Rusty nodded. 'Ya sheikh, I would be honoured to serve you.'

The sheikh smiled. 'Then the matter is settled, providing Mr Parker can make the necessary arrangements.'

'I'm sure there will be no difficulties with that, sir,' Parker said. 'I will personally deal with any problems relating to Rusty's immediate discharge from the British Army.' He hesitated for a moment. 'Forgive me, but there still remains one other pressing problem to address: the fate of your cousin.'

'He cannot be executed,' the sheikh said. 'He deserves it, of course, and I know that he would have killed me without a second thought if it had suited his purpose. But to take my revenge by executing him would cause discontent among some sections of my people. In any case, I'm not sure it would be wise to encourage the belief in my subjects that members of the ruling house can be executed just like other men.' He gave a brief smile. 'Who knows where the axe might fall next? However, he cannot be allowed to remain in my country as a focus for discontent and sedition.'

After a further discussion, Parker finally agreed that he would arrange for the sheikh's cousin, like his father before him, to go into an involuntary exile, albeit a gilded one, in a Park Lane hotel in London. 'Then it is all agreed,' the sheikh said. 'And perhaps this time I can rely on the British authorities to take rather better care of him.'

Parker inclined his head in acknowledgement of the implied rebuke.

'You know what, Jonathan?' Shepherd said as they walked back down the marble stairs. 'I've only just realised that the root cause of the problem all along was the inability of the UK security services to keep tabs on a known serious potential threat. Not very reassuring is it? And you know what else? We've just saved your arse for the second time in six months. You owe us, big time. Make sure you don't forget it.'

'I won't,' said Parker. He took out a pack of small cigars and lit one. He offered the pack to Shepherd but Shepherd shook his head. 'Mind you, you have to understand that "alla sharifnee" is an Arab thing.'

'You mean there's no honour in MI6?'

'We do our best,' said Parker. 'But needs must, right? Still, you and the guys did a great job. When you get this soldiering thing out of your system, you should think about working for the security services.'

'That'll never happen,' said Shepherd.

'Never say never,' said Parker. He waved a languid hand and walked away.

Geordie, Jock and Jimbo came up behind Shepherd. 'Penny for them?' asked Geordie.

'Dark thoughts,' laughed Shepherd. 'Let's go get a beer.'

THE ROPE

Dan "Spider" Shepherd was sipping his first coffee of the day as the sweat from his morning run slowly dried on his skin. He'd take a shower in a moment, but for now he was content just to relax and take in the scene around him. To the far north, the listening station's gleaming white radomes looked like giant mushrooms growing out of the pine forest cloaking the flanks of the mountains. The summit of Mount Olympus had been dusted with the first snow of the winter during the night, but at Akrotiri, 6,000 feet below, it was already hot enough for heat waves to be rising from the shimmering white salt flats towards the north of the Sovereign Base Area. He looked over at Jock McIntyre. 'What is it they say about Cyprus?' he said. 'Ski before lunch, and you can be sunbathing and swimming in the sea couple of hours later.'

'Know what else they say about Cyprus?' growled Jock in his grating Glaswegian accent. 'It's even less exciting than kissing your grandma.' Craggy-faced and beginning to grey at the temples, Jock was several years older than his patrol mates. He'd grown up in the Maryhill district of Glasgow and delighted in conforming to every stereotype of the down-market Scot, right down to Irn-Bru and deep-fried Mars Bars. He gave a theatrical sigh. 'God, I'm bored. Just look at it.' The sweep of his hand took in the dusty runways, Hardened Aircraft Shelters and admin buildings of the RAF section which occupied most of the SBA. The SAS compound tucked away in a corner, separated by a razor wire fence. A cluster of tents and Portakabins with makeshift canvas awnings to screen them from the Cypriot sun served as accommodation for the two SAS men permanently stationed there, a couple of "scaleybacks" - signallers - and any SAS patrols, like Shepherd's, who were temporarily based there.

The tents were drawn up in a circle like a wagon train from the Old West, surrounding the concrete admin building, a Cold War hangover still protected by berms and blast walls. Shepherd and his patrol had sole possession of a converted shipping container with a wheezing air conditioning unit attached to the outside that offered some relief from the fiercer heat of mid-summer. Now it was December and the patrol members were happy to soak up the warm, early morning sunlight, perching on upturned crates or any other improvised seating they could find.

'I've run around it, through it, under it and over it,' Jock said, warming to his theme. 'And it still doesn't get any better. I thought Maryhill was dull but it has got nothing on this place. I'm fed up to the back teeth, but no matter how much I beg and plead for an op, or some training, or any kind of action, the Head Shed just ignores me.'

'God, I wish I could,' Geordie Mitchell said with feeling. 'Can you not change the frigging record, Jock? The only thing more boring than being at Akrotiri is listening to you whine about it.' Pale-faced, pale-eyed and with thinning, sandy hair, Geordie looked like everyone's idea of an unhealthy specimen, but appearances could be deceptive. He could carry a load in his bergen that would have crippled a lesser man, and would still be slogging onwards when many apparently fitter men had collapsed in shattered heaps. The two of them were best buddies, constantly bickering and sparring like an old married couple but at the merest hint of criticism of either of them by an outsider they would instantly close ranks.

Shepherd stirred himself. 'I hear you Jock, but I've spoken to Base every day with our Sitrep, and every day it has been the same: Nothing To Report. The Ops Officer doesn't even get back to me. He's supposed to be your mate, Jock, not mine, so if he's not talking to you, he won't be talking to anybody.' The Ops Officer, Jamie, an "Honourable" from an aristocratic family with a cut glass accent and a Hugh Grant hairstyle, had formed an unlikely friendship with Jock when they were serving in the South American jungles together, tracking down drug runners.

The fourth member of the patrol, Jim "Jimbo" Shortt, stretched his lanky frame and yawned. 'Like it or not, we're in Cyprus and people pay good money to go on holiday here, so slap on some Factor 15, Jock, park your grumbling Glaswegian arse in a deck chair and see if you can turn that rancid milk complexion a fetching shade of pink.' Jimbo stretched out even further and sighed. 'Seriously, this is the life.'

'I'll turn you a fetching shade of black and blue in a minute,' Jock growled. 'Sod Cyprus, if they've nothing better for us to do, why won't they let us have some home leave? It's been the neck end of a year since we last set eyes on Hereford.'

'You know why,' Jimbo said. 'As long as de Vale has any pull, he'll be keeping us in exile, well out of the way.'

'He's already home and hosed anyway,' Geordie said. 'His version of events has gone unchallenged and is now the official version, and once it's official...' He didn't need to finish the sentence. Shepherd knew he was right. De Vale, the former Squadron OC, was notorious among SAS men for never missing an opportunity to "big himself up" and for volunteering his men for any op, no matter how reckless or poorly planned. A training exercise De Vale had put together had cost Shepherd's best mate, Liam, his life. De Vale bore direct responsibility because not only had he ordered the exercise, but he had also overflown Shepherd's patrol in the support helicopter while they were clinging to a capsized raft in frigid, sub-Arctic waters. Even though they fired a series of distress flares, de Vale had ordered the heli pilot to ignore them and return to base, leaving his men to their fate. A Norwegian coastguard helicopter eventually picked up the other members of the patrol, with Shepherd on the point of death from hypothermia, but by the time the winchman returned for Liam, it was too late. He had slipped beneath the waves and his body was never found.

De Vale had claimed that he was defending the Regiment's 'warrior traditions' by leaving the patrol literally to sink or swim, but Shepherd felt the officer had risked their lives for some worthless point of principle and Liam had paid the price. His SAS comrades agreed with him and, faced with a near-mutiny, the Regiment hurriedly convened a Court of Inquiry. However, to no one's great surprise, despite damning evidence from neutral observers and participants and Shepherd's own furious denunciation of de Vale, it concluded that the death had been "a tragic accident for which no blame could be attached to any individual". Jimbo had summed up the feelings of the SAS men when the verdict was announced - 'the words "wash" and "white" spring to mind' he'd said, with venom.

Soon afterwards de Vale was promoted and posted to Special Forces HQ in London, where one of his first actions was to issue a "Warning Order" to Shepherd's patrol for an imminent active service operation. It meant that they were put into immediate isolation and quarantine, in the SAS's secret special training camp away from the regiment's Hereford base. Cut off from the outside world, with even their phone conversations to their wives or girlfriends monitored, they were then sent overseas and could not legally resign from the Army until they were back in the UK, having completed any active service commitments the Regiment required. It was a devious move, and pretty much fool-proof. Shepherd and his team had no choice other than to sit tight and wait it out.

That had been well over six months ago now, and they had been on active service in Sierra Leone and the Middle East, or on stand-by in Cyprus ever since. Shepherd had not seen his wife Sue, nor his new-born baby son Liam in all that time. Requests to return to the UK on leave were ignored and his attempt to fly Sue and Liam out to Cyprus for a visit had also been vetoed. The intense focus required while they were on active service had served to silence the angry clamour of his thoughts for a while, but now they were again just going through the motions in Cyprus, it left him with way too much time for reflection and resentment.

His thoughts were interrupted by a discreet cough. A scaleyback from the Communications Centre - the only soldier in the SAS compound wearing a regulation army uniform - was standing there. 'Bloody hell, you should be in the SAS, mate,' Jimbo said, with the ghost of a wink to the others. 'I never even heard you coming.'

The signaller gave him an uncertain smile and then switched his gaze to Shepherd. 'Sunray Ops wants a one-to-one with 528 on the Red Line at 15.30.'

In the spare, clipped jargon that ruled military life, he was telling Shepherd that the Operations Officer in Hereford wanted to speak to him on the Top Secret line at half past three that afternoon. Sunray was the Ops Officer and 528 was Shepherd's personal Operations Number. Everyone in the SAS was given an Operations Number on entry to the Regiment. On ops it allowed the individual to order resupply items over the air without giving any personal details, since the quartermasters department kept a record of sizes for every individual. The process was secure, easy and saved time, and it also meant that details of casualties suffered abroad could be transmitted quickly and securely back to the UK.

Shepherd had put in a request for a one-on-one with the Ops Officer the previous day, though without any great hopes of success. The fact that Jamie had set one up straight away gave him hope that something might finally be in the air. 'There you are,' Shepherd said to Jock. 'The answer to a maiden's prayer: we may have a job on at last.'

Just before three-thirty that afternoon, Shepherd sauntered into the Communications Centre and was waved towards the sound-proof booth used for communications on the Red Line. In the SAS "need to know" applied here as everywhere else: if you didn't, you would be kept out of the loop - hence the sound-proof booth. When the Scaley had patched him through, Shepherd found that he could hear the Operations Officer as clear as a bell.

'Right Spider, what's the story? And don't give me any bad news for God's sake, there's already a shit-storm going on around here.'

'There's no story, Jamie,' Shepherd said, 'and that's the problem. We've been stuck in Cyprus twiddling our thumbs for weeks now. The boredom's driving Jock mad and he's sending the rest of us up the wall by bumping his gums about it. Can you not find us an op or swing some leave back in Blighty? My son's first birthday is coming up soon and I've barely set eyes on him since he was born. I'm his dad and he won't even know who I am.'

'I hope you know that I would do something about it if I could, but the orders came down from on high to keep you guys on a permanent rotation of Ops and Standby until further notice, and I can't countermand them. You seem to have pissed someone off mightily up there.'

'You've got that right,' Shepherd said. 'I'll tell you the whole story one day, and when I catch the gentleman in question out of uniform, I'll be punching his teeth so far down his throat, he'll have to stick a toothbrush up his arse to clean them.' He took a deep breath. 'Is there really nothing you can point us at, even a bit of training, just as long as it's somewhere else?'

'Hold on,' Jamie said. 'There are no ops I can send you on, but I'll see what else is doing.'

As he waited, Shepherd could hear the faint rustle of papers and the clack of Jamie's computer keyboard down the line. 'It's not an op or training,' Jamie said at last, 'but you can have a jolly, if you like. There's a Hercules leaving Akrotiri for Kathmandu tomorrow morning. Get yourselves on it, if you like the idea. The Hercules will be staying in Nepal for a week and you'll then return to Cyprus with it, but take all your operational kit with you in case you have to redeploy from there. Otherwise the trip will just be a pleasure cruise. It's not Blighty I'm afraid, but it's better than nothing. Report to the Military Attaché at the British Embassy in Kathmandu and leave your military kit with him. Do some trekking, climb Everest if you want to, but make contact with an ex-Regiment climber called "Taff the Rope" while you're there, will you? We've lost track of him but he's somewhere in Nepal so the Military Attaché should be able to put you in touch with him. Oh and Spider? You think you're the only one who's getting earache from Jock? I've been listening to his moaning every day for the past month as well, so tell him I hope this will shut him up. Enjoy your holiday.'

Shepherd thanked him and hurried back to the others to break the news. 'Great news, ladies,' he said.

'Where are we off to?' asked Jock. 'Singapore? Bangkok? Vegas? Sydney?'

'None of those, Cinderella. There's a Herc flying to Nepal tomorrow morning and we're booked on it, Club Class.'

'Club Class in a Herc,' Geordie said. 'That will be when they warm the steel floor before they make us lie on it, will it?'

Shepherd raised an eyebrow. 'Not complaining, are you? You can stay here if you want.'

'Hell no,' Geordie said. 'We can get some high altitude trekking and climbing in while we're there and after a week of that, even a miserable Scots git like Jock might be glad to be back in Cyprus with his feet up.'

'I'll check in with Air Movements right now,' Jock said. 'Just to make sure we can really get on that flight.' He hurried off.

They were still sitting on empty crates outside the shipping container, having yet another brew, when Jock came back. 'You'll never guess who I've just seen over by Air Movements,' he said. 'Gul the Gurkha. He's on his way to Nepal on that Hercules and he's overnighting in the transit accommodation.'

'Who's Gul?' Shepherd said.

'You won't know him. He was before your time in the Regiment and he only did one tour and then left because he wasn't comfortable with the individual thinking philosophy. He was much more comfortable in the group relationships of the Gurkhas, but he was a brilliant soldier, as brave as a lion, and he sailed through the Selection course.'

'Never heard of him,' said Shepherd.

'He's a living legend,' said Jock. 'He did a lot of operations when he was here and developed a great reputation. It was a shame he didn't stay longer. And I tell you what, you'd much rather have him as an ally than an enemy, because he was a real warrior. When the Falklands war was on, Gul used to infiltrate the Argentinian lines during the night. He'd by-pass or kill their sentries, sneak into one of their eight-man tents and slit the throat of one of the sleeping soldiers. Then he'd gut him and spread his entrails all over the floor of the tent, and then exfiltrate back to his own lines. They say you could hear the screams when the Argentinians woke up in the morning from a mile away. Did wonders for their morale.'

'I'm guessing the rest of them wouldn't sleep too easily after that,' Geordie said. 'You wonder who'd greenlight something like that.'

'I'm guessing he was using his initiative,' said Jock. 'Anyway, I said we'd see him for a few beers tonight. You can ask him yourself.'

'After a build-up like that, I'm not sure how wise that would be,' Shepherd said with a laugh.

'No danger,' Jock said. 'The funny thing is, off-duty, you couldn't meet a nicer, gentler guy.'

They met Gul in the Transit Mess that evening. He had the typical Gurkha build: short and wiry, with dark skin and jet black hair. He could have been anywhere between his early forties and his mid fifties and the only outward signs of his fearsome reputation as a warrior were his fierce, challenging stare and the proud way he carried himself. But he also had a ready smile and a dry sense of humour, and Shepherd warmed to him at once. The others drank beer as they chatted, but Gul stuck to the customary Gurkha drink of dark navy rum that he gulped rather than sipped.

'I don't know how you can drink that stuff,' Shepherd said. 'To me it looks, smells and tastes like engine oil.'

Gul shrugged. 'All Gurkhas drink it; it's even written into our terms of service that we're entitled to a tot of rum a day. On dark nights it keeps out the cold and we also believe that it stops the mosquitos from biting us.'

'You might be right about that,' Shepherd said. 'One whiff of that and I'd definitely be buzzing off somewhere else.'

'So why are you heading for Nepal, Gul?' Geordie said. 'Bit of home leave?'

'No, I'm on my way home for good. I've served my full twenty-two years now, but I'm still on the payroll for a few more weeks, helping out on the MoD's annual Gurkha remittance and recruiting flight. We're taking the pension payments out to the retired Gurkha soldiers in Nepal. It's like Christmas, New Year's Eve and the fourth of July rolled into one for Nepalis, because the Gurkha pension is often the only cash income for a man's entire village. The army money is absolutely vital for the local economy.'

'That's pretty much how it goes in Hereford,' said Shepherd. 'A big chunk of the local economy depends on the Regiment.'

'At the same time, the Army Gurkha Team is running the annual selection courses for potential recruits to the Brigade of Gurkhas,' Gul continued. 'As the Army has downsized, the competition for places in the recruitment process has got tougher and tougher, but to be a Gurkha soldier is still almost every young man's ambition in Nepal.' He smiled. 'And of course we remain the world's most ferocious fighters.'

'Present company excepted,' Jock said, grinning.

Gul's smile widened. 'Perhaps, although it would be an interesting contest. In the Anglo-Nepal war of 1814-16, Gurkhas so frightened the British soldiers that they decided to recruit us to fight alongside them, instead of against them, and we've been part of the British army ever since. We Gurkhas fear no one and our war cry remains the same: "Jaya Mahakali, Ayo Gorkhali" - Glory to Great Kali, Gurkhas approach.'

'Who's Kali?' Geordie asked, pronouncing it to rhyme with "alley".

'A four-armed god, whose hands hold a trident, a sword, a severed head and a bowl for catching the blood from the head.'

'A nice friendly god then,' Jimbo said with a laugh. 'My favourite sort.'

'Are there no other jobs for Gurkha boys than soldiering?' Shepherd asked.

Gul shrugged. 'There are some in the commercial security sector but those are invariably reserved for ex-Gurkha soldiers. The only other source of cash income is in the tourist climbing industry but that's a closed shop to anyone outside of the Sherpas. So the pressures on my country's young men are already considerable and the political situation in Nepal is only making that worse. The Ruling Family is imploding, dogged by constant claims of corruption, and the main opposition is a Maoist Party with a violent revolutionary agenda. There have already been a number of bloody attacks on remote police stations and district headquarters, and the unrest has now spread to the capital, Kathmandu. In fact things are so desperate that I've even been approached to enter Nepalese politics myself.'

'Why you, Gul?' Geordie said. He paused for a moment and then hastily added 'No disrespect intended but, well, you're just a squaddie like us.'

'Well, in other countries retired people watch football, but in Nepal we watch soldiering, and though I don't want to sound like I'm bragging, I am quite well known in my country.'

Jock interrupted him. 'Quite well known? Do me a favour, you're bloody famous and you know it: the first ever Special Forces Gurkha, with a string of citations and decorations for bravery. I don't know how you'll do in politics though. From what I know of you, you're straight as a die and a man who tells it like it is - an honest man, in fact, and if Nepalese politics is anything like ours, that's not exactly a qualification for the job.'

Gul smiled. 'Perhaps you're right. Anyway, I've not made up my mind yet. I'm going to travel round the country with the pension payment delivery and the Gurkha selection courses, sound people out in different parts of Nepal and try to get a feeling for whether they think that I should run for office or not. There will be some risk if I take that path, but if I can help to save my country from civil war, I have to do it. It's my duty.'

Jock disappeared behind the bar and re-emerged with a bottle of whisky and what was left of the dark rum. 'A toast then, to Nepal's next Prime Minister,' he said, filling their glasses to the brim.

A series of increasingly incoherent toasts followed: to Anglo-Nepali friendship, the Brigade of Gurkhas, the SAS and the "Toon Army" - the last a sop to Geordie who had just heard the previous day's football results from England and was celebrating a derby win for Newcastle United.

It was well on the wrong side of midnight when they stumbled off to grab a few hours sleep and they took off aboard the Hercules the next morning with dry mouths and pounding heads. As usual Jock and Geordie spent much of the flight asleep. Both had the soldier's knack of grabbing a few minutes shut-eye whenever the opportunity presented itself and on a long-range flight on a ponderous Hercules, those minutes would stretch into hours. They could drop off almost anywhere - even standing up, Jimbo used to joke - and could sleep through everything including the thunder of the Herc's engines. Yet at a whisper or a touch on their shoulder, they would both be instantly awake and alert, reaching for their weapons even as their eyes were opening.

Jimbo was also dozing in his netting seat, his chin nodding onto his chest, but Shepherd was wide awake, staring unseeing at the Herc's metal roof, his mind thousands of miles away, imagining Sue bathing their baby, feeding him and putting him to bed. The ache in his heart was almost unbearable and he had to force himself to think about something else.

After transiting Saudi Arabia, they overnighted in Dubai. There was no crew change-over - the same crew would stay with the aircraft for the duration of the trip. Before leaving Dubai, a number of ammunition boxes were loaded onto the Herc. 'Why the ammo, Gul?' Shepherd had asked. 'Is there a war on?'

'They're old boxes, they're full of cash now,' said Gul. 'It's actually the cash for the Gurkha pensioners. They prefer US Dollars because they can get a better rate of exchange.'

After leaving Dubai and flying over part of northern India, the Hercules seemed to be climbing forever before reaching the height of Kathmandu. On the final part of the flight, they had tremendous views of the high Himalayan peaks, with the stunning panorama of Annapurna, K2, Everest and many other nameless snow-capped peaks laid out before them.

The flight was uneventful but the landing at Kathmandu was hairy to say the least. The city sat 1,600 metres above sea level in Nepal's central valley, where the warm air rising from the plains met the sheer wall of the high Himalayas. The resulting turbulence threw the Hercules around like a rag doll in a hurricane as the pilot fought to land the giant aircraft and bring it to a halt before he ran out of runway. After landing and bypassing customs and immigration, courtesy of their Nepalese hosts, Shepherd looked around him with interest as they made the short drive into the centre of Kathmandu.

'Welcome to my beautiful country,' Gul said, beaming with pride. The patchwork of emerald green rice-paddies and vivid yellow-green millet fields on the valley floor alongside the fast-rushing river gave way to terraces of crops clinging to the precipitous hillsides. Above them rose an endless array of snow-capped peaks, filling the horizon from east to west. Shepherd could pick out the shark's tooth outline of Kangchenjunga and the sloping summit plateau of Annapurna, but to his disappointment, the highest of all, Everest, was obscured by the whirling cloud of a snow storm engulfing the summit.

He switched his gaze back to the river flowing alongside the road. 'What river's that, Gul?' he asked.

'The Bagmati, it's a holy river to Hindus and Buddhists alike. Its waters are believed to purify us and there are many temples alongside it. According to our traditions, the bodies of Hindu dead must first be dipped three times into the river before being cremated on its banks. The chief mourner, who lights the funeral pyre, must also bathe in the river after the cremation.'

'I was just fancying a dip until you told us that,' laughed Jock.

As they approached the city Shepherd could see the copper and gold pagoda roofs of the Hindu temples glinting in the sunlight. Kathmandu was much bigger than he had imagined, with a dense urban sprawl of four- and five-storey apartment blocks, many painted in vivid colours - lime green, lavender, orange - that dazzled the eye against the deep azure blue background of the sky. However at street-level the dust and traffic fumes created a brown haze as bad as any smog he'd ever seen.

After they had been dropped off in the city centre, they strolled around for a while, with Gul pointing out some of the sights. 'Most of the tourists stay in the Thamel district where all the guest houses, restaurants, and shops are concentrated,' he said.

'Do we look like tourists?' Jimbo said with feigned disgust. 'We want to see the real Kathmandu.'

Gul grinned. 'Maybe Jhochhen Tol would be more your style then; it used to be known as "Freak Street" in the days in the 1960s and 1970s when Kathmandu was on every hippy's itinerary... But on second thoughts, maybe not, "Love and Peace" isn't really SAS style is it? Nor Gurkha-style come to that.'

Shepherd and his mates parted company from Gul outside the British Embassy, but arranged to meet him that night for a meal. They found the Military Attaché, George Jenner, in his office at the Embassy. An urbane, Sandhurst-trained career officer, he greeted them with a broad smile.

'Welcome to Nepal,' he said. 'Anything I can do to help you, just ask. You will need to keep in touch with us, of course, and if you're going trekking up-country, you will find that comms are a bit of a problem - as you may have noticed, there are quite a few mountains around here and they do tend to interfere with communications. But you can reach this department at any time, day or night, from anywhere in Nepal by using the communications system in the Nepalese Police Posts; there's one in every town and village. I'm afraid I won't be available in person after today because I'm going trekking with the Gurkha recruitment team.'

'Sounds like fun,' said Shepherd.

Jenner grinned. 'I'm an ex-Gurkha Officer myself, I simply wouldn't miss it for the world. But my clerk will look after all your kit and will pass on any messages that come in from Hereford. So if you can make contact through one of the police posts on a daily basis, he'll keep you updated. Now, anything else I can help you with?'

'There might be,' Shepherd said. 'Do you happen to know a guy called Taff the Rope?'

'Dai Evans? Yes, I know him. I think he is usually to be found at the Tilcho Hotel, a cheap hotel in Pokhara. It's three or four hours drive west of here. He's not a regular visitor to Kathmandu and certainly not to the Embassy; he seems to prefer Nepalese company to ours.' He hesitated for a few moments, studying them over the rim of his china teacup before continuing. 'Just one other thing before you go: I believe your old comrade, Gul, was on the same plane as you today.'

'Not an old comrade of mine,' Shepherd said, 'but yes, he flew in with us.'

'Just a word to the wise then,' Jenner said. 'By all means be friendly if you happen to bump into him again, but my advice would be not to get too close to him.'

'Any particular reason why?' Jock said, his Glaswegian growl as usual sounding like a declaration of war.

'Just that I hear he may be harbouring political ambitions,' Jenner said with a disarming smile, 'and it wouldn't do for us to be seen to be actively favouring a member of the opposition in what is quite a sensitive political situation.'

'Yeah?' Jock said. 'Well, he's a mate and we're having dinner with him tonight. Get used to it.'

'It's nice to see that you haven't lost any of your diplomatic charm,' Geordie said to Jock as they walked away from the embassy.

'Diplomacy my arse,' Jock said. 'A mate's a mate, and that's all there is to it.'

'Guy's got a point, though,' said Shepherd. 'By hanging out with him, it might look as if the British Government is giving him their support.'

'So what?'' said Jock. 'He'd make a better politician than the shower we've got back in the UK.'

'No argument here,' said Shepherd.

They spent the rest of the day exploring Kathmandu and that evening they met up with Gul in a Chinese restaurant. 'Bloody hell, Gul,' Jock said, as soon as they were seated. 'I've really been looking forward to my first proper Gurkha curry in years and here we are eating bloody Chinese.'

Gul laughed. 'Most of the upmarket restaurants in Kathmandu are foreign, my friend, and the best of them are Chinese, so here we are. But next time we meet, we'll eat Gurkha food. You must come to the recruiting day at the Gurkha base in Pokhara tomorrow. It's really something to see and there we will eat the real Gurkha food, I promise.'

They left the restaurant much later, after a big meal and quite a few beers and black rums, and strolled back through the still-crowded streets. 'Bloody hell, will you look at that?' Jimbo was pointing up the street. Shepherd followed his gaze and saw an aged Nepali carrying a six foot by four foot steel security cabinet on his back up a steep hill. 'I know from bitter experience that one of those is a four-man lift,' Jimbo said, 'but there's an elderly gent managing it all on his own.'

Gul gave a proud smile. 'Never underestimate the strength and determination of the Gurkha, my friend. Many of our enemies have made that mistake down the years, and always to their cost.'

Even as they were sauntering along, deep in conversation, Shepherd was still keeping a wary eye on their surroundings. It was so deeply ingrained a part of SAS training that it had become second nature. Now his antennae had detected something in the ebb and flow of the people around them: a group of young men, moving through the crowds behind them with a common purpose.

He double-checked, using the reflection in the windscreen of one of the few cars parked in the street and then alerted the others. 'We've got company,' he said.

Suddenly sober, everyone's survival instincts kicked in. From the surrounding alleys a gang of teenage thugs had appeared, armed with a variety of weapons, including Gurkha khukris - vicious knives with a curved blade. The next moment, Shepherd, Gul and the others were locked in a vicious, bloody street brawl with no quarter given, as they fought for their lives. As a thug ran at him, slashing at his face with his khukri, Shepherd swayed back to let the wickedly curved blade whistle past his chest, then doubled his attacker up with a kick to the groin and sent him down and out with a chop to the neck and a stamp with his booted heel to the Nepali's face as he slumped to the ground.

The next one was already on him, but Shepherd dispatched him with a series of rapid-fire blows: the heel of his hand to the thug's nose, a raking stamp down the shins and onto the instep - agonising for the victim - and then an elbow to the head put him down.

His last assailant turned and ran for it, even dropping his knife as he did so in his panic to get away, but Shepherd at once turned to target one of the three thugs still surrounding Gul. The Gurkha had already flattened one attacker but was being hard-pressed by the others until Shepherd poleaxed one of them with a blow to the back of his head and spread another's nose all over his face with a vicious straight-arm punch. Gul meanwhile dealt with the other one, letting out a blood-curdling war cry as he rained down a fusillade of blows on him. Jock, Geordie and Jimbo were finishing off the remnants of the attackers. Battered and bleeding, they scrambled to their feet and stumbled away into the maze of surrounding streets, the last one sped on his way by Jimbo's Size 12 boot up his backside.

'That was fun,' Jock said as they got their breath back. 'Kathmandu's a lot less boring than Akrotiri any day of the week.'

'Anyone hurt?' Shepherd said.

'Just me,' Geordie said, examining a deep cut in the side of his hand. 'Bloody hell, it's through to the bone. Some of those little bastards had khukris!'

'Well you're the patrol medic, aren't you,' Jock said, showing not a trace of sympathy. 'Physician heal thy bloody self, as Shakespeare once said.'

'In fact that quote comes from the Bible, you ignorant Scots git,' Geordie said. ' And anyway, I've got a better idea. It's a two-handed job, so I'll tell you what to do while you bloody suture it up for me.'

While Jock patched Geordie up, Shepherd turned to Gul. 'What was that about?'

'I don't know. Street violence like that is almost unknown here. Perhaps they just saw a group of Westerners and thought they'd rob you.'

'They didn't seem like they had robbery on their minds,' said Shepherd. 'And they can't have been targeting us deliberately because nobody knew we were in town. Besides, they seemed to be focusing on you, which suggests that you were their target.'

'He's right, Gul,' Jimbo said. 'They'd followed us from the market area and tried to set up an ambush. It was planned.'

Gul brushed their concerns away. 'Well, if they were targeting me, it was probably just a case of mistaken identity. Don't worry about it.'

The following day, Shepherd was coming back from his morning run, chest heaving with the effort required in the thin air, when he saw the Military Attaché striding towards their quarters with a face like thunder. 'Get your men together,' he said, ignoring Shepherd's greeting. When they were all assembled, he let rip. 'I told you to keep your distance from Gul, but I now discover that not only did you ignore my request but you were also involved in an ugly street brawl with him last night.'

'News travels fast,' Shepherd said. ' But we were attacked without provocation. What do you expect us to do, let them cut us to pieces?'

'You should not have been with Gul. As I expressly warned you, it's an implicit message of British support for his political candidacy, which is not at all the message we wish to send. The Nepalese government is furious and the ambassador has already been summoned to receive a bollocking in person.'

'So what about our attackers?' asked Shepherd. 'What's being done to trace them? They shouldn't be too hard to find because they'll be nursing a few broken noses and black eyes.'

Jenner gave an impatient shake of his head. 'The Nepalese authorities are keeping a tight lid on the whole affair, because they're terrified about the detrimental effect that reports of street violence might have on the tourist trade.' He paused. 'So, the sooner you four are on the Herc back to Cyprus, the happier I'll be, and meanwhile I would be grateful if you could avoid making any further waves around here.'

'So the next time we're attacked, you'd just like us to lie back and take it, would you?'

Jenner's eyes hardened. 'No, I'd like you to make sure there isn't a next time. And do not see Gul again, that's an order.'

'Tough,' Jock said. 'You're not part of our chain of command, so we don't take orders from you, and we're seeing Gul this afternoon in Pokhara.'

After their frosty confrontation with Jenner, Shepherd used the Diplomatic Service telegram secure signals system to speak to Jamie, the Ops Officer, back in Hereford and obtain permission to go west.

They then borrowed the MA's Landrover - without his knowledge, for he'd now left Kathmandu with the Gurkha recruiters. They loaded their operational kit into the Landrover, stocked up with food from the market and then set off for Pokhara. That chilly December afternoon found them on a sports field alongside a spectacular river gorge on the outskirts of Pokhara.

A group of five hundred young Nepalis, all dressed alike in British Army issue physical training kit - blue shorts with a red top and brown canvas shoes - were sitting cross-legged in an atmosphere dripping with tension. They were patiently waiting to be processed, issued with an identifying number and then put through a gruelling series of physical and mental tests. Those that passed would be eligible to join the Brigade of Gurkhas. They were being watched by an audience of several thousand spectators

'This is just the final stage,' Gul said. 'They started with several thousand volunteers and the competition is so fierce that there are always about 25,000 applicants a year, competing for just 200 places. That's more than 100 for every single place. Recruiting is like the bloody Pied Piper. We send "Galla Wallahs" - former Gurkhas - up into the hills and each of them comes back with a few hundred would-be Gurkha recruits trailing behind him. Most still come from the martial castes: Gurungs and Magars from central Nepal, and Rais and Limbus from the east. They've bred soldiers for centuries, but we make sure that Gurkha Selection is free and fair - no one is chosen or excluded because of their caste or their family's influence. In fact it's almost the only thing in Nepal that isn't governed by an accident of birth, geography or caste. Becoming a Gurkha remains a great source of pride and families sacrifice a lot to help their sons prepare for Gurkha Selection. The earnings of those who succeed are enormous by Nepalese standards, enabling their parents to retire and securing the future of their families, but it's a brutal process; those who fail, return to their villages with only their bus fares.'

'What's with the red dot?' Geordie asked with his usual irreverence, pointing to the mark that many of the young candidates had painted on their foreheads. 'Is that to help the snipers sight on them?'

'It's what we call a tilaka,' Gul said. 'It's a religious thing, before they travel here for Selection - and some have travelled day and night for three days from their villages to get here - they are blessed by a Brahmin who paints a red tilaka on their foreheads. Most of them get a haircut as well.'

Gul explained that the applicants were sorted into groups of fifty and each group rotated through the assessment, ranging from a timed run over an army obstacle course, press-ups, pull-ups, carrying a man over a hundred yard dash using the fireman's lift, and finally a lung-bursting "doko run".

'What's a doko run?' Shepherd said.

'It's a three mile run carrying a seventy pound doko or rucksack, over dusty, rough and rocky tracks, up a gradient that climbs 1500 feet. The doko is the traditional wicker basket carried on our backs, with most of the weight borne by a broad strap across our foreheads. It's the toughest physical challenge any British Army recruit has to face, but most applicants succeed.'

'In the SAS we have the Fan Dance, where we run up and down a mountain,' said Geordie. 'It separates the men from the boys, all right.'

'All the Gurkha applicants are fit to start with,' said Gul. 'Fitness is never an issue. The hardest tests to pass are the mental and written ones. The candidates may never have heard English spoken by a native speaker, but if they join the Gurkhas they have to respond instantly to orders in English. So even before they start training we need to be sure that they have the ability to understand and respond instantly to orders. It's a ruthless process - a bit like SAS Selection.'

'Not really,' Jock said. 'Because if there'd been an intelligence test in SAS Selection let alone a written one, Geordie would never have got through it. He can't add two and two without a calculator and his handwriting looks like a spider has had diarrhoea and then crawled across a piece of paper.'

'At least I can write and talk,' Geordie said. 'All you and your fellow Picts do is grunt at each other.'

'What happens if they fail?' Shepherd said. 'Is that it?'

'Not immediately, they can reapply up to three more times until they're twenty-one, but after that, it's over for them. It's heart-breaking to see the faces of those who've failed for the final time, because they know that for their families, so much depends on them.'

They fell silent as the tests began. Many in the crowd were former Gurkhas themselves and they watched every move with critical eyes. The group being selected carried out the tests impassively, their faces revealing none of the physical strain and psychological pressure they must have been feeling. 'Hell fire, Gul,' Shepherd said, 'none of them have even broken sweat.'

Gul shrugged. 'We're used to living and working at altitude, and everything here is man-carried because our mountain tracks aren't well-suited to vehicles or horses and carts. But there are a lot of other things for us to get used to. When I joined the Gurkhas, I'd never seen Western food - I brought a piece of yak's milk cheese with me, wrapped in a leaf, in case I couldn't eat the Army food.'

'You weren't wrong there,' Shepherd said. 'You don't have to come from Nepal to find Army food inedible.'

'I and many of those selected with me also had to be taught to use a knife and fork,' Gul continued. 'And after a lifetime of wearing sandals or flip-flops, or going barefoot, we had to adjust to wearing army boots and learn to tie shoelaces. We'd never seen flush toilets or showers either; we used to wash every morning in the icy meltwater of the river. And of course Nepal is a land-locked country, so none of us had ever seen the sea. But do you want to know the strangest thing of all? We live our lives within sight of snow - Annapurna, Everest and the Himalayan peaks fill our northern horizon - but it never snows here in the valleys and the first time most Gurkhas ever experience snow is when they arrive at Catterick for their basic training. Selection is always in December so they do their training in January and February every year.'

'Poor sods,' Geordie said with feeling. 'Catterick's a shit hole at the best of times, but in winter it's the arsehole of the world.'

After completing the other tests, the candidates did the doko run, sprinting and scrambling up the steep slopes, indifferent to the magnificent backdrop of the Himalayas. Many collapsed as soon as they reached the finishing line.

'When do they find out if they've passed Selection?' Jimbo said.

'Not until later,' Gul said. 'There is such pressure to succeed and the price of failure is so high, that some young men have killed themselves after failing. So rather than risk of them throwing themselves into the gorge, we wait until we can break the news in a slightly safer, more controlled environment.'

The applicants were sent off in batches and after watching the first two groups, Jock suddenly said, 'I'm going to see how they measure up.' He stripped off his jacket, grabbed one of the spare weighted packs and joined the next group as they began their run up the hill. He trailed in half way down the group and returned, mortified to his friends. 'Bloody hell,' he said, drenched in sweat and still struggling to regain his breath. 'They would all pass the SAS Selection course easily.' He paused. 'Though I would have beaten them all, of course, if it hadn't been for the altitude.'

'Yeah, yeah, the altitude,' Geordie said, rolling his eyes. 'That and a dozen beers and a five course dinner last night. That's what you get for being bleeding greedy.'

With all the candidates now sitting in rows back on the sports field, the Gurkha recruiters conferred and then began calling out the numbers of the successful ones.

'I hate this part,' Gul said. 'I can't stop myself thinking about the heartbreak for those who aren't called. The lucky ones will be on their way in a few hours; they'll be issued with their kit and measured for their "mufti" - the civilian suits we wear when off-duty and off-base. But the rest have to go back other villages and dash the hopes, and probably break the hearts, of their families.'

An officious looking Nepali was addressing the crowd through a megaphone. After thanking the candidates, the recruiters and seemingly, everyone else who happened to be in Pokhara that day, he ended by calling on Gul to stand up. The ovation their friend received almost but not quite, drowned out the Nepali's next words. 'And please show your appreciation for our British friends from the famous SAS Regiment for coming to Nepal to show solidarity with Gul, as he sets out on his new chosen career path in politics.'

There was a thunderous burst of applause, but the SAS men remained in their seats, with faces set like stone. 'Bloody hell, we've been set up,' Shepherd said. 'Gul, did you know anything about this?'

There was a flash of anger in Gul's eyes. 'Of course not. I'm hurt that you should even think that I would be party to this.'

'Then I apologise,' Shepherd said, 'but I can tell you the Military Attaché is not going to be too thrilled by this. He says that we can't be seen to be playing favourites. I'm sorry Gul but I'm afraid it means that we're going to have to keep our distance from you from now on. I hope you understand.'

'Of course, my friend, I completely understand, and I can only apologise for the incident. I'm sure the gentleman meant no harm. He was just pleased that you were here. It's an honour and he wanted to share it, I'm sure.'

They parted firm friends and went in search of Dai Evans - "Taff the Rope". They soon found his hotel, in a run-down area of the city. 'Not exactly salubrious, is it?' Jimbo said as he took in the crumbling plaster and sagging timbers of the low-ceilinged room that served as reception, bar and restaurant for Evans and whatever other guests there might be.

Evans was sitting at the bar with a glass of beer in front of him. He was a man of indeterminate age, with grey hair, washed out blue eyes and a face tanned like shoe leather and so lined and wrinkled that he could have been any age from forty to seventy. He broke into a broad smile when they introduced themselves. 'I thought I'd dropped off the Regiment's radar,' he said. 'But you've managed to track me down. There really is no escape, is there?'

'So why are you called Taff the Rope?' Jimbo said climbing onto a stool and waving a barman over. 'You a hangman then?'

'Not quite. In my squadron, among others, there was Taff the Pill, who was a medic, and Taff the Valve, a signals technician. I was a climber so they called me "Taff the Rope", but the nicknames always wound up getting shorter and shorter, so in time, Dai Evans aka Taff the Rope, became known simply as The Rope.'

'So what's your story?' Geordie said. 'How do you come to be living in this...' He paused, groping for a tactful word. 'Erm, this boutique hotel in downtown Pokhara?'

Evans laughed. 'Boutique as in "The Pits" you mean? Well, I was raised in the valleys of South Wales and like every other male in my valley, as soon as I was old enough, I left school and went straight down the pit; I don't ever remember any other possibility being mentioned, that was just what we did. I was a strong lad so before long they made me a tunnel ripper, all hand work with pick and shovel, driving tunnels through solid rock. It nearly killed me at first but it gave me the upper body strength that I've never lost and that in turn helped me to become a good rock climber.'

The barman plonked bottles of Carlsberg down on the bar and the men grabbed them.

'The colliery would probably have been the story of my life,' Evans continued. 'Twenty years hewing rock and coal, and another twenty wheezing and coughing my way to an early grave from emphysema. But then I discovered that my childhood sweetheart was having an affair with a clerk on the local council.' He shook his head as if still unable to believe it. 'I mean, I ask you - a steelworker, a farmer, another miner, fair enough, but a bloody milk and water pen-pusher on the council, that was really adding insult to injury! So I thought sod this for a game of soldiers, I'm not hanging around here to be humiliated. I'm going to join the army, see the world, and get as far away from Wales as I possibly can. So I took a bus to Cardiff and enlisted in an English Infantry Regiment.' He gave a rueful smile. 'Big mistake. I only found myself being posted to bloody Brecon, didn't I? I could practically see my home from there. But while I was serving there, I saw some mysterious soldiers who kept themselves to themselves, away from the others in the camp, and who were attempting a mysterious quest known only as "Selection". I decided I'd give it a go. I was naturally lean and mean, and highly motivated to get out of Wales, and to my own, and probably everyone else's surprise, I passed the mysterious Selection and found myself as one of the youngest ever members of the SAS Regiment.' He raised his bottle and Shepherd clinked it with his own. 'A few weeks later I was in Malaya, working deep in the jungle chasing the last remnants of the Malayan Emergency. Now that was different to the valleys, I can tell you.'

'Malaya?' Jock said. 'Bloody hell, Taff, that was back in the 1960s, wasn't it? How old are you exactly?'

'It was the late 1950s actually, but like I said, I was one of the youngest back then, and anyway, don't you worry, I could still beat any of you to the top of a rock face with one hand tied behind my back.' He paused and his stare challenged them to disagree. 'On my way back to the UK with my squadron we found ourselves in Oman, involved in what later became famous in the Regiment as the Jebel Akhdar campaign. For an ex-coal miner to find myself at the top of a ten thousand foot high peak was unbelievable. The views, the clean, clear air and the sense of being almost literally out of this world had a profound effect on me. From then on I was absolutely addicted to climbing. As the SAS began organising itself into troops with various methods of entry into a battlefield, I managed to wangle a position in Mountain Troop. I did every climbing course the military had to offer including the Royal Marines and the RAF Mountain Rescue Training Courses. I spent every spare moment in North Wales at Capel Curig, climbing with the best civilian climbers in Europe, including some who had been on the Coronation climb of Everest in 1953, the first ever successful summit ascent.'

He sipped his beer before continuing. 'I was so passionate about climbing that I even managed to persuade the SAS Head Shed to send me to train with the French and German military regiments in the Alps, and I kept on and on at them until finally they agreed to finance the long and very expensive training course for me to qualify as an Alpine Guide. But at that point - Sod's Law - I found myself falling out of love with everything I was doing. Every climb was becoming more and more technical. All I was doing was putting up fixed lines so that non-climbers could carabiner onto the rope and get over the highest cliffs and mountains. I put in place hundreds of fixed lines for the SAS so they could take men and equipment into and across terrain where the enemy least expected them to be. But then, at the point where I had achieved my greatest skill-set, I found...' He paused, then took a long pull on his beer. 'I dunno, I suppose you could call it a religion of sorts, but I came to believe that every climb and every mountain should be treated with respect and should be climbed without any artificial aids. So without even realising it at first, I had become a free climber.'

Shepherd had been studying the man as he spoke. Physically he was pretty short and wiry, but the most notable thing about him was the cross-hatching of scar tissue on his hands, arms and legs, so dense that there was not an inch of skin visible that did not bear the white trace-mark of a scar.

Evans intercepted his gaze. 'Not pretty are they? he said. 'But I've come to like them. They're souvenirs of my climbs and every one tells a story to me.'

Shepherd laughed. 'You must know a lot of stories then, that's for sure.'

'I've climbed more than my share of mountains, that's true. I never wear gloves or shoes when I'm climbing, but use my extremities - hands, feet, fingers and toes - forcing them into cracks in the rock and using them as anchors or bracing points while I pull the rest of my body upwards to the next hold.' He paused and gave a rueful smile. 'As you may have noticed, once you wind me up and start me going, I'm capable of talking non-stop for hours at a time. Let me get some more beers and then you can tell me about yourselves and what brings you to this beautiful lost world of mine.'

After a long night of non-stop talking they persuaded The Rope to take them for a few days recreational climbing in Western Nepal. 'You've missed the best times of year for trekking here,' he said. 'Spring is the time for rhododendrons - the colours of the flowers in this pure air and dazzling sunlight, under a sky so dark blue it looks almost purple, are absolutely jaw-dropping, but the clearest skies of all and the best views of the Himalayan peaks, are found after the monsoon in October and November. However, we'll make the best of it while you're here, though it's a shame you can't stay a bit longer. We could do the Annapurna Circuit, one of the world's great treks, or even climb the mountain itself, though it has the worst fatality rate of any, even worse than Everest itself. About one in four of the people who attempt to summit Annapurna die in the attempt.'

'We'll pass on that one then,' Jock said. 'If I'm going to die I want it to be with a gun in my hand, not freezing my tits off on some godforsaken mountain summit.'

'Fair enough,' The Rope said with a smile. 'But apart from Annapurna, another two of the world's ten highest mountains are also right on our doorstep, Dhaulagiri and Manaslu, along with some of the best rock-climbing you'll find anywhere, so we're not short of other challenges. Dhaulagiri is my favourite, it's name means "dazzling white, beautiful mountain" in Nepali. It's the most striking and solitary of all the Himalayan peaks, rising almost sheer.'

'That doesn't sound too great either,' Geordie said. 'Maybe we should just stick to rock climbing and trekking!'

'Where's your sense of adventure?' asked Shepherd.

'Mate, mountains kill people,' said Geordie.

'Not if you know what you're doing, and you treat them with respect,' said The Rope.

'That there's the problem,' said Geordie. 'You know what you're doing. You've had a lifetime acquiring the skills. Me, I'd just be a dead weight on the end of a rope.'

They set off later that morning, driving west with The Rope navigating. The dirt road they were following, flanked by Himalayan Wild Cherry trees, climbed steadily higher, through dense thickets of rhododendron and, higher on the slopes, stands of blue pine. Eventually, well above the tree-line and still climbing higher, it dwindled to a rock-strewn track and then petered out altogether by a police post near the head of a long valley.

'We'll use this as base camp,' The Rope said. 'You can use the police communications system to keep in touch with the embassy and the Head Shed in Hereford, and if you leave our rations with the Nepalese police, they'll turn them into delicious curries for us.' He smiled. 'The crime rates are pretty low around here, so they're glad of something to do and a few dollars won't go amiss with them either.'

Shepherd had brought a climbing rope for each of them, much to The Rope's disgust. They also had a carabiner on their belt kits. The Rope had nothing but a pouch of resin attached to his belt. 'So,' he said, surveying their climbing aids and making no attempt to hide his disapproval, 'we can be reasonably confident that we have Health and Safety covered, can we?'

'And what exactly do you do when you fall?" asked Geordie.

The Rope grinned. 'I don't.'

'Well there's always a first time,' said Geordie.

'Aye,' agreed Jock. 'And a last.'

The Rope led them off up the track into the mountains, walking alongside the river gorge. To his surprise, Shepherd found himself struggling for breath almost at once. 'Bloody hell, you sound like my grandad,' Geordie said unsympathetically, 'and he died of emphysema.'

'We're at almost 15,000 feet here,' The Rope said. 'It takes a while to adjust to the altitude and some people take longer than others. There's no shame in it and no apparent pattern either; sometimes the strongest blokes are the first to suffer. Most people acclimatise fairly quickly but if you do really start to suffer from altitude sickness, the only cure is to go down to a lower level.'

'Don't worry, I'll be fine, but tell me, why is the water that aquamarine?' Shepherd said, playing for time while he got his breath back. 'I've never see water that blue before.'

'It's caused by billions of tiny flakes of schist and mica ground from the Himalayan rock by the glaciers and carried down by the meltwater that feed the river,' The Rope said. 'When the sunlight strikes the water it makes the whole river sparkle like a jewel.'

As they walked on, Jimbo pointed to a series of cables spanning the chasm ahead of them. 'What the hell's that?'

The Rope smiled. 'It's called a rope-way, and it's the only way across the gorge other than climbing down one side and back up the other. Don't worry, it's not quite as perilous as it looks.'

'For some reason, the word "quite" in that sentence, doesn't reassure me,' Jimbo said. As they got closer, they saw that the rickety wooden lean-to at the near end of the ropes housed a precarious looking cable car barely big enough for two of them to squash into.

'Is this thing safe?' Geordie said, eyeing it with suspicion.

'It's still up in the air at the moment, isn't it?' The Rope said.

'That's what worries me - it's an awful long way down.'

'Don't worry, it's not the fall that'll kill you,' said Geordie. 'It's hitting the ground that does the damage.'

The Rope ended the discussion by clambering into the cable car and Shepherd joined him. They pulled another rope to begin winching them across the gorge. It wasn't the most relaxing of journeys because the car shook, rattled and wobbled from side to side as it made its slow, jerky journey across the gorge. Looking down, Shepherd could see the river so far below them that it looked like an aquamarine thread. 'These rope-ways are an absolute lifeline to the people here,' The Rope said. They move people, and every conceivable kind of goods, even livestock, by them.'

They waited while the others hauled the cable car back and crossed, and then moved on. Further up the valley, the gorge ended in a sheer cliff down which a waterfall plunged hundreds of feet in a foaming avalanche of white water that raised a cloud of spray that hung in the air for hundreds of yards around it. 'The first climb,' The Rope said, gesturing to the rock face alongside the waterfall. 'I though we'd start with something gentle and build up from there.'

'Blood and sand,' Geordie said. 'If that's gentle, I'm not sure I want to be around when we get to severe.'

The Rope went first, dipping his fingers into his pouch of resin from time to time to aid his grip as he scaled the cliff, moving with a smooth confidence, pausing briefly to scan the next stretch of rock and then moving upwards again, making use of the smallest cracks and projections as hand- and foot-holds. He free-climbed but trailed a safety rope for the others as they followed him, their movements slow and hesitant by comparison.

Shepherd was barely aware of the biting cold of the air because he was concentrating so intensely. When he reached the top, the muscles of his forearms were still trembling from the effort and he was finding it hard to breathe again. He looked around while he waited for the others to follow him. Beyond the head of the waterfall, the river ran through an ice-gouged hanging valley, weaving a braided course around the vast drifts and moraines of grey gravel and ice-shattered rock swept down from the mountains in the spring floods caused by the snow-melt. At the far end of the valley, right against the wall of the mountains, he could see the sunlight reflecting from the black, still waters of a lake.

'There are hundreds of those glacier lakes hereabouts,' The Rope said, following his gaze. 'But they all want watching. Every now and again one bursts without warning, with catastrophic consequences for those living further down the valleys.'

'Thanks,' Jock said, as he hauled himself over the edge of the cliff. 'You're a real bundle of joy, you know that?'

The light was beginning to fade and they turned back at that point, using their ropes and carabiners to abseil back down the rock face they had so laboriously climbed and trekking back down the valley to the police post where the Nepali police had indeed prepared a curry for them, served up with the Nepali beer, Chang, and the fiery spirit, Raksi, distilled from fermented millet.

They spent the next few days enjoying their splendid isolation. They left early each morning and spent each day climbing a different virgin rock face with The Rope. Each time he went first, then lowered a safety rope and encouraged the rest of the team to follow him, making as little use of the rope as they could manage. Whenever one of them got into difficulties over a move, The Rope would give them a little time to solve it themselves and if that failed he would then use his incredible body strength to pull them over the snag until they could start climbing again. Slowly all of them gained in skill and confidence.

They arrived back at the police post on the fifth night to find the garrison on stand-to with the road barricaded and all passers-by were being stopped and searched. The Rope spoke to them in Nepali and then relayed the information to the others. 'There's been an incident to the east,' he said. 'They won't say what it was, but it was clearly pretty serious. They are searching for a band of terrorists who are believed to be heading in this direction.'

Shepherd immediately contacted the Embassy from the radio in the police post and when he broke the connection, his face was grim. 'The Gurkha recruiting party has been ambushed and Gul has been killed, along with several others,' he said. 'The Gurkha pension money's been stolen. The perpetrators are a gang of about twenty Maoist terrorists who are now thought to be heading back towards the tribal areas in the west of Nepal.'

'No bloody way,' said Jimbo.

'Yeah, this is my attempt at humour,' said Shepherd. 'Gul's dead. The bastards killed him.'

'And so are they,' growled Jock. 'They just don't know it yet.'

The Rope and the patrol had a quick Chinese Parliament to sort out a plan of action; whether they contributed to the discussion or not, everyone took joint ownership of the plan, ensuring that there could be no recriminations after the event.

The Rope took a map from his backpack and traced a route with his finger. 'They won't come this way,' he said. 'The most likely route for them to take is the parallel valley to the south of us.'

'So can we intercept them?' Shepherd said.

'We would need to climb a three thousand foot sheer wall of rock, but it can be done, if we're lucky.'

'Any objections to that idea?' Shepherd said, but one look around the circle of grim, determined faces was enough to answer his question. With the exception of Jock, they had only known Gul for a handful of days, but they had formed a strong bond with him in that time. But in any case, as a former member of the Regiment they owed him the same duty that they would owe to any SAS man: vengeance on his killers. One look at Jock's ferocious expression told Shepherd that any Maoist terrorists they encountered were unlikely to continue breathing for long.

They tooled up at once, travelling very light with only their belt kits and weapons. Shepherd, Geordie and Jimbo carried an AR-15 Colt Commando model with a retractable butt. Jock had the patrol heavy weapon, an M-203 Armalite with an underslung grenade launcher.

Almost the first thing every SAS soldier learns is that weapons are never slung except in the most unusual circumstances. They must always be ready for immediate use, so the sling swivels on their weapons were invariably removed to make the weapons lighter. But the fact they were climbing meant that the weapons had to be carried on their backs so they quickly made makeshift slings from parachute cord. They had fixed up The Rope with a spare Sterling 9mm sub-machine gun from the Nepali police post, the boss insisting Spider sign a ledger for the weapon and three magazines of ammunition to satisfy the bureaucracy in Kathmandu. Each of them - even The Rope - also had a coiled climbing rope slung over his shoulder.

They arrived at the foot of the cliff in darkness and The Rope began climbing even before it got fully light. All of them struggled at times, but Jimbo found it the most difficult, struggling to haul his big frame up the often sheer rock face. They paused to eat some rations, clinging to a narrow ledge, then carried on climbing. Shepherd's fingers were bruised and bleeding and his forearms and shoulders were sore with the effort of hauling himself upwards. But with a cold, furious determination he kept on moving up, working his way from handhold to handhold, each one marked by the faint traces of resin that The Rope's fingers had left as he pioneered the route.

Shepherd was moving up fast, gaining in confidence, but had just released his hold with his left hand when the flake of rock he was gripping with his right suddenly sheared off. He shouted a warning as the rock plummeted towards the others climbing below him, and felt himself beginning to fall away from the cliff. He made a frantic grab with his left hand and his fingers scrabbled at the rock, then caught. There was a stab of agonising pain as a fingernail was torn off, but his grip held. He hung there for a few seconds, his heart beating wildly, then found a hold for his right hand and, having checked that his comrades below were unhurt by the falling rock, began to climb again.

Snow flurries blew around him from time to time and ice that had formed in shaded crevasses was another hazard, but he kept working his way upwards, focusing only on the next hold, the next move, and avoiding the temptation to keep looking up to see how far there still was to climb.

About a hundred feet from the top they encountered a smooth slab with few visible handholds at the top of which was an overhang - a ledge jutting out at right angles to the cliff. The SAS men paused while The Rope moved slowly ahead, feeling for any tiny crevice or projection from the rock face that would serve as a handhold, inching slowly upwards.

'Bloody hell,' Jock said, his chest heaving. 'The guy is like Spiderman.'

'Or Spiderman's dad anyway,' Shepherd said. 'We're in our twenties and he'll be drawing his pension in a year or two, but he's leaving us for dead on this climb.'

It took The Rope forty minutes to negotiate those few feet of smooth rock, but at last he had reached the underside of the overhang. He paused there for a couple of minutes, giving his aching muscles what rest he could and bracing himself for the next effort, then he jammed the fingers of his left hand into a narrow crevice, using his thumb to wedge them in place, and launched himself outwards and upwards. The first time his scrabbling fingers fell just short and he dropped back, crashing against the cliff face with an impact that made Shepherd wince, but The Rope merely steadied himself, took a deep breath, and then launched himself again. This time his flailing fingertips caught the very tip of the ledge and held firm. He adjusted his grip a fraction, braced his feet against the smooth rock face for what little extra traction they could give and then, in one movement, pulled his left hand free of the crevice and grabbed at the ledge. He was now hanging, parallel to the ground almost 3000 feet below, but in another astonishing demonstration of his upper body strength, he pulled himself up as easily as a man doing chin-ups in the gym, swung a leg over the ledge and next moment was kneeling on it, lowering a rope to Shepherd and the others, waiting below.

Half-climbing, half-hauled by The Rope, each man in turn joined him on the ledge and from there to the ridge line was a relatively easy climb up a deeply-fissured rock face. It had taken them all day but they finally reached the top. They inched their way forward to look down the other side and in the fading light they could see faint smudges of smoke drifting up from camp fires on the valley floor below them.

They ate the rest of their rations as darkness fell and then, using the ropes, they descended the rock face in stages. Enough moonlight was filtering through the cloud cover to help them navigate their way down the cliff, but the dense thickets of rhododendrons and clumps of scrub alders along the valley floor made the darkness there almost impenetrable, though the faint smell of wood smoke on the breeze showed that the terrorists' campsite was not far away.

They held a brief whispered discussion at the foot of the cliff. 'The terrain and the vegetation may make it difficult for us to infiltrate undetected,' Shepherd said. 'Without a recce, we don't know what sentries they've got posted and twenty of them will be a challenge if they're alerted before we get to them. So I think we'd be better moving a little further west. We'll lie up there and intercept them as they move off after daybreak.'

'Agreed,' Jock said. 'A linear ambush: minimum effort, maximum results.'

They moved away from the cliff, threading their way around the densest patches of rhododendrons, until they reached a track, the dusty ground underfoot shining pale grey in the moonlight. Shepherd turned to The Rope. 'We'll set up the ambush here, you stay in cover while we deal with the bastards that killed Gul.'

'Like hell I will,' The Rope said. 'He's family, I'm family. I'm in this with you.'

Shepherd grinned. 'I thought you'd say that, but I had to make the offer!'

They chose a place where the track ran through a broad clearing and lay up in cover at the edge of the undergrowth, forming a linear ambush, all on the same side of the track, in a long line and spaced at twenty-yard intervals. Shepherd and Jock stationed themselves at either end with The Rope in the middle, flanked by Geordie and Jimbo.

As the first greying of the sky signalled the approach of dawn, they settled themselves, lying prone with their weapons at the ready and began the long wait.

About an hour after the sun had risen, Shepherd, closest to the terrorists' camp, heard the first faint sounds of movement and a few minutes later, the first of them came into view, moving cautiously, the barrel of his gun tracking his gaze as he scanned the ground ahead and to either side. Shepherd lay motionless as the man passed, unseeing, within twenty yards of him. He could have killed him in an instant but that would have alerted the rest of the gang and instead he allowed him to pass by. He watched man after man move past in single file, with the two in the middle of the line carrying bulging sacks over their shoulders. Shepherd kept his finger resting on the trigger, waiting for the first shots from Jock that would trigger the ambush.

As the last gang-member came level with him, Shepherd heard the first whip-crack sounds of shots as Jock opened up. Shepherd began firing a heartbeat later, and heard the rattle of gunfire from the others in the same instant. Cool and methodical, Shepherd fired short, targeted bursts, killing man after man. Some returned fire but they lacked the SAS men's discipline and accuracy, and most of the rounds merely shredded the undergrowth around them. Half a dozen turned and ran, three of them cut down instantly as they did so, but the others plunged into the rhododendrons and were lost from sight.

As the last of the remaining terrorists caught in the open was cut apart by simultaneous bursts from Jock and Jimbo, the SAS men leapt to their feet and sprinted across the clearing, diving into the undergrowth in pursuit of the escaping terrorists. The rhododendrons were almost impenetrable in places, but Shepherd could follow the track of one escaper easily by the bruised and broken leaves and stems he had caused as he ran for his life. There were bloodstains on the ground and a few leaves he had brushed against too, showing that he was wounded, but Shepherd was taking no chances. He checked as he came to an open area surrounded by more thickets of rhododendrons and began scanning the vegetation, using all his jungle fighting experience to refocus his eyes, looking through the foliage rather than at it. On the far side of the clearing, he saw a brief flash of fabric, pale against the dark green leaves and an instant later Shepherd's rifle barked twice and the body of the terrorist crashed backwards, his own weapon sending a burst of fire upwards into the sky. Still cautious, Shepherd moved forward and made certain with a double-tap to the man's head.

As he made his way back towards the clearing where the ambush had been set, he heard another double-tap away to his left.

He paused, calling to the others to warn them of his approach, before emerging into the open, rather than risk being shot by mistake. He found Jock, Jimbo and Geordie in all-round defence with one of the sacks on the ground beside them. 'Where's The Rope?' Shepherd said.

'He went that way, in hot pursuit,' Jock said gesturing towards the undergrowth. A moment later they heard another double-tap and soon afterwards The Rope appeared, carrying the other sack over his shoulder. 'I reckon it was the leader carrying that one,' he said, 'but I put paid to him.' He opened the sack, peered inside and then brandished a fistful of hundred dollar bills at them. 'Life can be a bitch sometimes,' he said. 'All through my entire career in the Army and then the Regiment, I used to pray that I'd get a chance to ambush a paymaster one day. Now I've finally done it and got my hands on a bloody fortune, and I've got no option but to give it back.'

'Gul's people need it more than you do,' said Shepherd. 'And let's be fair, none of us are in this for the money.'

'Ain't that the truth,' laughed Geordie.

PLANNING PACK

ARABIAN GULF.

November 1998.

Dan "Spider" Shepherd was standing on the flight deck of an RAF Hercules C-130, leaning on the back of the pilot's seat and anxiously scanning the horizon ahead of them in the first faint light of dawn. The plane's two pilots and the flight engineer were also scanning forwards, but it was the navigator, head down over his instruments, his face lit an eerie green by the light of his radar screen, who was the first to break the silence. 'The target should be on the nose now, range two and a half miles,' he said. He had a soft West Country accent that made Shepherd think of sheep and rolling hills.

Shepherd strained his eyes even more, squinting into the growing glow of dawn light, and at last spotted it: the long sleek shape of a modern warship, its grey hull at first barely distinguishable from the water around it and marked out mainly by the curl of white water at the knife-like prow slicing through the waves. The ship had slowed as the Hercules approached and was now barely making headway through the waves. 'I see it,' he said. 'Eleven o'clock.'

Shepherd watched the outline of the sleek, streamlined grey superstructure and the huge stars and stripes flag fluttering from the stern grow sharper as they closed rapidly on it. His thoughts were interrupted by the captain of the Hercules who was pointing at another C-130 that was already circling the almost stationary destroyer. 'They've already started the drop,' he said, 'you'd better get to the rear and prepare to jump. Wouldn't want you being late.'

The op had landed in their laps out of a clear blue sky just the previous day. Shepherd and his patrol mates - Jock McIntyre, Geordie Mitchell and Jimbo Shortt - had been making a leisurely return to Cyprus from Nepal, a journey that had begun on a sombre note with the funeral of their Gurkha mate, Gul, killed in an ambush by Maoist terrorists in Nepal's "Wild West". A few days earlier, Gul had been telling them about the Bagmati river that flowed through his native city of Pokhara - a holy river to Hindus and Buddhists alike - and the Hindu tradition of the dead being dipped into the river three times before being cremated on its banks. Only a few days later, they found themselves having to stand and watch as Gul's own dead body was ceremonially bathed and then placed on his funeral pyre and burned to ashes.

Shepherd's patrol had exacted a full measure of revenge on Gul's killers - within forty-eight hours of his death, none of them remained alive - and the grief that the SAS men felt for their lost comrade was no less intense for having to be so brief. Like soldiers the world over, they had to put the loss of their comrades and mates behind them almost at once despite the bonds formed by men who had looked death in the eye together. To spend too long mourning lost comrades was merely to invite reflections on their own mortality, and in the crucible of close-quarter combat those distracting thoughts could all too easily lead to it becoming a self-fulfilling prophecy.

Neither Shepherd, nor any of his patrol mates were in any hurry to return to twiddling their thumbs in the SAS compound at Akrotiri in Cyprus. When they were offered the chance to break the journey with a stay in a luxurious hotel in the Gulf, courtesy of the RAF, they did not need a second invitation. As soon as he got to his room, Shepherd's first thought was to phone Sue in Hereford. It would still be early evening in England and he imagined her giving Liam his tea, spooning baby food into him. The phone rang and rang, and he was about to hang up when Sue answered. 'It's me,' he said. 'Sorry I've not been in touch.'

'Where are you? England?' He winced at the excitement in her voice, knowing that he was going to have to disappoint her.

'I'm afraid not.'

'So where are you then?' Her voice was markedly colder now.

'I can't tell you where we've been - need to know and all that, but let's just say that communications weren't the best, and as far as a signal for a mobile goes, forget about it. This is the first chance I've had to call you.'

'Don't worry about it,' she said. 'It's all right, I'm used to it by now.'

He winced at the flat, faintly angry tone in her voice.

'Will you be home for Liam's birthday?' she said.

'I don't know. I hope so.'

There was a pause. 'Is this how it's going to be, Dan? Liam growing up and his father never being there for his birthdays, his first words, his first steps, his first day at school, for anything at all?'

'Come on, Sue. No, of course it won't be like that.'

'Are you sure about that? Because whenever it comes to a battle between Liam and me on one side and the SAS on the other, it seems to me that the Regiment always wins.'

Shepherd swallowed what he was about to say, realising that it would only fuel the fires, and instead said 'It's my job, Sue, but once I'm back in the UK, it'll all be different, I promise.'

'And when will that be?'

Shepherd grimaced. 'I'm not sure.'

'Can't you ask someone?'

'It's not as easy as that.'

'Someone must know? An officer?'

'They're moving us around. As soon as I know something concrete, I'll let you know.'

'But even then, you and I both know that nothing will change. As long as you're in the Regiment, it'll always be your first priority.'

Shepherd didn't argue with her because he had a feeling that she was probably right. There was a long silence and when Sue spoke again, her voice was even more flat and expressionless. 'I'll have to go, the baby's crying.'

Shepherd had not heard any sounds of crying down the line, but he didn't challenge her over it.

'I've got to go,' she said again. 'Just let me know when you're coming home.'

'Of course I will....' he started to say, but the line had already gone dead. He swore loudly to himself as he slammed the phone down, then went down to the bar to bury the memory of the strained conversation with a few beers.

He slept fitfully and woke early, taking his customary six-mile run at dawn. Afterwards he showered and relaxed over breakfast by the pool, drinking coffee and eating croissants with his patrol mates. As usual in hot countries and fierce sunlight, Geordie's skimmed milk complexion was turning pinker by the moment and he was continually arranging and rearranging the strands of his pale, thinning hair, trying to cover his scalp.

'Will you stop fiddling with that comb-over,' Jock said. 'If you need to cover your bald patch, I'll buy you a yarmulke.'

'I haven't got a bald patch,' Geordie said, as his mates stifled laughs and snorts of disbelief. The patrol medic and an unchallenged expert in battlefield trauma, Geordie's wispy hair, pale skin and general air of diffidence sometimes led men to underestimate him - always to their cost, for he was as tough as the sole of an army boot, and in a fight, almost as skilled as inflicting injuries as he was at healing them.

'You're right,' Jimbo said, stretching to his full six-foot plus height to peer down at the top of Geordie's head. 'It's more of a hair patch on the edge of a bald desert.'

Jock took a bite of his croissant as he stared out over the hotel's palm-fringed gardens, watching the streams of high-end Mercedes and BMWs speeding along the motorway towards the gleaming steel and glass towers of the city. 'It's amazing,' he said. 'I came here on a job years ago and none of this was here at all. There were no buildings taller than three stories - and most of them were built from mud bricks. The roads were dirt or potholed concrete, and the airport was a landing strip with a so-called terminal that was just a prefab building and a cluster of Portakabins. Now look at it.'

'I know, it's incredible isn't it?' Geordie said. 'Mind you, Maryhill, where you come from, is the same. It was a complete shit-hole a few years ago and now look at it: a complete shit-hole.' He ducked as Jock launched the half-eaten croissant at his head.

'I'll tell you something about Maryhill,' Jock said. 'A Geordie git like you would never...' He broke off and his face darkened as he caught sight of a familiar figure making his way towards them. 'Look what the cat just dragged in,' he said, his voice showing his contempt. 'Is there no bloody escape?'

Tall, urbane-looking and wearing a linen tropical suit and a panama hat, no one would have mistaken the newcomer for anything but an Englishman. He had a nonchalant, slightly distracted air, but those who watched him closely would have noticed that Jonathan Parker's sharp eyes missed nothing going on around him. His cover was as a businessman - 'a little import-export, old boy,' as he liked to say - played up to the stereotype of the gentlemen amateur Englishman abroad, but in reality he was an MI6 agent. Shepherd and his mates had already crossed paths with him more often than they would have wished, including having to repair the damage from a botched MI6 operation in Sierra Leone. His arrival was always greeted by them with groans, for they knew it was almost invariably the harbinger of difficult and dangerous work for them. More often than not - as in Sierra Leone – it involved clearing up a mess that Six themselves had created.

'Bloody hell, Jonathan,' Shepherd said. 'We didn't even know ourselves that we'd be here until yesterday evening. How did you track us down?'

'You seem to turn up everywhere,' Geordie said. 'The proverbial bad penny.'

'Like a bad dose of the clap that even antibiotics won't shift,' said Jimbo.

'Nice image,' said Shepherd. 'But appropriate.'

'Pure coincidence old chap,' Parker said, ignoring the insults. 'I just happened to be out here on business.' He smiled as he saw their looks of contempt. 'Business that won't involve you, you'll be sorry to hear. But something else has cropped up which will require your urgent attention.'

Geordie scowled at him. 'I thought you said it wouldn't involve us.'

'My business won't. Today I'm just a messenger boy for someone else, but I'm afraid it still means that your sunshine holiday is about to be interrupted. You are to report to the British Embassy immediately. A car is waiting outside to take you there.'

'What's that all about?' Jimbo said.

Parker raised an eyebrow. 'Surely you know better than to ask? Even if I knew, I couldn't tell you. But I'm sure your "Head Shed", as you so charmingly put it, will enlighten you.' He glanced at his watch. 'Now chop, chop, chaps, tempus fugit and all that.'

'Tempers what now?' Geordie said.

'He means time's pressing,' Jock said, whose carefully cultivated image as a monosyllabic Glaswegian hard case was rumoured to conceal a mind sharp and well-tutored enough to be able to read the Classics in the original Greek and Latin.

It was Standard Operating Procedure for Shepherd and his patrol mates always to leave their kit ninety per cent packed and ready so that they could make a fast exit whenever a call to action came. Within a few minutes of Jonathan Parker's unwelcome arrival, the SAS men were in a car with smoked windows and diplomatic plates, speeding towards the British Embassy.

It was an old stone colonial-era building with a fountain playing in its manicured gardens, but the perimeter wall and the gates had been reinforced against the perils of a more modern age, with coils of razor wire along the top of the wall and arc lights and CCTV cameras at regular intervals. There was a group of heavily-armed guards manning the gates. Even though the SAS men were travelling in an Embassy car, they still had to wait while the guards ran a mirror on a steel pole underneath the vehicle, looking for bombs. The guards then scrutinised their IDs minutely before allowing them through. Even though the country was a long-standing British ally, it also played host to its share of potential jihadists - any one of whom would happily launch an attack on the embassy.

As soon as they had announced themselves at the reception desk, they were taken to the secure communications room, a windowless concrete box, deep in the basement below the building. '528 to speak to Sunray Ops,' Shepherd said to the signals technician manning the equipment - his personal Operations Number and the radio codename for the Ops Officer at Hereford. Shepherd then entered the sound-proof booth, preventing even the technician from overhearing anything that was said. When the technician had made the connection, Shepherd found that it wasn't only the Operations Officer who wanted to speak to him. The Commanding Officer was also on the diplomatic secure line. There was no preamble, no enquiries about his health and well-being, no wasted words at all. 'A situation has developed which you and your patrol will have to deal with,' the Operations Officer said. 'The Hercules you came in is waiting to fly you to an RV with a US warship at the following co-ordinates.' Shepherd scribbled down the latitude and longitude references, noting immediately that it was somewhere in the southern Mediterranean. 'You are to make a water para-drop to RV with the warship, and will then carry out your assigned task. The operation is being planned for you in Hereford by the Operations Oversight Team.'

Shepherd frowned to himself. The Operations Oversight Team was a group of respected elder statesmen from the SAS ranks whose usual job was to ensure that the patrol planning for active service operations was robust and professional enough to give the patrols carrying them out every chance of being successful. Over the years the system had saved many lives by reining in the more gung-ho patrol commanders and concentrating on efficiency and results. He knew that any plan they came up with would be fine, but he would still much rather have been in control of his own destiny, planning the op with his own patrol rather than relying on the input of outsiders, no matter how skilled and experienced they might be.

'The matter is so sensitive,' the CO said, 'that no further information will be transmitted to you at this point. When you make the RV, you will be supplied with everything the Operations Oversight Team has calculated that you will need, and you will also be joined there by an additional patrol member, who will be bringing the Patrol Planning Pack by hand.'

The fact that the Planning Pack was being couriered to them rather than communicated over the secure line reinforced the sensitive nature of the operation, whatever it was.

'One final point,' the CO said. 'While you are in-country where you are now, you are to liaise with General Said, the head of the local Royal Guard. He is a friend of HMG who we have trained in the past and he will supply you with any logistical support that you need to get you to the RV.'

Shepherd remained silent while the Embassy car drove them back to their hotel - need to know applied to chauffeurs even more than signals technicians - but he broke the news to his patrol mates as soon as they were safe from prying eyes and ears.

While Shepherd rounded up the RAF Hercules crew, Jock and Geordie jumped into a taxi waiting on the rank outside the hotel and set off to meet the General.

'Don't forget we need ammo,' Jimbo shouted at them as they were clambering into the taxi. 'We're almost out after the contact in Nepal!'

A couple of hours later Jock and Geordie returned, driving a Royal Guard pick-up truck. Loaded in the back were four state-of-the-art steerable static line parachutes and a stack of boxes of .223 ammo for their Colt Commando model AR-15's: the lightweight, air-cooled, semi-automatic ArmaLite rifles that, due to their accuracy and reliability were their weapon of choice on many of their ops. Jock carried the M-203, an AR-15 with an underslung 79mm grenade launcher that used the same ammo, to give the patrol a bit of short-range punch if it were needed. Thoughtfully, they had also called in at the souq - the market - in the ancient heart of the city and had managed to buy an assortment of rubber waterproof bags. The para drop would be into the sea alongside the US Navy warship and the waterproof bags would protect their weapons and equipment and save them having to waste a lot of time cleaning and drying it.

They spent the rest of the day preparing for the drop and later that night they set off for the air force base where there Hercules was waiting. The flight to the RV was the usual Herc experience: long, boring, noisy and uncomfortable, and it was a relief when Shepherd at last saw the US warship ahead of them. As he watched the other Hercules dropping its parachutes, Shepherd was surprised to see that the single personnel chute floating down was followed by six much larger cargo parachutes with heavy loads swinging beneath them. 'How much kit do they think we need?' he muttered. 'It looks like they've sent the entire Quartermaster's stores.'

Each of the containers was efficiently collected from the sea by the men manning one of the powerful ship's boats and winched up to the deck of the destroyer. When the first Hercules had finished its drop, it wheeled away and departed to the north in the direction of Cyprus, the black smudges of the wash from its props staining the sky behind it.

'Right, let's get on with it,' said the loadmaster, whose world-weary expression was designed to show that he'd seen it all and done it all and wasn't remotely impressed by having an SAS patrol aboard. He swung the door open and at once the noise in the loading bay redoubled, the thunder of the engines sounding louder than ever, but still almost drowned by the roar of the slipstream.

The patrol hooked their bergens onto the parachute harness and then hooked the static line onto the overhead cable, ensuring they were safely anchored. After a cursory safety check, the Loady shouted to them 'Stand by! Watch the lights!'

Shepherd had done hundreds of Para jumps in his time, first with the Paras, and then the Regiment, and probably knew the drill better than even the loadmaster himself. He nodded and fixed his gaze on the light panel above the open door.

Shepherd kept staring at the red light and the instant that it changed to green he propelled himself through the doorway. Immediately he was riding the slipstream as the lumbering shape of the Herc disappeared ahead of him. He felt the jerk as the static line triggered the ripcord and his chute deployed above him. After the deafening noise inside the aircraft, the silence was stunning. He took a moment to check that the three other chutes had also opened safely, then concentrated on his own tasks. He lowered his container on its rope below him, and looking down, he began steering towards one of the waiting boats. The container entered the water just before he splashed down into the sea himself, and almost as soon as he broke surface strong hands were reaching down and pulling him aboard.

When Shepherd and the others had all been transferred to the mother ship, they assembled on the forward deck where the fifth member of the patrol was waiting to greet them. He was a Fijian, Joe Lavatani, who, though a new face to Shepherd, Jock and Geordie knew well. He was dark skinned and, like most of the Fijians that Shepherd had met, seemed to have a permanent smile on his face. The Fijians had a fierce warrior tradition of their own and a long history in the British Army and the SAS. In the early 1960's British commanders recruited a total of 200 Fijians into the newly created Regular Army. Over the next few years, twelve of them had gravitated to the SAS in Hereford. They proved to be prodigious warriors.

Of the twelve, one was killed in action in 1972 in the Battle of Mirbat during the Dhofar Rebellion in Oman. He single-handedly wielded a twenty-five-pounder gun that normally required a gun crew of four to six men to fire, in a battle against overwhelming odds that had gone down in SAS legend. He was subsequently awarded a posthumous Mention in Dispatches for his heroism, but it was an award that many of his comrades in the Regiment felt should have been a Victoria Cross, and probably would have been, had the man in question not been firstly, a "mere" sergeant, and secondly, a Fijian. The 25-pounder, renowned as the Mirbat gun, was on display in the Firepower Museum of the Royal Artillery in Woolwich. Almost all of the remaining eleven Fijians were also decorated for their gallantry and by the time they returned home most had been wounded in combat while on active service.

After shaking hands with Shepherd and Jimbo, Joe hugged Jock and Geordie like long lost brothers and they then launched into a bout of reminiscences about past ops and escapades, and a round-up of everything they'd all been doing since the last time they met.

Shepherd waited patiently for a few minutes, then called them to order. 'Okay guys, let's save the rest of the catch-up until we've all got a glass of beer in our hands. Let's focus on the op instead for a few minutes, shall we?'

Joe grinned. 'Sorry, I sometimes get a bit carried away when I see old friends.' He produced the Patrol Planning Pack from his bergen and handed it to Shepherd, who skim-read it at once.

The mission was a daunting one: to rescue two American students who had been kidnapped by a group of terrorists close to the Valley of the Kings in Egypt. The two boys, in their late teens, were the sons of a very senior member of the Administration in Washington DC.

'We can't be 100 per cent sure,' Joe said, 'because the intelligence is understandably patchy, but it looks as if, so far at least, the terrorists are unaware of the identity of the youths. Fortunately they appear to have left their passports in the hotel safe when they went out sightseeing for the day, and it seems that they were targeted and captured purely because they were US citizens.'

The Planning Pack also contained a summary of the available intelligence on the kidnappers. 'Not exactly War And Peace, is it?' Shepherd said, gesturing to the handful of lines of text that was all the information supplied. The little that was known indicated that the kidnappers were part of a large group of desert tribesmen who roamed the Western Desert of Egypt and Libya. They travelled in pick-ups that were armed with Russian ZSU anti-aircraft guns, 12.7mm NSV heavy machine guns and some SAM missiles. Although little known in the West, they were such a formidable group and so heavily armed, that the Libyan and Egyptian armies had evidently decided that discretion was the better part of valour and, rather than try to confront them, they preferred to leave the terrorists well alone. As a result, they had the freedom of the Western Desert and the Great Sand Sea, staging raids on tourist sites like the Valley of the Kings or the towns of the fertile strip flanking the Nile, and then disappearing into the vastness of the desert.

The plan put together by the Operations Oversight Team in Hereford involved a helicopter insertion into the Egyptian desert as close to the target area as possible. AWACS and satellite surveillance had identified an area close to the Nile where it was believed the group was now lying up. The patrol were not to transmit any signals when in country; instead they would be monitored by AWACS and would be given a "GO" or "NO GO" command for each phase of the operation from higher up the chain of command.

Jock gave a cynical smile. 'The Yanks are obviously worried that if Israel cottons on to the fact that Special Forces troops are on the ground in Egypt on a clandestine mission, they might well choose to escalate the situation for their own ends.'

'It wouldn't be the first time,' Joe said. 'There are also many in the US military who harbour serious doubts about the security of the US covert communications systems and suspect that the Israelis have the ability to monitor them.'

'That's probably true,' said Shepherd. 'Much of the US equipment was developed jointly with Israel and many in the American forces believe that the systems contain covert monitoring circuits which transmit directly to Tel Aviv. Since the UK's military communications also pass through American facilities or contain American-manufactured components, what we know, the Yanks will know. And if the Yanks know it, we have to assume that the Israelis will, too. Hence the restrictions on our comms when in-theatre. Better safe than sorry.'

'Hell's bells,' Geordie said, 'with friends like those, who needs enemies?'

'You know what they say,' said Shepherd. 'Keep your friends close and your enemies closer.'

'So this is an American-led operation, to rescue American boys, and making use of American assets,' Jimbo said, 'and yet they've given the job to us.'

Joe nodded. 'The US Administration knows it would take too long to get Delta Force on the ground and in any case very few in Washington would have much confidence that Delta Force are really up to the task.'

'They've got that right,' Jock growled. 'By the time Delta's lot have finished their pre-op Bible reading and prayer meeting, and made arrangements for Burger King and Dunkin Donuts franchises to be set up to keep them supplied while in-country, we'll already have finished the task and be on our way home again.'

'At least it looks like we won't be short of equipment for the job,' Shepherd said, gesturing towards the cargo parachute loads stacked on the deck nearby.

Joe nodded. 'Part of that is my fault. After I read the Planning Pack, I added a Packet Easy to the stores list as well. We might need it, and if not, we can always burn it to heat our rations.'

A Packet Easy was SAS shorthand for a pack of one hundred standard plastic explosive charges, each weighing one pound. It came with a variety of detonating card, primers, timer switches and detonators enabling the user to take on a large variety of targets. However, the plastic explosive was also so stable that, without a detonator, it would not explode and could even be set on fire and used as fuel.

'So that explains one of the cargo chutes,' Shepherd said. 'But what was in the other parachute loads?'

'Desert sand buggies,' Joe said. 'They are being tested by the Operational Equipment guys for Delta Force. They are tricycles with a silent petrol engine, and a seriously good bit of kit if you ask me. We're lucky to get it. But the Yanks want everything to go smoothly so it's money no object.'

'A silent petrol engine? That would be a first,' Jock said.

'Virtually silent anyway,' Joe said. 'The exhaust vents into the aluminium frame rather than into the air, and they are so quiet that you can be standing next to them and not even realise that the engine is running. They are fitted with sand tyres, the whole thing weighs just a few pounds, and they will run forever on a jerry can of petrol, so they are pretty much ideal for where we're going.'

Shepherd nodded, impressed. 'It seems like the Yanks are developing the kit for something big in this part of the world pretty soon.'

He'd been thinking furiously about the task ahead of them and had already come up with a few ideas of his own but, as was the SAS custom he initiated a "Chinese Parliament", allowing every member of the patrol to contribute ideas that would, if necessary, refine the plan. Those who chose to remain silent forfeited any right to complain about the plan or its results afterwards.

After a long discussion they decided on an approach to the target by water, reasoning that the kidnappers would be expecting any attack to come from the landward side. Having fine-tuned the plan a little more, Shepherd led them up to the bridge of the ship. Expecting a difficult meeting - relations between Brits and Yanks weren't always silky smooth and the traditional rivalry between the Navy and the Army only added another layer of complications - they were pleasantly surprised to find that the ship's skipper could not have been more helpful if he'd tried.

'Welcome aboard, guys,' he said. 'I obviously don't know what you're up to, but it's clearly top priority because I've received orders from "on high" that I am to co-operate with you to the fullest possible extent.' He spread his hands wide, as if encompassing the ship around him. 'So you've got a blank cheque. Anything we've got, you can have... within reason anyway.'

'Thank you Captain,' Shepherd said. 'There are just a couple of things you can help us with. We need a Sea Dragon heavy lift chopper here as soon as possible. If you don't have one on board, can you summon one for us?'

If the ship's commander was surprised by the request, he didn't show it and didn't even blink before replying, 'You've got it. Anything else?'

'We'll also need five of the dry suits that your ship's divers use.'

'Not a problem. Nothing else?' He smiled as Shepherd shook his head. 'If only all the requests we receive for assistance were as easily satisfied. I'll get those sorted for you right away.' He turned away and began barking orders as the SAS men returned to the deck and started cleaning their weapons and preparing their equipment.

SAS Standard Ops Procedures dictated a lower limit to the amount of ammo that each member of the patrol had to carry, but there was no upper limit. The use of .223 rounds meant the patrol could carry more ammo to support themselves than would normally be the case. Spider and the others knew that if push came to shove they could not expect the cavalry in the shape of Close Air Support or friendly artillery fire to come to their rescue. They would be on their own.

'Dry suits?' Jock said. 'Aren't those a little old school even for an old-fashioned guy like me? What's wrong with wet suits?'

'As a general rule, nothing,' Shepherd said. 'But once we've vented all the trapped air through the waterproof cuffs on them, using dry suits will give us a negative buoyancy and that will allow us to float just below the surface, making us virtually invisible.' He paused. 'Except to the Nile crocodiles of course.'

As the others burst out laughing, Jimbo tried and failed to smile at the thought. 'Bloody hell, don't even joke about stuff like that?' Sensing that he had just laid himself open to a lifetime of piss-taking, he hastily tried to back-track. 'I mean, hell, I'm not scared of them but I'd rather go into a contact with the enemy armed with nothing more than a pea-shooter than have to swim down a murky river that could be crawling with crocodiles.'

'It's the not knowing, isn't it?' Jock said, apparently sympathetic. 'Not knowing if you're going to scream like a girl and then burst into tears, I mean.'

'And look on the bright side,' Geordie said joining in with relish. 'If a croc gets you, we'll make sure we get the croc in revenge, so even if she's lost a husband, at least your widow will get a nice handbag and a pair of shoes out of it.'

Mercifully for Jimbo, his tormentors were distracted as the Sea Dragon was brought up from below decks and crewmen began swarming all over it, preparing it for its mission. The Sea Dragon was the largest and heaviest helicopter the US military had - bigger even than the US Army's Chinook. Its triple engines gave it huge lifting power and the massive sponsons on either side of the fuselage carried enough additional fuel to give it a range of well over 1000 miles. And if that was not enough, it was fitted with a probe to enable in-flight refuelling.

'Right, Joe,' Shepherd said. 'Let's take a look at these buggies you've brought and give them a test drive. I'd hate the first time I rode one of them to be during a contact with a bunch of terrorists with heavy weapons.'

Joe unpacked one and began tinkering with it while Shepherd and the others unpacked the rest. They were strange, skeletal-looking vehicles with a thin, tubular aluminium frame, a relatively narrow front wheel and two fat rear tyres.

'Start one up then,' Jimbo said, and let's see how quiet it really is.'

'I already have,' Joe said with a grin. 'It's running now.' The bike's engine was running but it barely made any sound. As Joe had said, the exhaust gases were vented into the frame's aluminium tubing before eventually being released through a series of small holes at the rear of the frame. The effect was remarkable. The engine was virtually inaudible.

Shepherd gave a nod of approval. 'Good kit, providing they work.'

'Let's see what they can do,' said Joe. They started up the engines of all of them and began testing them, riding in circles round and round the flight deck at the rear of the ship, and then gunning the engines to test their speed, zooming half the length of the ship, inches from the guard rail, then manhandling them around and speeding back to the prow. Joe glanced at Shepherd. 'Happy?'

'I'll be happy if they run as well on desert sand as they do on a steel deck, yes.'

'They should run better on it, that's what they're designed for.'

Once they had finished their preparations, the SAS men stacked their flimsy-looking desert buggies in the loading bay of the Sea Dragon, and then went off to the mess decks to fuel up with some food. They would be travelling as light as possible, with maximum ammunition and minimum rations. Even if the op went to plan and was trouble-free, it would be at least forty-eight to seventy-two hours before they were back within range of anything other than their belt rations to eat.

Shepherd and the patrol embarked on the Sea Dragon at last light, having spent the previous couple of hours doing work-up training with the chopper crew. The Navy pilots were very gung-ho and did not appear to be at all fazed by their mission, even though it involved a covert insertion into a country that, although technically a US ally, could not be expected to take kindly to the violation of its airspace.

'I'm getting the strong impression that the US Navy don't view international boundaries as things to be respected,' Shepherd said with a smile.

'Except where the boundaries in question belong to the United States,' Jock said, 'when they tend to take them very seriously indeed.'

'One of the benefits of being a superpower, I guess," said Shepherd.

They took off immediately after nightfall, heading south over the Eastern Mediterranean. As they flew towards the Egyptian coast the bright lights of the coastal resorts pierced the darkness ahead of them.

Guided by an AWACS aircraft flying thousands of feet above them, the Sea Dragon flew at wave-top height. They reached land and skimmed over the low coastal cliffs, the massive rotors churning up a sand and dust storm as they flew on at low level, disappearing into the black void of the Western Desert, where the original SAS had made such a mark during World War Two. They were heading in a southerly direction, and there was nothing to see in the unrelieved darkness below them but the occasional flare of light from an oil installation, and the flicker of cooking fires in isolated Bedouin encampments.

Eventually, about an hour after crossing the coast, the helicopter swung on to an easterly course and before long, peering down at the ground through their Passive Night Goggles, the SAS men could see the desert giving way to the fertile strip flanking the river Nile. The transition was abrupt; one minute they were still passing over featureless desert, the next, as if someone had thrown a switch, they saw a lush patchwork of crop fields: cotton, wheat, maize, clover, sugar cane, groves of olive and citrus trees, date palms, and, nearer to the river itself, extensive rice paddies. Reflecting the moonlight, each crop seen through their goggles glowed a different vivid and eerie shade of yellowish-green.

In the distance ahead they could now see the gleam of the river Nile. Mud-brown in daylight, it glowed silver by the light of the moon. Immediately they began their preparations to disembark, as the pilot began counting them down towards their landing site.

The Sea Dragon went into a hover above a dusty, arable field, and as soon the helicopter's wheels touched the ground, the loadmaster lowered the rear loading ramp. The SAS men disembarked at once, driving their dune buggies off the ramp through the blizzard of sand and dust raised by the whirling rotors of the helicopter. They went into all-round defence while the loadmaster dumped out the rest of their equipment. A few minutes later the Sea Dragon was rising back into the air, whipping up a fresh sand- and dust-storm as it did so. It swung away to the west, streaking low over the crop fields and the desert sands beyond, and again keeping well clear of the settlements of the Nile Valley before turning north to make for the rendezvous with the US warship waiting offshore.

After the thunder of the helicopter's rotors had faded, Shepherd and the patrol waited a further twenty minutes before moving, both making sure that their arrival had not been detected and allowing their eyes time to become accustomed to the darkness, and their ears to the faint, subtle sounds of the desert at night. They then spent the next hour cacheing their spare fuel and explosives, before beginning to make for their objective.

Shepherd felt strange not sending out radio messages with his situation reports, but the device on his shoulder was constantly relaying their position to the satellite tracking them. This in turn was relaying the information directly back to a bunker in the SAS base in Hereford, where the guys from the Operations Oversight Team were evaluating the information coming in, not just from Shepherd and his patrol mates, but from every available intelligence source, before deciding what further course of action they should take. Their orders were then relayed back to Shepherd's patrol through their ear-pieces, with each stage of the operation potentially subject to a "NO GO" veto. Shepherd wasn't too happy being under the thumb of the OOT, but he realised that it was the future, the way that all SAS operations would one day be carried out. He was sure that eventually every facet of every SAS operation would be subject to planning, control and veto in real time by the Head Shed back in Hereford. It wasn't a future he was looking forward to – he much preferred to be in charge of his own destiny.

They left the buggies hidden in a wadi while they approached the Nile a mile upstream from the site of the kidnapper's camp. They quickly donned their dry suits and secured their weapons and ammunition in waterproof rubber bags that they then strapped across their chests so that the outline of the bags would not break the surface of the water once the SAS men had submerged.

They waited on the bank of the river, screened by the crops growing around them, until Shepherd's earpiece crackled a single word: 'Go!' Then, one by one, they slipped silently into the water up to their necks. They paused, waiting while each man in turn vented the trapped air from the cuffs of his suit, before they pushed off from the bank. Shepherd was pleased to see that, just as predicted, their negative buoyancy allowed them to float just below the surface of the river, invisible to any watchers on the bank as they drifted downstream with the current. Only their heads briefly showed above the surface from time to time as they checked their bearings.

After drifting downstream for twenty minutes, Shepherd checked his GPS, then led the way into the shallows at the edge of the river where pools of deep shadow cast by a plantation of date palms growing next to the bank screened them from view. 'If the intelligence we had was right,' he whispered. 'And if they haven't moved in the meantime, the terrorists' camp should be about 300 yards west of us now.'

They emerged from the water without a sound and then stole towards the terrorists' camp. Peering from the shadows beneath the date palms, they could see the dark forms of an array of heavily armed pick-ups, their gun barrels and rocket-launchers visible as blacker outlines against the darkness of the night sky. They were drawn up in a semi-circle and watched over by a couple of sentries whose hunched shoulders and lowered, nodding heads suggested that they were at least half-asleep. A few indeterminate shapes were also lying around a pile of embers glowing in the dark, but even using their Passive Night Vision Goggles it was impossible for the SAS men to identify the hostages among them.

'We must get the kids out first,' Shepherd whispered, 'but which ones are they? I can't make them out from here.'

Joe was already stripping off his dry suit. 'I look and speak like an Arab, I'll go and find them,' he said, as nonchalantly as if he was discussing a trip to the off-licence to buy a few bottles of beer.

He moved off before Shepherd could argue. He watched Joe slip away through the darkness, moving silent as a ghost from shadow to shadow, evading the sentries and passing the vehicles without a sound. However, when he reached the fringes of the group of sleeping men, he began to noisily and clumsily blunder around, trying to look for all the world like a half-awake Arab going for a piss in the middle of the night. As he did so, he kept tripping over sleeping bodies and muttering unintelligible Arabic replies when the aroused sleepers cursed at him. Eventually he found what he was looking for. Shepherd heard an aggrieved and boyish-sounding American voice muttering 'Fuck off will you? Leave us alone'. Straight away Joe lay down where he was, next to one of the boys and Shepherd then belly-crawled over to join him.

'Who the hell...' the boy said, but got no further before Shepherd clamped a hand over his mouth, put his own lips very close to his ear and hissed 'We're the only friends you've got in the world right now. If you keep your mouths shut and do exactly as we tell you, there's a very good chance that we'll be able to get you out of here and have you safely on your way back to the good old US of A before the sun comes up. But if you make any noise, or argue, or refuse to do what we tell you, or piss us off in any other way, you're on your own and we'll leave you here to the tender mercies of the terrorists. Understood? Don't speak, just nod.' He waited until he got an answering nod, then repeated the message to the other boy.

He and Joe then protected the boys by covering them with their bodies, and Shepherd raised his hand a few inches as a signal to the other members of the patrol, watching from the shadows. A moment later there was the staccato chatter of semi-automatic fire as Jock, Jimbo and Geordie opened up, picking off the two available targets, the half-awake sentries, and firing bursts of rounds at the pick-ups.

The noise of the gunfire, the metallic thwock of rounds piercing the pick-ups' metal skins and the whine and howl of ricochets was terrifying to men who were still barely awake. The result was instant panic, with the terrified terrorists scattering in all directions. Some of them jumped into their pick-ups, started them up and disappeared at high speed into the desert, trailing clouds of dust. But others, having also scrambled to their vehicles, brought their heavy weapons to bear and began opening up with them at the fleeing terrorists, apparently oblivious to the fact that they were shooting at their own comrades. In the continuing panic and confusion, Joe and Shepherd were able to stealthily guide the two boys away, belly crawling across the ground while the rest of the patrol kept the terrorists' heads down with further barrages of fire.

While Jock, Geordie and Jimbo continued to cover their retreat, Shepherd and Joe reached the riverbank with the two boys and slid quietly into the water. They began making their way slowly downstream, soon followed by the other three, with Jock announcing their arrival by quietly moaning, to himself as much as to the others, 'I hate fucking water ops'.

'Of course you hate water ops,' Geordie said. 'You're from Glasgow, you're allergic to water, full stop. That's why there's probably no bathroom in that hovel you call home.'

They emerged from the river a couple of miles downstream, crossed the fields to a farm-track heading north, parallel to the river, and began cautiously moving along it in classic patrolling style, with Shepherd as lead scout, the boys shielded in the middle of the line of SAS men, and Joe as "tail end Charlie" bringing up the rear, checking constantly behind him for signs of pursuit.

Moving by the little-used paths and tracks crossing the crop fields to avoid passing through settlements, by later that morning, the patrol had moved well downstream and brought the boys close to a ferry crossing, where a party of American and Japanese tourists were waiting, their eyes fixed on the ferry that was just setting out from the far bank. Just beyond the jetty on that side, Shepherd could see the flags fluttering above the luxury hotel where the boys had been staying.

They waited with them until the ferry had docked on the near bank and the tourists began to board. 'Right,' Shepherd said. 'You need to get out of Egypt as quick as you can. Do not speak a word to anyone about anything, particularly about the people who helped you escape. If anyone asks - and they will - you tell them that you did it on your own. You managed to undo the ropes they'd tied you up with and slipped away from the terrorists' camp while they were sleeping. Now get your arses on that ferry. Once you're on, sit down and stare straight ahead. Stay on the fringes of the tourist party until you reach the hotel, then go inside, pack your bags, grab your passports and check out. Take a taxi straight to the airport, get on the first flight back to the USA and, if you've got any sense, this will be your first and last visit to the Middle East.'

Numb with fatigue, the younger boy merely nodded, muttered 'Thank you,' and began to head off towards the ferry, but his older brother stood his ground. 'You can't just dump us here,' he said in a nasal East Coast whine. 'It's not safe.'

'It's perfectly safe,' Shepherd said, 'as long as you do what I've just told you to do.'

'And I'm telling you that we're not doing that,' the boy said, folding his arms defiantly. 'Do you have any idea who my father is? You'll take us to the US Embassy now or my father will get to hear of it.'

Shepherd exchanged a world-weary glance with his comrades. 'Let me handle this,' Jock said. He picked the boy up by his lapels, so his feet were dangling above the ground. 'Now you listen to me, you ungrateful little shit,' he said, his mouth just inches from the terrified boy's face. 'We just saved your miserable lives back there. Do you think those terrorists were taking you out into the desert for popcorn and movies? And you know what? We're not even looking for any gratitude from you for risking our lives to save yours. All we want you to do is to do as you're told: get on that ferry, get your passports and get out of here. And don't bother threatening us with what your big bad daddy might do. We know exactly who he is and the person we answer to is a lot higher up the food chain; he'd eat your father for breakfast and shit him out afterwards.'

He paused, holding the boy's gaze and keeping him lifted off the ground, feet dangling. 'So,' Jock said at last. 'If you're still standing here, arguing the toss, by the time I've counted to three, I'll either shoot you where you stand or, even better, we'll take you back up the river and hand you back to your new best friends. And, having had their nights sleep disturbed and at least a couple of their friends shot dead, I don't imagine that they are in the best of tempers. Ready? One... Two...' He didn't get to "Three" because the boy and his brother were already sprinting for the ferry as if their lives depended on it.

'Ever the diplomat,' Geordie said.

'No more and no less than the little prick deserved.'

They watched to make sure the boys actually boarded the ferry and waited until it begin to pull away from the jetty, then turned to retrace their steps towards the south. 'Now the real fun starts,' Shepherd said.

They trekked back along the river, avoiding well-used roads and tracks and skirting the settlements they encountered, until they reached the place where they had cached the buggies the previous night. They collected the spare fuel, explosives and ammunition, and then set out to track the terrorists, wherever their trail might lead.

They first rode south for a couple of miles, aiming to pick up the trail from the terrorist encampment where they had rescued the boys. All of them found riding the desert buggies a strange experience at first. Apart from a few circuits of the US Navy warship's foredeck, none of them had ridden the buggies before, and it took a while to get used to their handling characteristics. Even more disconcerting, though, was the lack of engine noise and Shepherd found himself checking the speedometer, just to be sure the buggy really was responding to the throttle.

When they reached the site of the previous contact with the terrorists, they found that Egyptian vultures were already feasting on the spoils, tearing at the sun-blackened flesh of the bodies of three dead terrorists, while jackals prowled the fringes, wary of the vultures' cruel, hooked beaks, but seeking the chance to steal some of the carrion for themselves.

Jimbo shuddered and looked away. 'Jesus, I'm not sure even a terrorist deserves to end up like that.'

Jock shrugged his broad shoulders. 'You're not going soft on us, are you? Just be glad that it's not you on the menu.'

After circling the campsite, they picked up the terrorists' trail from the pattern of tyre treads their pick-ups had cut into the earth. They were pointing west, towards the desert, just visible beyond the fertile lands of the Nile valley floor. They went slowly at first, picking their way along the dusty tracks flanking the crop fields and palm plantations, and pausing frequently where two tracks intersected to make sure that they were not losing the terrorists' trail.

The crops thinned and grew more stunted as they travelled further from the river behind them, with the irrigation channels increasingly silted with sand blown in from the desert.

Finally they reached the edge of the fertile zone: a line straight as a ruler drawn across the terrain. Behind them were green fields, tall palms and trickling water. Ahead of them there was only sand and rock with the burning heat of the sun rising from it in shimmering waves. Shepherd paused long enough to wind a scarf around his mouth and nose, in an attempt to keep the dust and fine sand out of them, then led the way as they gunned their engines and headed out across the desert wastes.

They followed the tyre tracks, still running arrow-straight towards the west. They were travelling at speed, reaching up to fifty miles an hour over the hard, rocky surfaces, though moving slower over the patches of soft sand and dunes. But even when travelling flat out, they were doing so in almost complete silence with even the faint whisper from the buggies' exhausts carried away on the breeze. Disconcerting to him at first, Shepherd had now adjusted to it and was enjoying riding the buggy, which seemed to take all the different desert terrains in its stride. Its lightweight and broad, soft tyres made light work of the low sand dunes they crossed, and it was also stable and powerful enough to speed across the stony plateaus, swerving around the boulders that dotted the surface.

They climbed steadily away from the Nile Valley, crossing some dunes, but mainly traversing rocky, exposed terrain known as hamada - wind-stripped plains of loose rock and gravel, that would have made the trail harder to follow had it not been for the tyre treads imprinted in the frequent patches of dust and soft sand.

They were able to travel much quicker on their tricycle buggies than the terrorist pick-ups, heavily laden as they were with the weight of men, supplies, heavy weapons and ammunition that they were carrying.

The SAS men were rapidly beginning to overhaul the terrorists, and eventually they began glimpsing the dust-trail the column of vehicles left as they headed west across the desert in front of them. All the time Shepherd's earpiece stayed suspiciously quiet. The Head Shed would know exactly where they were from the AWACS monitoring their movements and though there had been no 'Go' for a pursuit of the terrorists, nor had there been a 'No Go' either. Shepherd and his patrol mates took that silence as acquiescence.

They had been travelling across a high, stony plateau for some time when Shepherd saw the land ahead of them dip steeply away. They found themselves on the edge of a steep escarpment, dropping almost sheer for a thousand feet. Through his binoculars, Shepherd could see the terrorists pulling to a halt a couple of miles away from the foot of the escarpment, and beginning to "laager up" their vehicles, like Boer trekkers in South Africa, parking them in a classic, circular formation deep inside a wadi running due west. They were clearly preparing to camp there for the night.

Around them, stretching away to the west and south as far as the eye could see, was a strange, almost lunar landscape in a patchwork of colours and textures: areas of yellow and white sand, and the pink-tinged exposed rock, giving way to the dark, crescent-shaped shadows cast by steep sand-dunes, and then mud-brown areas, gleaming white salt pans and in the distance, the glint of what might have been a lake, or a mirage. In places Shepherd could also see strange, rounded rock columns, rising like giant mushrooms from the desert floor. 'What the hell is this place?' Jock said. 'It's like no desert I've ever seen.'

'It's called the Qattara Depression,' Joe said. 'It's a massive area, something like 7,500 square miles stretching across the Libyan border to the west and to the edge of the Great Sand Sea to the south. It's about 450 feet below sea level and most of it is a wilderness of salt pans, salt marshes and treacherous stretches of dunes and soft sand. Nothing grows in the Depression except acacia groves in the drier areas and reed beds in the swamps.'

'Swamps? In the desert?'

'Don't forget that it's well below sea level, so what water there is all drains into the Depression and it retains all the water that flows into it; there's no outflow at all, though obviously there's a fearsome loss to evaporation. No doubt one day there'll be nothing here but a vast salt-pan, but for the moment there's enough water to form a brackish lake covering about four square miles in the north-eastern corner of the Depression and, as well as the swamps, there's also an oasis on the south-western side that's so big that if you stand at one end, the far end is invisible beyond the horizon.'

'Even so, how do the trees survive?' Jimbo said.

'They put down very deep tap roots and use the run-off from the rains, when they come, and the groundwater deep below the surface to survive.'

'So does anybody live here?'

'There are a few hundred people, some nomadic Bedouins and their flocks, but mostly Berbers, living in small, isolated oases, and maybe a few thousand people in the Siwa oasis. Oh and there are a few oil prospectors as well and a handful of oilfields. The Berbers grow huge quantities of dates and olives, and there are goats and Barbary sheep and quite a bit of game around the swamps and acacia groves - hares if you can get to them before the desert foxes and jackals, and gazelles if you can beat the cheetahs to them.'

'How come you know all this, Joe?'

'I'm an Arabist, I spent almost all of my time on active service in the Middle East, a lot of it in the Libyan Desert.' He showed them the gold signet ring he wore, with a translucent yellow-green stone set in it. 'One other strange thing about this desert. The stone is Libyan desert glass; Tutankhamen had a piece of this in some of his jewellery, so I'm in good company. You can find pieces of it scattered over an area of hundreds of square kilometres of the desert. It's tens of millions of years old and some people say it was formed when meteorites crashed into the earth or exploded in mid-air, though no one really knows where it comes from.'

He paused. 'Anyway, we need to overhaul the terrorists before they get much further into the Depression, because the terrain from here on in is very difficult. In the Second World War, the first and second Battles of El Alamein were fought between here and the coast. Both commanders constructed their defensive lines there because they could not be outflanked - the Depression and its surrounding cliffs were thought to be impassable, not just to tanks but to any military vehicles. That wasn't quite true - there are ways through and the Long Range Desert Group, who often guided the original SAS across the Western Desert to their targets, sometimes used them - but the terrain is treacherous. Do you know what fech fech is?'

He was greeted with blank looks and he grinned. 'It's the Arabic word for a very fine powdery soil - as fine as talc - that's been eroded from the rock of the surrounding plateaus by the desert wind and then washed down by flash floods into the Depression. It forms a subsoil like quicksand, but it is not easily detectable from the surface because it's usually hidden beneath a thin crust, so it forms a huge hazard for people and particularly for vehicles. You can be driving along and suddenly find the ground disintegrating beneath you, burying your vehicle - and any people inside it - in quicksand. Fech fech is very common in the Qattara Depression, making it almost a no-go area for vehicles - probably even lightweight buggies like these - unless you know the safe routes. There are dry lakes too, with a hard crust covering deep, cloying mud, which can be equally hazardous.'

'But then it's potentially hazardous for the terrorists too.'

'True, but they've been operating in this area for some time, and it would be surprising if they had not discovered at least one safe route through it.'

'Then we just have to follow them,' Jimbo said.

Jock shook his head. 'Except that following them along a narrow, well-defined track would just be laying ourselves open to ambush.'

'We could outflank them then, go north of the Depression and intercept them at the far side.'

'We could,' Joe said, 'but to do that we would have to cross "The Devil's Gardens", as they're still known: the minefields that stretch from the edge of the Qattara Depression all the way to the Mediterranean. Around three million mines were laid before the battle of El Alamein and most of them are still there beneath the sands, growing more and more unstable with every passing year. They reap a steady harvest of Bedouin herdsman and others crossing the desert, and I'm not anxious to add ourselves to the total.'

'So, no time like the present,' Shepherd said. 'We'll deal with the terrorists tonight, before they get the chance to move any further into the Depression. How does that sound?'

Everyone nodded in agreement. Still riding their buggies, the SAS men began moving down the escarpment, moving slowly to avoid raising dust and using every ounce of tradecraft and every scrap of cover to avoid detection by the terrorists a couple of miles away. At the foot of the escarpment, they passed through the ruins of an abandoned settlement, perhaps once the site of a small, now dried-up oasis, with the crumbling remnants of the walls of the mud brick buildings looking more like collapsing termite mounds as they slowly returned to the earth from which they'd come. The patrol moved on, closing to within half a mile of the terrorist camp and then set up an OP and watched them covertly for the remaining hours of daylight, before finalising their plan of attack.

At last light, the gang, evidently confident that they were now so far from civilisation that they were totally safe, lit a large fire in the centre of the laager and began to prepare their evening meal. Despite the hostage rescue the previous night, they evidently now felt so secure, deep in their own desert heartlands, that they didn't even bother to post sentries.

As always, darkness fell in the desert with the suddenness of a light being switched off. Shepherd and his patrol mates remained watching and waiting as the terrorists prepared and ate their meal, and they stayed in cover while the flames from the campfire died down and the terrorists eventually settled themselves on the ground to sleep.

The SAS men waited another hour until all was quiet then, following the agreed plan, they split into two groups and began working their way around the outside of the circle of parked vehicles, placing a standard charge of plastic explosive from the Packet Easy on the fuel tank of each vehicle.

They connected them all with detonating cord to form a large "ring main", with a trigger wire leading back to their OP Position. The patrol then settled down and waited for dawn.

'Did you know that the Arabic word for dawn is Fagr? It means "explosion",' Joe whispered to Shepherd as the first light began to illuminate the eastern horizon. 'Because when it arrives, the dawn comes up like a bomb.'

Shepherd smiled. 'Very appropriate in this case, then. Because it's definitely going to be like that this morning.'

As the first rays of light appeared in the east, and the group of terrorists began to show the first signs of stirring, Shepherd pressed the fire button on the Shrike exploder he was holding. In a heartbeat the pick-ups disappeared, engulfed by an eruption of flame and smoke, as the explosive charges detonated the fuel tanks. Even as the thunderclap sounds of the explosions were still rumbling across the desert, the SAS men were already mounting their desert buggies. Like Apaches attacking an Old West wagon train, they circled the laager at high speed. Steering with one hand, and firing indiscriminately into the inferno with the other, they unleashed such a barrage of fire that it was almost impossible for the terrorists, cramped in the tight area inside the circle of burning vehicles, to avoid being hit. Barely awake, and blinded by the smoke and flames of their burning vehicles, the terrorists themselves had no targets to aim at and what ragged and sporadic return fire they produced flew well wide of the speeding SAS men.

Only one man attempted to escape the inferno. A terrorist, driven by desperation or panic, leapt to his feet despite the relentless firing from the SAS men, sprinted towards the circle of burning vehicles and dived through the wall of flame. His hair, beard and loose robe were instantly ignited by the flames and he became a human torch, staggering blindly forward, screaming his agony until Shepherd slewed his buggy to a halt and put him out of his misery with a double tap. No other terrorists emerged from behind the curtain of flames and after several more minutes of carnage, Shepherd stopped firing and signalled to the others to withdraw.

They reassembled at the RV point a couple of miles away at the foot of the escarpment. 'The Third Battle of El Alamein,' Jock said. 'Shame it won't be as famous as the first two.'

'Pity you called us off, Spider,' Geordie said, 'I was just starting to enjoy that. Ee, there were more fireworks than the fifth of November on the Town Moor.'

Jock gave him a pitying look. 'Is there anything, anywhere in the world, that you can look at and not be reminded of some aspect of Newcastle?'

'Yeah, your face,' Geordie said. 'That just reminds me of my arse.'

'We didn't finish them off,' Jimbo said. 'And there are bound to be a few survivors. My mum always taught me to tidy up after myself, so should we not be mopping up?'

Joe shrugged and glanced up at the sky, where vultures, circling high on the thermals, were already beginning to gather. 'What we didn't kill, the desert will,' he said. 'With no transport and no water, even those who weren't killed or wounded are not going to last for long.'

'Strange we didn't hear any dissent from up above,' Shepherd said, gesturing to the radio at his shoulder. 'They'll certainly know where we've been and if they've managed to get a satellite overhead will know what we've been doing too. I hope we haven't upset them so much that they won't pick us up. It's a long ride back to civilisation from here and, I don't know about you, but I've got a feeling that when you've seen one desert, you've seen them all.' They wheeled away and began gunning their buggies along the steep track back up the escarpment. Behind them, the vultures, having circled lower and lower, were already landing and beginning to squabble over their prey.

FRIENDLY FIRE

THE UNITED ARAB EMIRATES.

November 2001.

For eight hours Spider Shepherd had been lying up in a sand dune overlooking the six-lane highway that slashed through the desert like a knife. It was a moonless night, the blackness dotted with so many stars that looking up made his head spin. He lay motionless, peering through his sniper scope, watching and waiting for any movement in the shadows. To his right, far off in the distance, were the lights of a city and beyond it, close to the sea, the diffused yellow glow of the oil terminals that gave the Gulf state its immeasurable wealth.

To his left, about a hundred yards away, was a clump of small concrete buildings and rusting pick-up trucks. Several of the buildings seemed to have been abandoned but, in some, oil lamps flickered behind wooden shutters. From time to time, Shepherd heard the reedy cry of a sick baby.

'Target mobile, said a voice in his ear. There was a faint double-click in his earpiece as he acknowledged, still peering through his scope towards a jumble of concrete and mud-brick houses flanking a narrow, high-walled passage. The houses were half a mile away, on the other side of the highway, but that wasn't a worry. The rifle he was using was accurate at well over double that distance.

At first he saw nothing, but then a black-clad figure slipped from the passage, crossed the street and disappeared again into an alley at the far side. Shepherd continued to track the man and focused on his face. 'Target acquired. Positive ID,' he murmured into his throat-mic. Shepherd's memory was photographic and one quick look at the surveillance photograph in his top pocket had been enough.

'Wait out.'

He saw the shadowy figure disappear and then reappear where the mud brick walls and buildings gave way to the empty scrub and desert beyond the city. There he paused and made a final scan of his surroundings before moving across the open ground towards the road that led from the airport into the city. Tomorrow was the ruler's birthday and other heads of state, including a representative of the Queen, would be traveling along this road from the airport to the palace. MI6 had come across intel that one of al-Qaeda's top bomb-makers had arrived in the Gulf state on a mission to attack one of the VIP convoys. The ruler was a close friend of the British Prime Minister and had agreed to allow the SAS to operate in his country, provided the mission remained totally covert.

As he checked out the target through his scope, Shepherd saw he was carrying a mobile phone. It would be the trigger for the massive bomb that two days earlier had been buried at the roadside. There were four oil drums full of explosives and it had taken three men the best part of two nights to dig the hole, taking cover every time they saw headlights heading their way. Now the bomb was buried and ready to be armed and that was the job of the bomb-maker. The three other members of the bomb-maker's team were being taken out by other teams. There would be no arrests, no trials, no publicity, just three bodies buried deep in the desert.

Slowly, deliberately, he took a series of deep breaths, preparing himself for the shot. The man came to a halt again, peering along the dusty road, then crouched down in the shallow ditch at the roadside. Shepherd murmured into his throat mic. 'I have the target. Positive ID. Clear engage?'

'Clear engage. Stand By, Stand By. Fire when ready!'

It had to be a head shot, a clean, instantaneous kill, to stop the bomb-maker activating his device. Shepherd sighted on the bridge of the man's nose, took up the first pressure on the trigger, then exhaled in a long, slow breath, and squeezed the trigger home. He barely felt the recoil, but the bomber dropped to the ground like a puppet whose strings had been cut.

'Target down,' said Shepherd.

Two dark shapes emerged from the darkness and ran to the body. One of them turned it over with the toe of his boot. There was no need to check for vital signs. The bullet Shepherd had fired had drilled a neat hole in the bomber's forehead and punched a fist-sized exit wound in the back of his head.

Shepherd slung his rifle across his back and ran towards the men, just as the dark shape of a Puma helicopter, flying without lights or markings, came skimming in over the sea. As he reached the men, the helicopter went into a hover a couple of feet above the ground, throwing up a whirlwind of dust. Shepherd and the other troopers jumped aboard, dragging the body with them. They were airborne in seconds, flying back towards the sea. When the helicopter was half a mile from land, one of the troopers kicked the body out of the open door. 'God bless all who sail in her,' he scowled as the body spun through the air and splashed into the waves far below.

* * *

Back at base, Shepherd was disassembling his rifle, carefully wrapping the telescope mount and the scope in foam rubber to protect them, and then slipping his scope into his grab bag. He looked up as a grizzled-looking figure in shorts and tee-shirt walked over to him. 'All right, Spider?' It was Billy Armstrong. He'd gone through selection with Shepherd five years ago and, like him, was a keen runner. It was Armstrong who had thrown the bomb-maker's body out of the chopper.

'Like shooting fish in a barrel... and just about as interesting.'

Armstrong grinned. 'They tell me the entry hole was an inch and a half northeast of his nose. You're losing your touch.'

'And you'd know?' Shepherd said, laughing. 'A man who couldn't hit his own arse with a shovel.' He rubbed his chin with his hand. He hadn't shaved in four days. 'I'll be glad to get back home,' he said. 'Only two more days.'

'Wishful thinking, mate,' said Armstrong.

'What? You're shitting me.'

'Fraid not, you're on your way to Doha.'

'To do what?'

'You know better than to ask and, even if I knew, I know better than to tell you, but I'll bet any money that wherever you are going, it isn't Hereford.'

'Are you coming?'

'Apparently not. They've got something for me but they're being all secret squirrel about it.'

'When do I go?'

'You should have left already.'

Shepherd groaned. 'I need to call my wife. She's going to hit the roof when she hears this.'

'No time, Spider. Seriously.'

* * *

Shepherd flew into the Doha International Air Base, better known as "Camp Snoopy", later that morning. Twenty years before, Doha had been a small town in a dusty, desert kingdom of Qatar with a lot of oil and not much else. Now it was a city of a million citizens with a cluster of gleaming tower blocks rising out of the desert sands. The American base was next to the international airport and was used as the main jumping-off point for troops and equipment heading into Afghanistan.

Shepherd had had no sleep other than a quick catnap during the two-hour flight, but the adrenaline was pumping as he looked around, taking in the hive of activity. Trucks and forklifts roared across the concrete as crates of ammunition and supplies, and more trucks and armoured vehicles were loaded into giant C5s and C17s. As each was loaded, it taxied out to the end of the runway and took off, its engines belching black fumes as the aircraft laboured upwards under maximum load. Before it was out of sight, the next C5 had taxied into position, ready to begin its own take-off run.

The sprawling base was the hub for the U.S. Central Command (CENTCOM) area of operations that included Iraq and Afghanistan. The invasion of Afghanistan had begun just four weeks earlier and the base was a hive of activity. There were vast areas of concrete hard-standing, acres of toughened hangars and warehouses, shielded by concrete blast walls, and communications centres and control rooms deep below ground in air-conditioned, blast-proof chambers carved out of the solid rock. Above ground there was the usual US base sprawl of McDonalds, Burger King, Starbucks and all the other home comforts US forces expected wherever they deployed. It wasn't like that in the rather more homespun British section, a small corner of the base allocated to the trusted partners in George Bush's "war on terror".

As Shepherd stood on the concrete next to the Hercules transport plane, easing the stiffness from his limbs, a Land Rover pulled up. 'You Shepherd?' asked the driver, a Geordie lad who looked as if he was barely out of his teens.

'Guilty as charged,' said Shepherd. He tossed his kitbag into the back of the Land Rover and climbed in. The driver set off across the airfield towards the SAS sector, a compound within a compound, a functional collection of tents, Portakabins, shipping containers and two breeze-block buildings, all surrounded by a double razor-wire fence, and shielded by berms bulldozed out of the sands. Three times on their way across the base, they were flagged down while their ID was examined by gum-chewing men in unbadged combat fatigues.

The driver dropped Shepherd at the gates of the SAS compound and sped off. As Shepherd showed his ID to the guard on the gate, he heard a shout. 'Spider! They've not got you on this Sunday school outing as well?'

One of the group of men sitting on upturned crates and sun-faded chairs next to a shipping container got to his feet with a big grin on his face. He had the typical SAS build: no more than medium height and a body built for endurance rather than raw power. Next to the young troopers who were sitting around him, his lined face and hair flecked with grey made him look even older than his forty years.

'Fuck me, Spud,' Shepherd said. 'I thought you'd be drawing your pension by now.' Jake 'Spud' Edwards had been one of his trainers back at the SAS Stirling Lines camp in Hereford.

'So did I, Spider, so did I. Turned forty last autumn, got myself a cushy little number back at The Lines, keeping my nose clean and counting down the days till I can jack it in. But there are so many of the Regiment away, with so much kit - and fuck knows what you're all doing - that even old men like me, and babies like these boys, fresh from Selection - are being shipped out on active service now.

Shepherd shrugged. 'As long as they can do the job. So... where're we going then?'

'Where d'you think?'

'I'm guessing Afghanistan?'

'You know what Spider?' Spud said with a broad grin. 'You're not as thick as you look. But take your suncream, we're going on holiday. The Defence Secretary stood up in the House of Commons the other day and said he doubted if British troops would even fire a single shot.'

He introduced him to the others. There were a couple of other older troopers he knew from previous ops but as Spud had said, the majority were fresh from Selection. There was also a contingent of Paras from the Special

Force Support Group Battalion with the usual assortment of tattoos and shaven heads on display.

Spud beckoned to one of the Paras, a young-looking, sandy-haired corporal with a rash of old acne scars across his forehead. 'This is Lex,' Spud said. 'He's going to be your spotter.'

'What?' Shepherd said. 'Why not one of ours?'

Spud shrugged. 'Not enough men. We're thin on the ground, remember?'

'What about Billy? Why's he sat on his arse over there? He's spotted for me before.'

Spud shrugged. 'Ours not to reason why,' he said. 'All I know is Lex has been assigned to you.'

Shepherd glanced at Lex. 'You know what spotters do, Lex?'

'Bit of a clue in the name, isn't there?' he said. He had a Scottish accent and had a habit of thrusting his chin up as if looking for a fight.

'Up to a point. You're called a spotter and you may spot targets as well, but your prime role is to have your sniper's back. My back. You protect me, so I can concentrate on what I'm doing.'

'I get it,' said Lex.

'You're sure?' said Shepherd. 'I have to trust you with my life out there. Literally.'

Lex's jaw tightened but he didn't say anything. As the two men stared at each other, Spud broke the silence. 'Lex is good, I've worked with him before. He'll be all right, trust me.' He patted Shepherd on the back. 'Trust me,' he repeated.

Shepherd nodded. 'Okay Lex. If Spud says your okay, that's good enough for me.'

He settled down in a quiet corner, unpacked and sorted his kit and began cleaning his rifle.

Lex walked over and squatted down next to him. 'That doesn't look like a standard 7.62.'

'No, this is the Rolls-Royce of sniper rifles, an Accuracy International .50 cal, made in the UK and going for twenty-three grand a pop.'

'So what's so great about it?'

'It's state of the art kit. The traditional sniper rifle fires a lighter round with an arcing flight that makes it less accurate. The .50 is heavier and has a flatter trajectory, so it's a more accurate weapon, and it's beautifully engineered.' He flashed Lex a tight smile. 'How much do you know about the Afghans?'

'They're ragheads, that much I know.'

'They're just about the toughest fighters in the world, mate,' said Shepherd. 'And just because we helped them out against the Sovs a few years ago, doesn't mean we're best buddies now. We're invading their country, don't forget, and they've been fighting westerners pretty much non-stop since Queen Victoria was a nipper, so it's not going to change now. Plus there are a lot of al Qaeda around. So a picnic it definitely won't be.' He paused as he checked the action of the rifle.

'You know what the muj used to do to the Soviet soldiers they captured?' asked Shepherd. Lex shook his head. 'First they'd castrate them and then they'd flay the skin from them while they were still alive.' He shrugged. 'But you never know, you might be lucky. You might be captured and kept alive - a few Soviets were, some of them for years. It's like medieval Europe if you're captured. You become the property of your captor until somebody who outranks them comes along. But I wouldn't be holding my breath for that. That's why it's so important that I know you've got my back. Because in Afghanistan there are no POW camps and no Geneva Convention.'

'I won't let you down,' said Lex.

'You'd better not, that's all I'm saying.'

* * *

During the night they flew in a Hercules to Bagram airbase, 25 miles north of Kabul. Built and named by the Russians, it was the only airport in Afghanistan that could accommodate the huge C5 Galaxies that Shepherd had seen taking off from Doha, and one was landing every five minutes. Men swarmed around them unloading ton after ton of supplies, while trucks and armoured vehicles rumbled down the ramps from the vast holds of the aircraft. The night was cold and, fresh from the searing heat of Doha, Shepherd pulled his jacket close around him as Spud, Shepherd, Lex and two other SAS troopers who had joined them walked across the dusty compound and found a place to bed down for the night in a draughty tattered tent.

Everyone was up before dawn and Shepherd, Spud and the others were sitting on folding stools eating their breakfast of naan bread and grapes as they watched the sunrise inching down the western face of the mountains. Shepherd took a sip from his mug of watery instant coffee and grimaced at the taste. 'Any idea why we're here?' he asked Spud.

'I went to see the Major first thing,' said Spud. 'Nothing specific, they just want more bodies on the ground. The Yanks are keen to show that this is a joint effort so they want to embed us in whatever Delta Force are doing.' He looked up as an Afghan boy approached. He walked with a limp, his left foot twisted inwards. He could not have been more than ten or eleven years old, but the expression in his eyes, so dark they could almost have been black, suggested that he'd seen a lot of life, good and bad. He broke into a broad smile as he caught Shepherd's eye, 'Salaam alaykum, Inglisi. You want cigarettes?' He pulled two packs out of his sleeve. 'Only two dollars.'

Spud glanced up 'Fuck off kid.'

'Leave him be, Spud,' Shepherd said, 'He's just trying to make a living, like the rest of us.' He turned back to the boy. 'No smokes thanks, kid, but what else have you got?'

'Anything you want, Inglisi: grapes, mulberries, tea, sugar, songbirds, gold jewellery, a pesh kabz - an Afghan knife - or if you want to dress like an Afghan man, I'll give you good price on a beautiful salwar kameez. Or I can get you a Kalashnikov. Just tell me and I'll get it for you.'

'A Kalashnikov?'

'Sure. Cheap, too, same price as a half-kilo of sugar.'

Shepherd glanced at Spud. 'What have we got ourselves into here - a country where you can get a Kalashnikov for the price of a bag of sugar?'

He turned back to the boy. 'No guns, thanks, and I suppose a decent espresso is out of the question?'

The boy's face fell. 'That might be more difficult, but I'll try.' He paused. 'What is espresso?'

'I'm pulling your chain, but a mint tea would be good.'

'At once, Inglisi. At once.' The boy turned and ran off as fast as his limp would allow. Shepherd shouted after him 'And go easy on the sugar, no more than six spoons, okay?

'Be careful with the locals, Spider,' said Spud. 'You don't know who you can trust.'

'He's a kid.'

'They use kids as suicide bombers here.'

'He's okay,' said Shepherd.

'That's a dad talking, isn't it?'

Shepherd laughed. 'Yeah, maybe.'

'How's your boy? What is he, four?'

'Four next birthday,' said Shepherd.

'Never wanted kids,' said Spud. 'Or a wife. Didn't want anything or anyone to tie me down.' He sipped his coffee. 'How's the lovely Sue?'

Shepherd put a hand to his forehead. 'Shit, I still have to call her,' he said. 'She's expecting me back this week.'

'Talk to the Major, he might let you use his sat-phone,' said Spud. 'Still giving you grief, is she?'

'It was bad enough before this Afghanistan thing,' said Shepherd. 'Now she's really on my case. Wants me out and back in Civvy Street.'

'Women huh? Can't live with them, can't put a bullet in their heads.'

'That's not funny, mate,' said Shepherd.

Spud held up his hands. 'I take it back,' he said. 'But I'm serious about the Major's sat-phone, he's let a few of the guys call home.'

'Cheers, I'll give it a go,' said Shepherd. He took a sip of coffee and grimaced. 'This is foul,' he said.

The boy was back within five minutes with a cup of hot, sweet green tea. Shepherd took it from him and tossed him a dollar bill, which he tucked inside his shirt. 'I can't keep calling you kid,' Shepherd said. 'What's your name?'

'I am Karim, son of Qaseem,' the boy said, touching his hand to his heart in the traditional Afghan gesture of greeting.

'And he's Spider, son of a bitch,' Spud said, laughing loudly at his own joke.

'Pleased to meet you Karim,' Shepherd said, ignoring the interruption. 'I'm Dan, but everyone calls me Spider.' He held out his hand and the boy solemnly shook it.

The boy's brow furrowed. 'Spider? Like an insect?'

'Yeah, I ate one once for a bet.'

'And not just any spider,' Spud said. 'He ate a fucking tarantula.'

Shepherd shrugged. 'I killed it first though, so it couldn't bite me before I bit it.' He grinned. 'Tasted like chicken.'

'Really?' said Karim. 'Spider tastes like chicken? I didn't know that.'

'I was joking,' said Shepherd. 'Anyway, what are you doing hanging around Bagram?'

'My father is here working for the Americans as a translator. He used to be a teacher. But before that he fought with you Inglisi against the Russians.'

'That's why your English is so good? Your father taught you?'

Karim nodded. 'He is a very good teacher. I shall be one too when I'm older, but for now I am a businessman.' He paused. 'You want a watch?' He pulled up his sleeve to reveal four or five watches strapped to his forearm. The cyrillic lettering on the face of each one showed their Russian origin.

'I'm not even going to ask how you got hold of those,' Shepherd said.

Karim shrugged. 'The previous owners had no further use for them.'

'No watches, thanks Karim,' Shepherd said, patting his arm. 'But you can keep the mint teas coming if you like. One every half hour till I tell you to stop.'

Karim grinned and then limped off in search of fresh customers. Shepherd began checking his rifle, cleaning it and wiping off the dust. Spud studied him for a moment. 'You keep rubbing that like you hope a genie'll appear,' he said. He was about to say something else when they heard a booming shout from across the compound. 'Spud! Spud my friend!'

A huge, black-bearded figure in a flowing, striped robe and a round cap lined with black lamb's wool was bounding towards them, showing a mouthful of crooked teeth in a broad grin.

He embraced Spud, planting a smacking wet kiss on both cheeks. 'It's been a long time, my friend.'

'And you're still an ugly bugger, Taj,' said Spud, entangling himself from the man's arms. 'And didn't I lend you a hundred bucks last time I saw you?'

Taj gave a piratical smile. 'Surely that was a gift, not a loan, my friend, and anyway it's long since spent.'

'Spider, this is Taj,' Spud said. 'He's one of us, I trained him and his men back in the late eighties when they were fighting the Sovs. Taught him to use Stingers.'

'Great days,' Taj said. 'We killed many, many Russians together.'

'You shot down a few helicopters, too,' Spud said. 'You know the Yanks are offering a reward for the return of the remaining Stingers, don't you? Any idea where they might be?'

Taj's expression was deadpan, but there was a glint in his eye. 'Why? Are the Americans worried that we will do to them what we did to the Russians?'

'Maybe. So you know where they might be? It's a very large reward. I'm serious, Taj. Be a nice bonus for you if you could bring a few in.'

'I heard rumours that perhaps the faranji fighters, the Arabs, may have some,' said the Afghan. 'I know no more than that, but I do have other information, Spud, valuable information.' The tip of his tongue moistened his lips.

Spud gave a cynical smile. 'How valuable?'

'The man the Americans seek? I know where he may be hiding.' He paused, glancing around to make sure no one else was within earshot, then beckoned Spud and Shepherd closer.

'You remember the White Mountains?' He pointed away to the southeast, where a range of towering, snow-capped peaks filled the horizon. 'That was our kick-off point and our main base when we made our raid on Bagram.' He laughed and slapped Spud on the back. 'A whole squadron of Mig 21s - their best aircraft - destroyed on the ground. What a day! From that moment we knew, and the Russians knew too, that they were beaten.'

'Aye, that was one hell of a scrap,' agreed Spud. 'We gave them a right bloody nose that day.'

'What about the White Mountains?' asked Shepherd.

'There are no roads there, but there are a handful of tracks and passes into Pakistan,' said Taj. 'The valleys are steep, twisting and very narrow, and a few men on the ridges above them can hold up an army. In the heart of one of the most narrow and inaccessible valleys of them all, there is a complex of caves. The main one is called Tora Bora in Pushtu, the Black Cave. We used it as our base. Russian aircraft and helicopters dared not penetrate those narrow valleys and those who did, we shot down. We could fire down on them from above. Then they sent ground troops against us, but we retreated before them, luring them on ever further into the mountains and then we struck. They sent five hundred men against us and we killed them all, except one.' He paused. 'The last one, we cut out his eyes so that he could not see the caves we used, or the passes and tracks to reach them, and we cut off his manhood, so that he should father no sons to seek blood revenge against us. Then we sent him back to the Russians as a warning of what would happen to any more they sent against us. There were no Russians in the White Mountains after that.'

Shepherd could see that Taj enjoyed telling stories, but he needed the man to get to the point. 'And why are you telling us this now, Taj?'

'Because no one moves in those mountains without me hearing of it, and recently many faranji - Muslims, but Arabs and Chechens, not Pushtuns, Tajiks or Uzbeks - have been seen there. Many pack trains of supplies have come through the mountains and a satellite dish has been installed on a ridge near Tora Bora.'

'So the Taliban are bedding in? Is that your big news, because that's no surprise. They're taking a pounding from American bombs and missiles on the plains, so why wouldn't they be retreating to the mountains?'

Taj shrugged. 'Because there are very few Taliban in the caves, according to men I trust. The Taliban are guarding the approaches to the mountains, but the valley itself is heavily guarded by faranji fighters, not Taliban, and they're fortifying it to resist a siege.'

'Any heavy weapons?' Shepherd said.

'They have RPGs, of course, plus heavy machine guns, mortars and perhaps even tanks.'

'And Stingers?'

'I do not know. It is possible.'

Shepherd thought for a moment. 'So what are you saying? You think they're protecting something - or someone - of high value?'

Taj crushed him in a bear hug, filling Shepherd's nostrils with the acrid stink of sweat and the oily smell of lanolin from his wool clothes. 'Exactly my friend,' he boomed. 'And who is worth that kind of protection, if not our honoured guest? He was with us when we fought the Russians but now, how do you say it? He has overstayed his welcome.'

The Afghan was talking about Bin Laden, Shepherd realised. The most wanted man in the world, the mastermind behind the 9/11 attacks.

'That's one hell of an assumption you're making,' said Shepherd.

'Who else would merit such activity?' said Taj. 'But if you do not believe me, let's go and we can look for ourselves.'

Shepherd studied him for a few moments. 'Why is this important to you Taj? Are you after the bounty on Bin Laden's head, is that it?'

Taj shook his head fiercely. 'You have heard of Ahmad Shah Masood?' he asked.

'The Northern Alliance guy who was killed by a suicide bomber? Sure.'

'He was a great man. I served him and my brother Mirzo served him. Mirzo was at his side when the bomber struck. He tried to shield Masood and....' His jaw clenched. 'He also was killed. So for me this is a blood feud. I shall not sleep until the blood debt has been repaid. They killed our leader and insh'allah, we shall kill theirs, even at the cost of my own life.' He looked at Spud and Shepherd. 'No man alive knows those mountains, and the tracks and paths through them, as well as I do. At Tora Bora we will have our revenge.'

There was a long silence. 'Give us a minute, Taj,' Spud said. 'Spider and I need to talk.'

Taj nodded and walked away across the compound.

Shepherd watched him go. 'You trust him, Spud? He looks like he'd sell his own grandmother for a few bucks.'

'Taj is okay, Spider,' Spud said. 'I'd trust him with my life - or yours.'

Shepherd gave him a dubious look. 'I'm hoping I won't have to, but if he's right about Tora Bora...'

'We'll need to take him with us,' Spud said. 'He knows the place like the back of his hand. He can lead us in and out.'

'I don't know Spud. He's on a one-man mission for revenge. That makes him a pretty loose cannon.'

'Trust me, Spider, I worked with the guy for three years back in the eighties. I'll personally vouch for him. He'll not go rogue on you and he's got local knowledge that it would take you and me a lifetime to acquire.'

Shepherd nodded thoughtfully. 'OK, let's see what the Head Shed says.'

Their CO was Major Allan Gannon, well over six feet tall with wide shoulders, a strong chin and a nose that had been broken at least twice. He was a good ten years older than Shepherd but was one of the fittest men in the Regiment, regularly running the SAS's selection course in the Brecon Beacons for the fun of it. He clapped Shepherd on the back when he saw him and congratulated him on his work in the Gulf state. 'You'd be up for a medal if it wasn't for the fact that it never happened,' he said.

'Can we have a word, boss?' asked Spud. 'We've just been given some intel that might make your day.'

Spud quickly outlined what Taj had told him. The Major listened in silence until Spud had finished. 'And this guy is trustworthy?' he said at last.

'No question,' Spud said.

'We need to be sure,' said the Major. 'This is big, but if he's setting you up a lot of people could get hurt. Or worse.'

'I'm happy to go, boss,' said Spud. 'I'd trust him with my life, no question.'

The Major looked across at Shepherd. Shepherd nodded. 'I'm up for it,' he said.

The Major nodded thoughtfully. 'Okay,' he said. 'Then let's use some of our drone time and see what's going on there. I'll give you a shout when I get the intel. Until then, mum's the word, obviously.'

Spud left but Shepherd stayed put. 'Boss, I need a favour.'

'You want to phone the missus?' Shepherd's jaw dropped and the Major grinned. 'I'm not psychic, Spud mentioned it earlier.' He went over to a metal chest, opened it and took out a bulky sat-phone. 'Take it outside, try to keep it below ten minutes, any longer than that and I have to do a memo. Crazy as it sounds, if you end the call at nine minutes and redial it counts as separate calls.'

'Cheers, Boss,' said Shepherd. He took the sat-phone outside and called his wife. 'Hi honey,' he said.

'Where are you?' asked Sue.

'I can't tell you,' he said. 'Sorry. It's classified.'

'You're still coming back this week, aren't you?'

'That's looking unlikely,' said Shepherd.

'Dan....' sighed Sue.

He could hear the disappointment in her voice. 'I'm sorry, honey. There's a lot going on at the moment.'

'It's Afghanistan, isn't it?'

'I can't say.'

'That bloody Blair. What's he doing sending our troops to that God-forsaken place? We need you here, Dan. Not in some bloody desert.'

'It won't be long,' said Shepherd.

'You're always saying that. And then I get the phone call saying that you'll be another week and another. And one day I'll get a phone call that says you won't be coming back.'

'Sue!'

She sighed. 'Okay, I'm sorry. But this isn't fair on Liam and me. You know that?'

'I'll make it up to you,' he said, A Chinook helicopter flew overhead, its twin rotors kicking up dust around him and Shepherd shielded his mouth with his left hand. 'Is Liam there?'

'Of course he's here. Where else would he be?'

'Can I speak to him?'

He heard Sue talking to Liam and then she came back on. 'He says he doesn't want to.'

'What?'

'He just shakes his head and says he doesn't want to talk to you.'

'That's stupid.'

'That's as may be, but I can't force him.'

'He's okay?'

'He's fine. But he keeps asking when you're coming home.'

'Tell him, soon.'

'I'll tell him, Dan. But you'd better mean it.'

'Honey, I'm sorry. Truly.'

'You'd better be here for his birthday, Dan.'

'I'll try.'

'You need to do more than try. You've missed his last two birthdays. And last Christmas. Last night he took one of your old sweatshirts and stuffed it with a pillow and slept holding it. He said it felt like he was hugging you.'

Shepherd felt as if he'd been punched in the chest. 'I'm sorry, Sue. Really. I'll make this up to you.'

'You need to think about what you're doing, Dan,' she said. 'I know how important the SAS is to you, but we didn't sign up for this.'

Shepherd rubbed the bridge of his nose. The Chinook had flown off into the distance and the air around him was still thick with dust but that only half-explained the tears that were pricking his eyes. 'Honey, I'm sorry.' He took a deep breath. 'I will make it up to you. I swear.'

'Just be careful. And come back in one piece, you hear me?'

'I hear you.'

'I love you. We both do.'

'I love you too, honey.'

There was a lot more he wanted to say but he knew that there was nothing he could tell her that would make her any happier and the longer he stayed on the line the more he risked upsetting her, so he ended the call.

* * *

The Major arranged for a US surveillance drone to be routed over Tora Bora, and later that day he called in Spud and Shepherd to examine the footage on a laptop. Mist and squally snow showers made it hard to decipher much detail but it was clear that Taj was right – something was going on in the mountains. The valley was so steep-sided and narrow it could almost have been a ravine, but there were fresh tracks through the snow, following the river and then cutting away at a steep angle up a narrow, precipitous path. The path, barely wide enough for two men to pass, lead to a series of caves. Geometric shapes that might have been stone-walled defensive sangers were positioned on the ridge above and at intervals along the cliff face overlooking the track.

'Something's definitely going on there,' the Major said, 'but it's hard to see exactly what. Someone's going to have to go in for a look-see.'

'We'll need a heli-lift for three two-man teams,' said Spud.

'I'm not sure about that,' said the Major. 'That terrain and altitude are iffy. The approaches to the valley are crawling with muj and Taliban, so we're risking compromise, and if they've got Stingers...' He left the rest of the sentence hanging. 'We'll go in over land. We can use ex-Sov vehicle, there are enough of them lying around Bagram. The Sov UAZ 469s are just like Land Rovers. I'll get the mechanics on the case.'

Twenty-four hours later, they had three UAZ 469s fuelled and ready and the Major called everyone in for a final briefing.

Major Gannon went over the map and the satellite imagery together, identifying possible sites for the OPs that the two teams would use to locate enemy sangers and defensive positions.

The dirt-track road leading to the valley where the caves were sited was heavily defended and there was no possibility of approaching that way. The Major traced the line of the dirt-track road running up the valley to the north of the Tora Bora valley, and stabbed his finger at a point where the faint line of a side-track could be seen, ending in a straggling clump of trees by what might have been the ruins of a house or goat pen near the river. 'You can leave the vehicles there,' he said, 'and climb the ridge, though it'll be a stiff climb. It's well over then thousand feet.'

'There is a track,' Taj said, pointing to a wavering line up the ridge, so faint as to be almost invisible.

'What's it used by?' asked Shepherd. 'Mountain goats?'

Spud's team and the other SAS team would be infiltrating the valley from the other side, crossing a lower ridge to reach their OP sites. The Para Support Group with the heavy weapons would move up to a Forward Operating Base near the entrance to the valley, outside the Taliban defences but close enough to make a rapid intervention.

The Major straightened up as he addressed the men. 'You know the prime target we're seeking is code name Muj 1, but snipers, if you make positive IDs on targets, make sure you have permission to fire from your Sunray before engaging. This may be highly sensitive and we don't want any cock-ups.' Shepherd and Spud exchanged a brief glance, knowing that the cock-ups usually came a lot further up the chain of command than the men in the front line.

'Comms. The usual call signs: Snipers prefix Sierra, assault troops Alpha, support groups Quebec, and all leaders are Sunray. Snipers, assault groups and the support heavy weapons, all have your own internal nets,' the Major said. 'Everything's encrypted so everyone can talk in real time and the only reason to use codes would be to shorten the time, so "Fetch Sunray" will do it instead of "I want to talk to the Boss". We'll keep you separate to stop the net from getting clogged up with traffic, but if you need mortars or other support, tell the Head Shed and we'll link you in with the other nets if necessary. The Head Shed on the ground will monitor and control, but we also have a link back to Bagram patched through to the UK, so they'll be exercising tactical control from there.'

Shepherd and Spud exchanged another world-weary glance. Signals traffic was always monitored in Bagram, where they would arrange any air- or heavy weapons support that was called for, but the army - the Green Army as SAS men dismissively termed it - would also be involved. Shepherd was far from happy about it as it smacked of too many cooks, but it was the way that wars were fought and there was no point in saying anything.

'I know you guys would rather work autonomously but that's not going to happen here,' he said as if reading Shepherd's mind. 'The Americans are running things so everything has to be run by them and that's done at a pay grade much higher than mine. So, again, you need permission to fire from Sunray. No excuses.'

'What if we come under attack, boss?' asked Spud, at the same moment it had occurred to Shepherd.

'I'm not going to say no exceptions, Spud. But if you fire without authorization, you'd better have a bloody good reason because you'll have to justify every round down the line.'

The comms system was secure but it was increasingly complex. Anything Shepherd transmitted in the field would be immediately encrypted. It went up to one satellite, where it was encrypted again, and then a second one, where it was encrypted for a third time, before being sent down to a recipient who might be two hundred yards or two thousand miles away. The Head Shed would consist of a couple of bosses led by the Major, with two or three signallers monitoring Shepherd and the other SAS crews, and a couple more sending back to Bagram. There would also be an overview in COBRA in London, and quite possibly the White House, since politicians tended to treat special ops as a spectator sport. Even if it wasn't patched through to the USA, since the comms system was licensed from the

US and used American satellites, all the SAS troopers knew that anything they said and did could be seen and heard by the US military. So pulling a fast one on the Americans was pretty much out of the question.

As they left the Major's quarters, Shepherd slapped Lex on the back. 'Got your own set of Passive Night Goggles yet?'

Lex shook his head. 'No.'

'Now's your chance. They're very expensive but easy to acquire. If we get in a fire-fight, when we're on our way out again, stash your PNGs in your grab bag and tell the quartermaster you lost them in the confusion; that way you'll have your own set in future - it's how I got mine.'

They headed for the weapons store and armoury, a small concrete bunker buried under a mound of bulldozed earth. Lex filled his bergen with ammunition for his M16, then watched as Shepherd collected his ammo. He held up a bullet for Lex to admire. '.50 ammo,' he said. 'High tech stuff. The rounds are precision-engineered with a titanium-tipped head. Plus I use two types of mass produced ammo: the ones with red bands around the business end are APTI - Armour Piercing Tracer Incendiary. The ones with yellow bands are APTP - the second "P" is for Phosphorous. I use them for target marking, you get puffs of white smoke where they strike.'

Shepherd had a small personal radio, like a sat-phone, on his right shoulder, so he merely had to take a sideways glance to see what channel and frequency he was on. Like the other old SAS hands, he also had a voice-activated, throat-mic, keeping his hands free. The new guys, still with much to learn, mostly opted for the hand-operated switch that they had to press to talk.

They set out in the early afternoon. All of them wore Afghan clothing and headgear. They were all fresh from tours in the Middle East and, with skin burned by the sun and at least a few days growth of beard, they could just about pass as Afghans to any villagers they passed. Shepherd, Lex, and Taj took the lead vehicle, with Spud in the next with one of the SAS rookies, and the other two-man team bringing up the rear. Taj had an AK74, the updated and smaller calibre version of the ubiquitous AK47, ammunition belts and a pack loaded with even more ammunition. Apart from the weapon and ammo he could have been dressed for a country stroll, with his rations - rice, almonds and raisins - in a small pouch around his waist. 'Is that all the kit you've got, Taj?' Shepherd said.

The Afghan nodded. 'It's all I need.'

'I've heard about traveling light, but you take the biscuit,' said Shepherd.

'I have no biscuits,' said Taj. Shepherd couldn't tell if the Afghan was joking or not.

They drove out of the base and took the road to the south, soon leaving the city well behind. The road was rough and the only traffic was an occasional vividly-painted, ancient Afghan truck rumbling past in a cloud of diesel fumes.

Signs of the country's perpetual war were everywhere: shell-blasted and bombed buildings, wrecked trucks and rusting military equipment, much of it from the Soviet era. The people they passed paused to stare at them, their expressions neither friendly nor hostile, merely watchful, and everyone they passed carried a weapon. 'Have you seen that, even the kids have got AK47s,' said Lex.

Paths at the edge of villages were marked by lines of white stones, showing cleared pathways through the minefields that covered much of the country.

They drove by a roadside stall, roofed with torn sacking, selling sandals cut from used tyres and cooking pots made from beaten, reclaimed metal that still bore traces of camouflage paint and cyrillic lettering, and a collection of wooden limbs, perhaps harvested from the dead for re-use. The only goods that looked new were the racks of Kalashnikovs and the boxes of ammunition. The shopkeeper was an old man, his face the colour of a weathered satchel, a steel hook where his left hand had once been.

There were brief glimpses of the rich, fertile country that had once been known as "The Crossroads of Asia", but there were few people tilling the fields and almost all of them were old men. 'This is what three generations of war has done to my country,' Taj said. 'The young men are gone either to fight for or against the Taliban or they are already dead. Only the old remain.'

As the valley narrowed, the road passed through an abandoned village, the mud-brick houses already returning to the earth from which they were formed. The crumbling mosque still had remnants of the shimmering blue tiles that must once have covered it, but it was pocked with bullet holes and blackened by fire. The pool for ritual bathing was dry and filled with rubble, and the mulberry and walnut trees that had once shaded it had been shattered by shellfire.

Just beyond the village, a spindly tree had been dragged across the road, and two figures stood behind it, an older man with a long grey beard and a boy who was barely as tall as the AK47 he was holding. 'What do you think?' Shepherd said, his hand resting on his rifle.

'They're not Taliban,' Taj said. 'Just a couple of villagers trying to levy a toll of a few Afghanis for crossing their land.'

'Then let's pay them,' Shepherd said. 'Why look for trouble before we need to? You do the talking.'

He slowed to a halt and Taj jumped out, walked over to the makeshift barrier and exchanged a few words with the old man. Whatever the old man asked for, Taj greeted it with a roar of laughter. He shook his head, thrust a few crumpled Afghani notes into the old man's hand, then turned his back without waiting for a reply and strode back to the vehicle. After a momentary hesitation, the two villagers dragged the tree off the road and Shepherd accelerated away.

'How much did he want?' asked Shepherd.

'A hundred dollars.'

'How much did you give him?'

Taj laughed. 'A lot less than that.'

The terrain grew ever more bleak and forbidding the farther they drove. The walls of the mountains rose higher around them and the soaring, jagged, snow-capped peaks were thrown into even starker relief by the low sun. Steep scree slopes were punctuated by mountain torrents and waterfalls tumbling down black cliff faces, the wind tossing the spray high into the air.

Just beyond a perilous stone bridge, a rough side-track split from the road. It led around a rocky crag and down towards a ruined house, sheltered by a stand of cedars and larches on the banks of a rushing green river in the valley floor. 'This is the place,' Taj said. 'The valley we want is beyond that ridge.' He pointed beyond the river at the rocky, scree-strewn slopes, rising to what looked like an almost sheer, snow-covered ridge line. Shepherd checked his GPS and nodded. They swung off the road and bounced and jolted down the track, coming to a halt at a point where they were screened by the trees from the road.

Taj got out, crouched on the banks of the stream and scooped up a few handfuls of water. Shepherd and Lex drank from their water bottles. 'What now?' Lex said.

'We wait for the sun to go down,' said Shepherd said. He gestured at the bleak mountainside above them, 'We'd be sitting ducks up there in daylight.'

They set out as soon as night had fallen. Shepherd had his sniper rifle on a sling leaving his hands free for an AK47. The sniping rifle was perfect for long distance but if the fighting got up close and personal he wanted something less fancy in his hands. Taj cradled his AK74 and Lex had the standard Para Support Group M-16.

All of them wore PNGs, turning the night into an eerie, yellow-tinted landscape. Shepherd watched as Lex prepared himself and stopped him as he began to put his trauma dressing into one of the pockets of his jacket. 'Word to the wise,' he said. 'Keep your dressing on your left chest or left arm where you can get to it straight away; even a delay of a few seconds while you fumble with your pocket could be fatal. And keep your morphine syrettes on a bit of para cord round your neck, that way you can get to it straight away if you're hit.'

The first obstacle was the narrow but fast-flowing river. The only way across was to get into the water and that meant taking off their clothes because wet clothes at night would be a killer. He stripped off his clothes and tied them in a bundle, gesturing for Lex to do the same. 'I'll cross first,' Taj said, 'I've been doing this since I was a boy.'

'What about my boxers?' asked Lex.

'Everything,' said Shepherd. 'You can dry yourself after you've crossed but wet clothes will stay wet.' He chuckled. 'Don't worry, Lex, you haven't got anything we haven't all seen before.'

Taj pulled off his clothes revealing a back as hairy as a bear's. 'Give me a rope,' he said. Shepherd handed him his tac line, a coil of nylon rope with a carabineer on one end. Taj secured one end with a quick release knot to the trunk of a larch just above the water's edge. He put his pack back on, hoisted his bundle of clothes onto his head and, holding his rifle aloft in his other hand, slipped into the river and moved away.

The bitterly-cold current was fierce but he never seemed to slip or stumble and soon afterwards Shepherd saw him clamber out on the far bank and secure the rope around a boulder. Shepherd sent Lex next and then began to edge across after him. He let out an involuntary gasp as he lowered himself into the icy water. It rose above his waist, lapping against the bottom of the bergen on his back, as he began to inch across, grateful for the rope, for the current tugged at him and the rocks underfoot were smooth and slippery.

As he approached the bank, he threw his bundle of clothes onto the ground ahead of him and pulled himself out. He heard Lex's teeth chattering and hissed to him 'Rub yourself dry with your shirt or you'll freeze.' He took his own shirt from his bundle and began to do the same, his flesh burning in the cold. Taj, impassive, had already dressed, as if a stark naked crossing of a freezing river was all in a day's work.

Shepherd retrieved the rope and they moved off. The ground sloped steeply upwards and the cold was soon forgotten with the effort of climbing. Taj moved with a slow, relentless stride. They climbed higher, a zig-zagging ascent as the track wound its way across the face of the mountain, pausing frequently to watch and listen, waiting for the blood to cease pounding in their ears as they searched for any trace of noise or movement in the darkness above them.

As the gradient increased, they had to use their hands to haul themselves upwards. They passed the snow line, clambering on across hard frozen snow and ice-covered rocks that made every step a gamble, and still the ridge was high above them. The Afghan winter was coming on and it was ferociously cold. The physical effort left Shepherd and Lex fighting for breath, but Taj, born and raised in the mountains, was totally unfazed by it.

After what seemed an eternity of crawling slowly upwards, his head pounding from oxygen deprivation and with the dead weight of his bergen making every step an ordeal, Shepherd saw the crest of the ridge no more than fifty yards above them. Taj had stopped, waiting and listening once more, and he now signalled to Shepherd and Lex to get down. The two men flattened themselves to the ground, pressing their faces into the gritty snow. Taj drew his curved Afghan knife and moved up the mountainside. He paused just below the ridgeline, and then moved forward again and disappeared from their sight.

The minutes dragged and Shepherd was about to move up the slope when a dark shape appeared on the ridge above and to their right. The next instant, it slid down the mountainside, gathering ice and stones in a miniature avalanche as it fell. A second later, another dark form followed it. As it fell, Shepherd heard Taj's voice in his earpiece. 'Come up, it's clear.'

When they reached the ridge, Taj was cleaning his knife. 'Two,' he said, baring his teeth in a savage smile. 'But both were sleeping.' He slid the knife back into its sheath.

'Did they have radios?' asked Shepherd.

'No, and the Taliban often sends sentries to such places for a week or more before they're relieved, so it may be some time before their disappearance is discovered.'

If Shepherd had had any remaining doubts about Taj's value and trustworthiness, they were now completely resolved. He had risked his own life to clear the way for Shepherd and Lex. A few moments later, they were looking down into the upper reaches of the Tora Bora valley. The rock-strewn slopes were as bleak and featureless as the surface of the moon. There were no trees or grass, just bare ice, rock and scree. They began the descent into the valley, moving even more cautiously now, inching their way, climbing down the rock faces and crossing the open slopes from boulder to boulder, using the natural cover and avoiding the loose screes that would give them away.

Two hours before dawn, they reached the position Shepherd had identified from the surveillance imagery and set up their OP overlooking the caves. Two huge boulders jutting from the mountainside provided cover and some shelter from the bitter wind. In front of them, a rock ledge a few metres wide, part-covered with a thin layer of gritty soil, gave them a platform from which they could observe the caves and the track leading to them.

Shepherd wormed his way forward, feeling the ammo vest on his chest catching on small stones and projecting edges of rock. Still wearing his PNGs, Shepherd scanned the area, searching for suspiciously regular shapes or movement that would give away the presence of enemy soldiers or equipment, but the goggles didn't have much magnification and the yellow tint blurred his vision.

He took off his goggles and used the sniper scope to focus first on the area surrounding the caves. The sniper scope had a twenty-five fold magnification without having the same distortion as the PNGs, and it picked up a lot of ambient light. He was able to identify a series of defensive sangers just above the track and what might have been the barrels of heavy weapons in some of them, clearly outlined against patches of fresh snow.

He turned his attention to the caves and saw something. Activity. Heavily armed men, some in turbans and black robes and others in what looked like white Arab robes, entering and leaving.

Shepherd wormed his way back to Taj and Lex in the deeper shadows at the foot of the boulders and checked his radio channel. 'Sunray, Sierra 5. Eyes on the target. Much activity, defensive positions and heavy weapons. At least fifty men visible outside the caves.'

He heard the other OPs checking in, adding their intelligence. There was now no doubt that, at the least, they were looking at a substantial Taliban or al Qaeda stronghold. But it was also possible - and Shepherd felt a jolt of adrenaline at the thought - that they had found Bin Laden's lair.

He could imagine the buzz of excitement at the Head Shed at Bagram and even more so in London and Washington. The intelligence was now not from rumour or satellite surveillance, but from eyes on the ground, and he knew that it would galvanize the Regiment into action. His earpiece crackled again. 'Sierra 5, Sunray. Maintain Eyes On and wait out.'

As dawn broke, he carefully removed the protective foam from his rifle, took his sniper scope from his grab bag and assembled the rifle, zeroing them to one point. He laid it down on the foam rubber, careful not to give it the least knock that might throw it off, then settled down for what experience told him would be a long wait. In theory, a Quick Reaction Force could be on its way, if not within minutes, at least within hours. In practice, days might pass before an order to attack was given, as the various arms of the forces of the two nations jostled for position, and the politicians and spin doctors in Whitehall and Capitol Hill positioned themselves to claim the credit if successful and deflect the blame if not.

Throughout the day they watched a steady flow of arrivals and departures from the caves. Near midday, one of the Taliban's red Toyota pick-ups pulled up at the foot of the track to the cave. The back was packed with soldier monks with kohl-rimmed eyes and the forked tails of their black turbans flying in the breeze. They looked like young boys, but each of them clutched an RPG or an AK47. While the driver painstakingly turned around, what appeared to be a delegation made their way up to the cave. They remained inside for forty minutes and then emerged and drove off again. Shepherd reported the sighting over the net, one more piece of the jigsaw in place.

Towards sunset the Major patched Shepherd into the net with the other teams. 'We're going in,' the Boss said. 'Alpha 1, can you set LTDs? I'm going to ask for top cover, the jet jockeys are the only heavy stuff we can use, we're out of artillery range.

The LTDs were laser targeting devices that would be used to bathe the target in a light visible only to the planes or choppers that would attack the stronghold.

Shepherd heard Spud's reply. 'Sunray, Alpha 1. I'll try but it might not work. We can set them up all right, but they need a level surface to reflect from and the rock face around the caves is as rough as they come. And the valley's narrow, steep-sided, and twists and turns like a corkscrew. I don't think the jets will be able to get close enough.'

'What about the attack helis?'

'We trained some of the guys down there, remember. We taught them how to catch the Sovs in a crossfire from the valley sides and shoot them down. They may or may not have Stingers, but they can do the job just as well with heavy machine guns and RPGs. They may be up on the ridges above where the top cover might fly and shoot down on them like they did the Sovs.'

There was a silence, broken only by the hiss of static, as the Major took instructions from up the line. 'We'll try with LTDs first,' he said at last. 'H Hour is 0500 hours. Suppressing fire to keep the Taliban heads down and the Support Group will move up at 0530.' He paused. 'One more thing. Our friends are running this operation, and they will be the lead teams going in.'

Shepherd gave a rueful smile. "Our friends" was the standard euphemism for US Special Forces. Not for the first time, it looked like SAS would do the spade work and Delta would get the gongs and glory.

Spud's voice interrupted him. 'Sunray, Alpha 1. We're here, they're not.'

'They will be, and they will lead. The decision is from the highest level.'

Shepherd glanced at Lex. 'Hear that? The White House has spoken, we're bag-carriers for the Yanks again.'

Just after eleven that night, Shepherd watched through his scope and his PNGs as Spud's team broke cover and inched their way down the valley sides, through the rubble of rocks and drifts of gravel washed down by the winter floods. One would move while the other covered him, ready to unleash an avalanche of fire if they were detected.

They slipped silently past the defences where Taliban and Arab mujahedeen dozed. He watched as they forded the river, then Spud took the lead up the facing slopes. They paused a quarter of a mile from the cave entrance and placed the first of the laser targeting devices, no bigger than a paperback book. They sited two more LTDs at intervals of fifty yards, then crept back the way they had come. They had covered no more than three quarters of a mile of ground, but it had taken them four hours to do so.

At five that morning, still a couple of hours before dawn, Shepherd heard the roar of jets and the first crumps of explosions as bombs began raining down on the Taliban positions further down the valley.

He looked towards the cave mouth where figures could be seen racing in all directions, like wasps buzzing around a shattered nest. Moments later the first A10 jets roared up the valley towards them, punching out clouds of chaff and flares to throw off any missiles. It pulled a sharp turn well short of Shepherd's OP, releasing its bomb load as it did so, before swinging away over the valley walls. He watched the parabola of the bomb's flight, but it fell well short of the caves and detonated harmlessly among the rocks on the valley floor. A second and a third followed and also fell short.

He spoke into the net. 'Sunray, Sierra 5. They're throwing bombs but they're not connecting with the lasers and falling well short. The valley's too tight, they can't get close enough.'

He could imagine the reaction from Spud and the other Assault Groups. They would now know this battle was not going to be fought from a distance – it was going to be up close and personal.

'Sunray, all groups. Intelligence from our friends: the cave system is a labyrinth of tunnels, sealed by iron or steel doors and extending deep into the mountain. They have concrete floors, a ventilation system, hydro-electric power and an armoury of weaponry and ammunition, that could supply an army of two thousand men.'

Shepherd looked across at Taj, who shook his head vigorously. 'They are natural caves and you would struggle to get more than two hundred men inside them,' hissed the Afghan.

'They could have been extended since the Soviet War,' said Shepherd.

Taj shook his head fiercely. 'My friend, I told you, I know these mountains and the people who live here or pass through here. Nothing happens here that I do not get to hear about.'

Shepherd nodded. 'Sunray, Sierra 5. Our man says that's BS. They're just small, natural caves, holding two hundred men, tops.'

'Maybe, but the friends are not going to believe that until they see it for themselves,' said the Major.

Just before zero hour, a fresh rain of bombs fell, dropped by B-52s so high above them they were only visible from the contrails in the icy winter sky. The explosions kept the enemy heads down but had little other impact.

It had taken the US seventy to ninety Cruise Missiles and a series of saturation bombing raids by B-52s to destroy four al Qaeda training camps sited in open desert in 1998. In this jagged, boulder-strewn terrain, a target could be within a few yards of an exploding bomb and suffer no more than a ringing in their ears. Shepherd knew that no matter what weight of ordnance the US brought to bear, they could not bomb the mountains into submission. If Bin Laden was here, he would only be flushed out by fighting troops.

At 5.30 am the percussive thud of mortar fire and the rattle of heavy machine guns showed that the ground battle was underway. As dawn broke, they could see the enemy fighters being slowly pushed back, but it was, literally, an uphill struggle for the Paras of the Support Group, attacking an enemy who was well entrenched on the higher ground. Even the air power that normally gave a decisive advantage in any pitched battle was almost nullified in this forbidding, almost impossible terrain. As Spud had warned, the surrounding mountain ridges were close to the height ceiling for attack helicopters and the approach up the valley floor would force them to run a gauntlet of anti-aircraft fire.

Shepherd heard the chopping sound of rotors and saw the dark shapes of a formation of Blackhawks inserting the guys from Delta Force. The attack choppers were laying down a barrage of suppressing fire from their rocket and machine gun pods, but there was a blizzard of answering fire from both flanks of the valley and the Blackhawks' array of electronic countermeasures were no defence against crude weapons like heavy machine guns and RPG's.

As Shepherd watched, an RPG streaked upwards and the lead Blackhawk erupted in flame. It slewed sideways, a rotor clipped the rock face in a shower of sparks, and the next moment the Blackhawk plummeted down, spinning crazily and exploded like a bomb.

The next Blackhawk in the formation emerged through the pall of black smoke and went into a brief hover as its cargo of troops spilled out and took firing positions in one fluid movement. The chopper was already speeding back the way it had come with bullets striking sparks from its fuselage. The next, hit by intersecting streams of HMG fire, made a crash landing and burst into flames. Shepherd counted the figures tumbling from it; only four of its ten-man payload emerged from the wreck. The remaining Blackhawks turned and flew back down the valley, still pursued by enemy fire.

He dragged his eyes away and, while Lex was on maximum alert scanning in all directions for risks, Shepherd began raking the enemy positions through his scope, searching out high value targets, those giving orders. He spotted one figure in black Taliban robes who was directing fire, and at once trained the scope on him and began the firing ritual that he had practised thousands of times. First, the firm but relaxed grip on the weapon, his eye glued to the scope, his mind closed to all distractions. Then the gentle first pressure on the trigger, the sighing exhaled breath and the final smooth, steady pressure on the trigger. Last, the recoil into his shoulder and the familiar sight of a target turning from a living figure one moment to a collapsing lump of dead meat the next.

Shepherd was also target marking for the Assault Teams. He spotted Spud's group, identifiable by the recognition markings they had placed to indicate their positions. Invisible from ground-level, they were primarily intended to identify their positions to supporting aircraft to prevent "blue on blue" casualties but, from his elevated position above the battlefield, he could clearly make them out. Spud's team were exchanging fire with muj fighters, but Shepherd saw an HMG in a sanger on the mountainside being brought to bear on them.

'Sunray, Sierra 5. Patch Alpha 1.' There was no time for courtesies or wasted words in the heat of battle.

A second later, he heard Spud's voice, almost drowned by the bark and rattle of small arms fire. 'Alpha 1.'

'Sierra 5. HMG, 350 yards bearing 020.'

There was a pause then 'Alpha 1. I have no visual. Repeat: no visual.'

'Sierra 5. Stand by. Stand by. Will spot it for you. Watch for my phos.' He reached into his ammo belt for two of the yellow tipped APTP phosphorous rounds. He aimed and fired and at once saw puffs of white smoke against the sanger where the machine gun was sited. A moment later there was the ferocious clatter of Spud's GPMG and Shepherd saw rounds chewing at the edge of the sanger, blasting stone chips in all directions and striking sparks from the enemy machine gun. There was a whoosh as an SAS trooper with an M203 launched a grenade and a fireball erupted from the sanger. Peering through his scope, Shepherd checked for movement in the sanger, then said 'Sierra 5. Problem solved.'

'Ta for that.'

Shepherd began to scan the battlefield again, when Lex suddenly grabbed his arm and pointed 'What the fuck is that?'

Shepherd followed his gaze and froze. 'And where the hell did it come from?' he said.

An armoured vehicle, like a miniature mediaeval castle on tank tracks, was rumbling towards the attackers, its turret swivelling as its heavy machine gun sprayed them with fire. Along each of its armoured steel sides there was a row of five small gun ports and the barrels of AK47s poked from them, spitting more fire. One of the SAS men fired his M203, but the grenade bounced harmlessly off the armour and exploded. A burst of fire from one of the gimpies was no more effective. The attacking troops were scattering as it roared towards them, and when Spud came on the net, Shepherd could hear the urgency in his voice, tinged with what might have been fear. 'Sunray, Alpha 1. Russian BMPI, tracked, armoured troop carrier. 76 mm gun, ten men firing AK47s from inside. We need support. We're pinned down and we've no Milans or even M72s. Who knew they had armour up here?'

'Sierra 5,' Shepherd said. 'Any weak points?'

'The tracks,' Spud said, 'but we've nothing can damage them enough. And the fuel tanks.'

'Where are they?'

'Bulbous shapes on the rear doors, but they're armoured too.'

Shepherd was already loading his .50 rifle with APTI incendiary rounds. As the BMPI halted, raking the SAS positions with fire, Shepherd took aim and began firing at the rear doors. The shots were marked by white streaks of tracer, and almost at once they drew answering fire from muj fighters, but Shepherd was shielded by the rock ledge and at maximum killing range for their weapons, though well within his. His first shot struck the top of the doors, the armour piercing round punching a hole in the plating. His next was a couple of inches lower. 'What are you doing?' said Lex, 'aim for the bottom where the fuel is.'

'You can't ignite the liquid fuel,' Shepherd said calmly, firing as he spoke. 'I'm aiming for the gap where there's a fuel and air mixture, not pure fuel.' He fired three more rounds and had a sinking feeling as each one failed to ignite the fuel.

He lowered his aim another couple of inches and fired again. The round struck home and in that instant, the armoured vehicle disappeared from sight, engulfed in a cloud of flame. As the inferno began to ease, he could see the vehicle ground to a halt, its machine gun silenced and tongues of flame licking from the gun ports. The hatch was half-open and a blackened limb, barely recognizable as a human arm, protruded from it. Shepherd could think of few worse deaths, but he closed his mind to that thought and raised the scope to his eye again, already seeking fresh targets.

The muj and Taliban fighters were pressing hard and the SAS and Para Support Group's flank was dangerously exposed, with the Delta Force troops pinned down as they tried to advance alongside them.

'Where the fuck are the rest of Delta?' asked Lex.

'They're inserting on foot,' said Shepherd.

The Delta Force troops who had survived the Blackhawk crash were pinned down by heavy enemy fire, and must have called in support from mortars, because two rounds came crashing down. They fell, not on the enemy, but close to where the SAS were.

'Stop-Stop-Stop!' Shepherd said. 'Abort mortars. They're hitting our guys.' He fell silent, horrified, as another pair of mortar shells fell. One dropped in dead ground twenty yards from the SAS position, but the other struck the rock they were using as cover and exploded at once. Shepherd saw a body thrown in the air, come crashing down several yards away. It lay exposed and Taliban rounds chewed the ground around it and struck the body, as a dark pool of blood spread around it.

Over the net, he heard the words they all dreaded: 'All stations. Minimize.' That meant 'Shut up, there's a crisis,' and was normally used only when there were casualties. It was followed at once by 'Oboe! Oboe!', SAS-speak for everybody get off the net right away. It was confirmation, if any were needed, that men were down. 'We have casualties. Alpha 1, Alpha 4, Alpha 7, Alpha 9. Two KIA. One serious trauma of the lower left limb. One major abdominal trauma. Request immediate casevac. Repeat two KIA. One serious trauma lower left limb. One serious abdominal trauma. Vital signs deteriorating. Request immediate casevac.'

Shepherd felt his heart lurch. Alpha 1 was Spud. He listened to the traffic on the net as, like an automaton, he continued to monitor the battlefield, even dropping another muj commander as he showed himself for a moment to urge his men forward. The mortars had stopped. When they resumed, they were landing among the muj and Taliban defenders, giving the Delta Force men enough respite to regroup and advance to close up with the Paras and the remnants of the SAS teams.

The light was beginning to fade - the battle had lasted all day - but it was now turning in the favour of the coalition forces. Delta Force Support Group were bringing up more and more heavy weapons and mortar shells were now raining on the enemy positions. The muj and their Taliban allies had already lost many men dead and wounded, and the remainder were slowly being driven back towards the caves.

As the battlefront moved away, Shepherd saw medics stretchering three SAS men away from the crater where the mortar shell had detonated among them. One lay motionless, face masked in blood, the other two were moving, but obviously badly wounded. 'Sunray, Sierra 5. Our guys were displaying ID markers I could see through my scope. We've lost four good men, wounded, crippled or killed, because some trigger-happy American fuckwit who thinks he's John Wayne fired first and thought afterwards.'

'Sierra 5, Sunray. This isn't the time for that. I understand your feelings, but we still need you to do your job.'

'Sunray, Sierra 5. Roger that. But when this is over...'

He broke off as Taj tugged at his arm. He had been a frustrated, peripheral figure throughout much of the fighting, firing his AK 74 at Taliban targets from near-maximum range, but he was now gesturing frantically at something further up the valley. Shepherd tracked his gaze, and through his scope he saw a small group of figures slipping out of a narrow fissure in the rock about two hundred yards from the main cave mouth, and making their way in single file along a narrow rock ledge leading away up the valley. Among them was one man well over six foot tall, who towered over his companions. He was grey-bearded and wore a camouflage jacket, with a white turban wound around his head, but he was moving away from Shepherd, so he couldn't make a definitive ID.

'Sunray. Probable Muj 1. Clear engage?'

'Negative,' said the Major.

'I can't see his face, but I'm certain it's him.'

'Negative. Permission refused. Do not engage. Repeat, do not engage.'

As Shepherd watched, the tall figure and the rest of the group rounded a buttress of rock and moved on out of sight.

Taj pulled at his arm again. 'Follow me.'

'Wait one,' Shepherd said and spoke into the net. 'Sunray, Sierra 5. Permission to move.'

'Negative. Hold position.'

Shepherd looked at Taj, then said 'Fuck it.' He turned to Lex. 'Follow me and keep my arse covered.' He slid back from the ledge, slung his sniper rifle on his back and, holding his AK47, followed Taj away from the battlefield, moving at a diagonal up the slope towards the ridge. A bitter wind was blowing snow flurries over the slopes and they battled against it up to the ridgeline, then turned east into the teeth of the wind, following the ridge through the gathering darkness. He looked over his shoulder. Lex was close behind him.

They paused to put on their PNGs and moved on with Taj still leading, picking his way among the rocks, as sure-footed as a goat. Some way ahead they could see movement, dark figures moving steadily upwards, outlined against the snow-covered screes close to the head of the valley. Shepherd thought about a shot but decided against it. He wanted to shorten the range to be certain of a hit.

They were now hidden from the battlefield and the sound of firing had faded, carried away on the wind. As they moved on, the upper reaches of the valley opened up to them and he could see a notch in the skyline, a narrow pass towards which the group was heading. As he stared towards it, Shepherd saw two figures waiting by it, holding the reins of a group of mountain ponies. 'Faster Taj,' he said, quickening his own pace. He looked back. Lex was falling behind but he didn't have time to wait for him.

Taj and Shepherd moved on at route march speed, no longer attempting to conceal their pursuit, the gap steadily narrowing. At last, Shepherd called a halt, trying to calm his laboured breathing as he took the sniper rifle from his back and once more sight-zeroed it, begrudging the time it took, but knowing the jolting it had taken on the march along the ridge would have thrown it off. He studied the group through the scope as they reached the horses and began to mount. The tall figure showed his profile as he was helped on to a horse and Shepherd made a positive ID. It was Muj 1 - Osama Bin Laden.

'Sunray, Sierra 5. Muj 1. Positive ID. 100%. Permission to fire.'

'Negative,' said the Major. 'Do not engage. Do not disobey this order.'

'What? I have him cold. He's the reason we're all here.'

'Negative. Permission refused. Do not engage.'

'Are you insane?'

'The Yanks want to do it. 9/11 gives them that right. We're the junior partner here.'

'So where are they - waiting for their helmet-cams so George Dubya and the boys back home can watch?'

'Delta Force are now in the caves but they can't find him.'

'That's because he isn't there. Muj 1 is almost out of the head of the valley. I've got him in my sights. I can take him right now.'

'Negative. Permission refused. Do not engage.'

Shepherd cursed under his breath, then dropped to the ground and lay still, calming his breathing as he brought up the rifle until Bin Laden's head filled the scope. He was in the middle of the line of horsemen and now almost at the summit of the pass, in a narrow defile between two rocky crags. It was now or never. He took up the first pressure, exhaled and fired. Bin Laden's head disappeared from the scope but there was no spray of blood. Instead, the rider in front of him now filled the scope, his back arched and arms flung wide as he slumped from his horse.

Shepherd swung the scope down. Bin Laden's horse was on its knees. It had stumbled in the instant that Shepherd had fired. Muj 1 was now scrambling from the saddle, stepping over the prone body of his comrade and scrambling for the summit. Three of his escorts ran with him. The others, heedless of their own safety, stood in the open firing at the point from which the muzzle flash had come.

Shepherd ignored the incoming fire. He found his target again in the scope and fired in one movement, but Bin Laden was already diving for the cover of the rocks at the summit, and he disappeared from sight as the round struck the rock face and ricocheted away.

Shepherd scrambled to his feet and he and Taj set off at a run, using fire and movement to keep the muj heads down, but they had gone a couple of hundred yards when the wind strengthened still more and the snow flurries became a blizzard. They struggled on but eventually Taj put his hand on Shepherd's arm. 'Even I cannot find my way in a white-out, my friend. We have to turn back.'

Shepherd hesitated then gave a grudging nod. 'Sunray, Sierra 5,' he said for the benefit of his radio. 'Call off the dogs. Muj 1's gone. He'll be in Pakistan before daybreak. Oh, and Sunray, be sure to thank Delta Force for me, won't you? There'll be a price to pay for this fuck up.' He switched off his radio and cursed under his breath.

Taj patted him on the back. 'You did your best, my friend.'

'It wasn't good enough,' said Shepherd bitterly.

'We'll get another chance one day, insh'allah,' said the Afghan.

'I bloody well hope so,' said Shepherd.

DEAD DROP

AFGHANISTAN

July 2002.

Dan 'Spider' Shepherd shifted position slightly, trying to ease the pressure from the rocks beneath him and the ammo belt pressing into his chest. He lay prone, scanning the terrain through his sniperscope. A rough dirt road ran along the foot of the hillside below their observation post, leading to the village away to the east, a cluster of mud-brick buildings, surrounded by terraced fields, thick with the vivid pink blooms of opium poppies. The heat was ferocious, rising in waves from the stony hillside around them, while high above vultures were circling on the thermals, the feathers at their wingtips extended like claws as they flexed in the updraft. Shepherd could feel beads of sweat trickling down his brow, the salt and the moisture attracting still more of the flies that had been buzzing around them since they set up the OP.

'Instead of lying there scratching your arse, Geordie,' Shepherd said. 'Can you not use your ninja skills to catch a few of these bloody flies?'

Geordie Mitchell, lying next to him on the rock ledge, gave him a sideways look. 'No chance,' he said. 'Your flies, your problem.' He was in his early thirties but looked older. His pale blue eyes seemed as sun-faded as his fatigues and the stress of continual active service had etched deep lines into his face.

'They're attracted to rancid smells,' Jock McIntyre said in the gruff Scottish growl that made every sentence sound like a declaration of war. 'So it's not surprising they've gone for you.' His round face and open features gave him a guileless look that had led many to underestimate him. It was a dangerous mistake to make for he was as hard as Aberdonian granite. 'Anyway, pal,' he said. 'Look on the bright side: if they're buzzing round you, at least they're leaving us alone.'

The fourth member of the group, Lex Harper, a Para who acted as Shepherd's spotter - part target-spotter, part-bodyguard - whenever he was on sniper ops, smiled to himself but didn't join the banter, keeping his gaze ranging over the terrain, alert for any movement or anything out of place.

Shepherd settled himself again, gently placing his sniper rifle on the rock. He'd already zeroed the rifle and scope but the least knock could throw it off a fraction of an inch which would be more than enough to turn a kill into a miss.

Mitchell gave a theatrical sigh. 'You're so precious with that bloody rifle it's a wonder you don't raise your pinkie when you fire it.'

Shepherd grinned. 'You'd be precious with it, if I was ever dumb enough to trust it to you,' he said. 'It's state of the art kit and it cost the Regiment well over £ 20,000 but it's worth every penny. I could drill you a new arsehole from a mile and a half away with it.'

'For fuck's sake don't do that,' McIntyre said. 'He does enough farts with the one he's already got. I don't think I could stand them in stereo.'

Harper and Mitchell chuckled. Banter and swearing was the norm in the Regiment – it was the glue that bound them together.

Shepherd put the spotter scope back to his eye. A temporary checkpoint had been set up on the road directly below them, manned by two Afghan troops and four of Harper's mates from the Para Support Group, who always supported the Regiment on ops. The site for the checkpoint had been well chosen. It was set in dead ground, where the road dipped down to ford a river that had been a torrent of snow melt in the spring, but was now as dry and lifeless as the landscape around it. Hidden in the dip, the checkpoint was invisible to people approaching from either direction until they were almost upon it. If, as the Intelligence suggested, Taliban insurgents were planning a raid on the village to kill or kidnap the local headman, they would have no more than a few seconds warning of the checkpoint and no time to take evasive action. If they then tried to shoot it out, they would be cut down in the cross fire from the SAS and Para Support Group troops on either side, or the close air support that they could call on.

So far only a few men on foot and a handful of vehicles - and most of those were farm carts - had passed along the road. Mitchell yawned. 'Quiet out there, Tonto.'

'Too quiet, Kemo Sabi,' McIntyre said.

As they watched and waited in the OP, an old man passed through the checkpoint, herding a small flock of scrawny goats, followed a few minutes later by a peddler with a donkey cart piled with cooking pots, bowls and water vessels, cut and hammered out of scrap metal. Shepherd noticed the faint markings on one large bowl and nudged Mitchell. 'Look at that,' he said. 'We're fighting a war that even environmentalists would approve of - the muj are recycling the bombs the Yanks drop on them.'

'The VC used to do something similar in Vietnam,' said Mitchell. 'They turned shell casings into lamps for their underground bases. Waste not, want not.'

Two Afghan men carrying AK47s provoked a brief heightening of tension as they approached the checkpoint, but it was far from an unusual sight - every Afghan male carried a weapon of some sort - and after being searched they were allowed through the cordon and walked on towards the village.

The road was now empty save for a heavily pregnant woman in a faded blue burqa, carrying a bundle wrapped in a shawl in her arms, and making her slow way on foot along the road towards the checkpoint. Shepherd's gaze had moved on, scanning the area relentlessly, eyes never still, always searching for potential threats. Then the hairs on the back of his neck stood up. 'Hold it. An Afghan woman traveling alone?' he said. 'Something's not right.'

Mitchell followed his gaze. 'Doesn't walk like a woman either.'

The woman – if it was a woman - was now close to the checkpoint.

Harper tapped Shepherd's shoulder and gestured back along the track. Shepherd shot a glance that way and saw that a Toyota pick-up had appeared on the brow of the hill a mile and a half away. The pick-up stopped but the engine was still running because they could see the blue-grey haze from its exhaust. The driver was making no move to continue along the road. Shepherd swung his scope onto it. Four figures were visible in the back of the pick-up, the barrels of their weapons outlined against the lapis blue of the sky. As he peered into the shadowed cab of the pick-up, Shepherd saw twin discs of reflected light as the man in the passenger seat trained binoculars towards the checkpoint ahead. Shepherd barked into his throat mic. 'Abort! Abort! Abort! Suicide bomber!'

The guards at the checkpoint started to shout as they swung up their weapons, but the figure had now almost reached them. Shepherd was already on auto-pilot, running through a sequence of actions so often practised that they were almost instinctive. The head of the burqa-clad figure now filled Shepherd's sniperscope - only a head-shot would stop a bomber triggering a device. He took up the first pressure on the trigger, but even as he exhaled, squeezed the trigger home and felt the recoil, he saw that he was too late. A micro-second before the shot, the burqa-clad figure's had slapped against its chest and in that instant, there was a blinding flash. A moment later Shepherd heard the thunder-clap of an explosion and the shock wave swept over them in a whirlwind of dust and dirt. There was the whine and whirr of shrapnel fragments overhead and then the spattering sound of softer, human debris falling to earth around him.

Shepherd lifted his head. The site of the checkpoint was now as blood-soaked as a halal butcher's yard. A pall of oily smoke was rising from a crater in the centre of the dirt road where the burqa-clad figure had been standing when the device detonated. The man – for Shepherd had no doubt that it had been man passing himself off as a woman - had disappeared completely, with only a few shreds of blood-stained and smoke-blackened blue fabric to show he had ever existed. The troops who had been manning the checkpoint were sprawled around the crater, their bodies contorted into unnatural positions by the force of the blast. The two men who had been closest to the bomber were so mangled as to be almost unrecognisable as human. Partially shielded by their dead comrades, the four others were still alive - so far at least - but all were wounded. Shepherd knew that suicide bombers routinely packed shards of steel, sharp stones and fragments of broken glass around their devices to increase the carnage from the blast. All the men were bleeding badly, one with blood pumping in spurts from the stump that was all that was now left of his right arm. Nearby, the severed limb was dangling obscenely from the branch of a stunted acacia tree.

In his earpiece, Shepherd heard Mitchell, the patrol medic, calling in a casevac as he broke cover and sprinted down the hillside towards the bomb-site, where the Paras' own medic was already working frantically to tie a tourniquet around what was left of the soldier's arm.

Shepherd swung his rifle back towards the brow of the ridge, and caught a glimpse of the pick-up as it reversed back out of sight. He squeezed off a quick shot but he was at maximum range and with no time to aim it would have been a miracle if he had hit the target. A moment later he saw a cloud of dust billowing above the ridgeline as the driver span the pick-up around and raced away.

Shepherd could already hear McIntyre in his earpiece, calling in an air-strike on the pick-up, but he knew that the response, whether a Warthog - an A10 Thunderbolt with a rotary cannon that could spit out almost 4,000 rounds a minute - or a stub-winged Blackhawk firing chain guns and Hellfire missiles ,would take four or five minutes to reach the area. By then the Taliban killers who had sent the suicide bomber to his death would already have hidden their vehicle from sight in some cover or abandoned it and gone to ground.

They saw the distinctive shape of a Warthog in the sky to the west a few minutes later but there were no rumbles of explosions nor bursts of distant cannon-fire; the Taliban had obviously made good their escape.

The helis arrived soon afterwards to casevac the dead and wounded. Shepherd and his team helped to load them onto the casevac helis and then clambered into the Chinook that would fly them back to the base at Bagram. Bagram was home to more than seven thousand troops, most of them American, housed in huge tented compounds. And while the area surrounding the base was nominally controlled by the coalition forces, it still came under daily rocket attack.

As soon as they landed back at Bagram they went into an immediate debrief with Major Allan Gannon who had been in overall charge of the operation. Gannon was a big man with a strong chin, his hair bleached from the unrelenting Afghan sun. He was in his shirtsleeves and had a black and white checked keffiyeh scarf tied loosely around his neck as he led the debrief in the windowless, underground briefing room, its air-conditioning a welcome respite from the furnace heat of the Afghan summer.

As the others focussed on the implications of the Taliban's new tactic of disguising suicide bombers in burqas, Shepherd found himself thinking through the sequence of events he had witnessed. As he did so, he felt a growing sense of unease. 'How did they know?' he said eventually.

Major Gannon frowned. 'How did they know what?' he asked.

'It wasn't a regular checkpoint,' said Shepherd. 'We'd never had troops there before and we hadn't been in position for more than an hour. So how did the Taliban know we were there? They don't have suicide bombers wandering around the countryside on the off chance they'll bump into a patrol or a checkpoint. They target them at places where they know troops will be.'

Mitchell nodded in agreement, his face still blood-spattered from working on the casualties.

'So the intel was planted?' said the Major. 'They lured our boys out there to blow them up?'

'Or the op was bubbled,' Shepherd said. 'Compromised before it had even started. Either way, there's something rotten in the state of Denmark.'

'It's not the first time either,' said Mitchell.

'Seems like everything's being bubbled at the moment,' said The Major. 'It looks as if all our air and ground movements are being monitored.'

'It's not surprising,' McIntyre growled, 'given the small army of domestics, barbers, cleaners, washers up, dhobi wallahs, chai wallahs, et bloody cetera, that we have hanging around the base.'

'You're not wrong there,' said Mitchell. 'There are fucking hundreds of them kicking around Bagram. No one notices them, they're just part of the furniture, which makes it all the easier for them to pick up information and pass it on to the Taliban. It'll only take someone to leave a memory stick lying around and they'll have the crown jewels.'

'But our ops are getting compromised too' Shepherd said. 'And our compound is a self-contained, sterile zone. We don't have any domestics because we do our own chores, so whatever the source of today's compromise, it didn't come from us.' He looked over the Major. 'I think you're right, Boss. I think they're clocking our flights in and out.'

Gannon shrugged. 'It's a big base, and they're not going to kick out all the Afghans. The place wouldn't function without them. All we can do is keep our own security water-tight and have everything on a need to know basis.'

'Which we already do anyway,' McIntyre said.

Shepherd nodded. 'Agreed. But if we need Green Army support on an op, let's give them the absolute minimum of notice.'

'Aye, right enough,' McIntyre said. 'The less time they know something, the less chance of it being compromised.'

* * *

Shepherd was up at dawn the next morning and before the heat of the day became too oppressive he went out for a run around the sprawling, six thousand acre base. As usual he did his running in his boots with a rucksack containing a concrete-block wrapped in old newspapers on his back. As he came out of the gates of the Special Forces' compound in the dim pre-dawn light, his eye was caught by a movement on the main runway. Lit by the harsh glare of floodlights and watched over by heavily armed American soldiers, a line of a dozen men, all hooded and dressed in identical orange jump suits, were shuffling towards an unmarked transport plane. They were shackled hand and foot, their chains clanking and rattling as they were hustled across the concrete hard-standing and up the loading ramp into the aircraft. By the faint light of the emergency lighting inside the loadspace, Shepherd could see each man being chained to a ring-bolt fixed to the steel floor. Then the ramp was closed and as Shepherd began running around the perimeter, he could hear the engines wind up and saw the plane taxi out and take off into the breaking dawn.

Shepherd had run ten miles and the sun was well above the horizon by the time he came back towards the gates of the Special Forces compound, sprinting the last four hundred yards flat out. He came to a halt, chest heaving, alongside a familiar figure, an Afghan boy squatting in the dust, with a kettle boiling on a small spirit stove. The boy beamed when he caught sight of Shepherd. 'Salaam alaikum, Spider. Mint tea?'

'Alaikum salaam, Karim,' Shepherd said between gasps. 'Hell yes, but give me a moment to get my breath back and drink some water first.' He drained the plastic bottle he'd been carrying, wiped the sweat from his brow and then took the cup of hot, sweet green tea from Karim, paying him with a dollar bill from the pocket of his shorts.

Only twelve years old, with dark, fathomless eyes, and a foot-dragging limp, the result of a broken ankle that had never been properly set, Karim was one of dozens of Afghan Artful Dodgers wheeling, dealing and hustling on the margins of the base. As well as mint tea, he changed money, sold cigarettes singly or in packs, and claimed to be able to lay his hands on almost anything else as well. The first time they'd met, he'd offered to sell Shepherd a Kalashnikov, and just the previous week he'd had a sackful of antiquities, small stone carvings that had been stolen by grave robbers from some ancient site or perhaps even looted from the wrecked Kabul museum. Shepherd liked the boy's spirit and cheeky sense of humour and had got into the habit of stopping to chat to him every morning. Karim was teaching him Pushtu and in return, although the boy already spoke excellent English, Shepherd was teaching him some English slang that wasn't in any textbook.

'So how's business, Karim?' he said.

'Slow, Spider, I need more customers like you.'

'So what's this week's special offer – gold bars? Stinger missiles?'

The boy pretended to be hurt. 'Don't mock me, Spider. I can be very useful to you. I don't just sell things,' He smiled slyly. 'I can sell you information too.'

'About what?' said Shepherd.

'About the Taliban. No one pays any attention to boys like me. I can go anywhere and everywhere, and I keep my eyes and ears open.'

'Oh come, on, Karim. You're telling me stories here. The Taliban don't go around talking in front of strangers.'

Karim broke into a big smile and spread his arms wide. 'Me? I'm just a simple cripple boy trying to make a living selling tea and cigarettes. No one pays me any attention, Spider. I'm invisible.'

Shepherd smiled despite himself. 'Simple is one thing you're not, Karim, but you need to be careful saying things like that. You're just a kid, you don't know what you're letting yourself in for.'

'I might be young in your country, Spider, but not here. We Afghans grow up fast - we have to. You pay others for information. Pay me and you will not regret it, I promise.'

'No, forget it, Karim. If the Taliban even suspect you of spying on them, it'll be your death sentence.' He pointed a finger at him. 'I'm serious now. The Taliban are dangerous people, you don't want to give them an excuse to hurt you.'

The boy grinned. 'They won't suspect - like you said, I'm just a kid.' He gave Shepherd a calculating look. 'I'll tell you something anyway - how do you say it? - a free sample. Don't pay me anything now, but if you find I spoke the truth, I'll trust you to pay me afterwards.'

'Karim, stop this.'

'I'm serious, Spider. I have some information that might be useful to you. How can you turn that down?'

'I can turn it down because I don't want to put you in the firing line.'

'But I already have the information. All I would be doing is to pass it to you.'

Shepherd thought for a few moments and then sighed. 'All right then, what do you know?'

'Some Taliban fighters will be coming to our village. They know that the American aid money is being delivered and they've told the head man of the village that they want half of it.'

'How do you know this?' Shepherd said.

'I heard the elders arguing about it. They don't want to pay, but they're frightened the Taliban will kill them if they don't.'

Shepherd thought for a moment. 'Do you know the name of the local Taliban leader?'

'There are two. One is Hadir, named for the sound thunder makes in the mountains. The other is Jabbaar. His name means "Cruel" in our language, and he's well-named. one of them is bound to be there with the fighters, because our head man refuses to negotiate with his underlings.' He nodded enthusiastically. 'That's good information, isn't it, Spider?'

'Yes, Karim, it is.'

'Worth money?'

'Possibly. But I want you to promise me that you'll be careful. Eavesdropping on elders is one thing, but keep well clear of the Taliban.'

Karim laughed. 'I will, Spider. I'm not stupid.'

Shepherd put his hand on the boy's shoulder. 'I'm serious about this, Karim.'

The boy looked into his eyes. 'I know you are, Spider. You are a true friend, I know that.'

Shepherd went straight over to the Major's tent and told him everything that he had learned from the boy. The next day at "morning prayers" – the daily briefing with the Boss – the Major announced that the intel appeared to be good. 'The Taliban know that they're losing the main battle and they're increasingly turning to coercing the local villages into giving them support, supplies and cash. And they certainly know that the US aid budget is distributed in cash, by the bucket-load, in an attempt to buy the support of the villagers.'

'And the names he mentioned?'

'Both check out.' The Major flicked through a series of images on his laptop until he found the ones he was seeking. 'Take a look at these.' Shepherd and the others leaned in to study the grainy surveillance imagery of two Afghan men. The Boss pointed to the first of them. 'Jabbaar seems to be a particularly nasty piece of work even by Taliban standards, and his side-kick, Hadir, isn't much better. The intel we have suggests they're living over the border, somewhere in the tribal areas, but as you know, it's a porous border hereabouts, so they won't have any difficulty infiltrating to carry out raids or do a bit of cash and carry – the villagers have the cash and the Taliban carry it away.'

'Then let's go take a look,' Shepherd said. 'But what about Karim?'

'The kid? Pay him a few dollars from the bribes fund. And if we get the Taliban head honchos, pay him some more. OK, final brief at 1600 hours. Insert by heli tonight, set up an OP and see what happens.'

* * *

As Shepherd was preparing his kit outside his tent later that morning the guard at the gate called to him. 'A local is asking for you,' he said. As Shepherd walked over to the gate, he saw a tall Afghan, dressed in an expensive looking shalwar kameez. 'Salaam alaikum,' he said. 'I'm Spider, what can I do for you?'

'Alaikum salaam,' the man replied, touching his hand to his heart in the traditional Afghan gesture. 'My name is Qaseem. You know my son, Karim.' His beard was long and straggly, rust-coloured at the bottom and greying close to his chin.

'Your son is a clever boy,' said Shepherd. 'Very entrepreneurial.'

'He is very enthusiastic,' said Qaseem. 'I am very proud of him, but I fear for him also, which is why I am here.' Qaseem hesitated and glanced around him. 'He talks about you a lot and that worries me.' He saw Shepherd frown and hurried on. 'I mean no offence and am suggesting nothing improper. I don't believe my son has anything to fear from you, but by being seen talking to you so often, he is putting himself in danger. Not all men here are what they seem. It would only take a word from one of them to those who are enemies of us both, to put my son's life at risk.'

'I understand,' said Shepherd. 'But he spends a lot of time in our compound, not just with me.'

'If he is trading, if he is selling you cigarettes or tea, then no one cares. But he spends time talking to you, and he behaves as if he was your friend.'

'I think of him as a friend,' said Shepherd. 'I have a young son myself. Much younger than Karim, but I would be very happy if my boy grew up to be like your son.'

The man smiled. 'I thank you for that, but you must understand that the friendship of a British soldier can be a dangerous thing during times like this.'

Shepherd nodded. 'Again, I hear what you're sending and I understand you. But you're talking to me now, in full view of other Afghans. And Karim has told me that you work for the Americans as an interpreter. Surely nothing that your son does represents any greater risk than what you do yourself?'

'I am a man, and I know the risks involved,' Qaseem said. 'I'm well aware that the fact that I work for the Americans means that my son will probably be an orphan before he is grown up; his mother, my wife - may she rest in the peace of Allah - died giving birth to him. I do not deceive myself that the Taliban cannot reach those who collaborate with the *faranji*, but I'm willing to take the risks for myself, because whatever happens to me, the money the Americans pay me will at least buy my son a better future… if he survives. But he is a child, still. If he is seen to be too close to the occupiers, or is suspected of passing information to *faranji* soldiers, there will be no future for him.' Qaseem placed his hand on Shepherd's arm, holding his gaze. 'Insh'allah that will not happen. Afghanistan is a poor country. A farmer may earn only a few dollars for an entire year's work. Even a teacher, as I used to be, earns only a pittance. Suddenly you Westerners are among us, scattering dollars like the chaff when the wheat is threshed. My son's head has been turned. He dreams of riches and neglects his education. He thinks that one day he will go to America, make his fortune, drive a big car and act like a movie star.' He paused. 'I do not blame him, he is young, but I am not as naïve as my son. I know that when the Americans tire of this war, they will leave without a backward glance, just like the Russians and, yes, like you British too in the past. And when they do, they will abandon their so-called friends to their fate, just as they did in Vietnam. We shall again be a forgotten country and what will become of my son then? So for his sake, I beg you not to encourage him in his daydreams nor put him at risk. Please send him away from you.'

Shepherd studied him for a few moments. 'If that's what you want, I'll do as you ask. You're his father, and I have no right to go against your wishes - but with your permission, I'd like to tell him face to face. I'll not mention that I've spoken to you, but I'll say it's not safe for him to be seen talking to me any more. OK?'

Qaseem nodded. 'Thank you. You are an honourable man. I doubt we shall meet again but-' Again he touched his hand to his heart. 'May you travel safely.'

Shepherd smiled, touched his own heart and gave the traditional reply Karim had taught him. 'And may you not be tired.'

When he'd finished sorting his kit, Shepherd took a stroll around the perimeter before setting off across the base to find Karim. He located him outside the American PX, selling Russian watches to a group of Yank new arrivals. 'Every one guaranteed to have been taken from the wrist of a dead Soviet soldier,' Karim was saying with gruesome relish, deep in his sales pitch. 'Only twenty dollars each.'

Shepherd waited until he'd clinched a sale, then led him off to one side, out of earshot. 'I've been thinking, Karim,' he said. 'You're going to have to more careful about being seen with me. It's putting you at unnecessary risk. It's one thing for you to be peddling stuff around the base, but being seen every day talking to a special forces guy like me is too risky.'

Karim gave him a suspicious look. 'My father has talked to you, hasn't he?'

Shepherd started to deny it, but Karim looked away and shook his head. 'You spoke to him,' he said flatly. 'Please do not lie to me.'

'OK, yes, he spoke to me. But what he said made sense to me anyway.'

Karim's eyes started to fill with tears, but he brushed them away with an angry swipe of his hand. 'I thought you were my friend.'

'I was – I am, I just don't want to be the cause of you getting hurt or worse.'

'I have done nothing wrong, Spider,' said the boy.

'I know that,' said Shepherd. 'But I can't put your life at risk. It's not fair.'

Karim looked at him with teary eyes. 'And what if I hear something useful;? Something that might save the lives of you and your friends? What would I do with information like that? Just forget it, and see you die? Is that what you want?'

Shepherd thought for a few moments. 'I'll tell you what. There's a way for us to stay in touch without putting you at risk. I'll set up a dead drop – a dead letter box for us to use.'

'A dead drop? I do not understand.'

'If you want to get in touch with me or you have information, you can put a note in the dead drop and I'll take it and leave money for you there. And if you're ever in danger, you can also use it as a live drop - a live letter box - to tell me that you need to meet.'

Karim beamed, his anger forgotten. 'I have read of this.' He rummaged through his sack of items for sale and produced a battered Cold War spy novel. 'An English officer gave me this.' He grinned. 'Or anyway, it used to belong to him. I read it. Spies use these dead drops, don't they?'

'Well we don't do it quite like the characters in novels,' Shepherd said. 'But you've got the general idea.'

'So I will be your spy?'

'Karim, no. I'm just showing you a way that you can continue to talk to me without anyone seeing you, that's all.'

The boy nodded seriously. 'I understand,' he said.

'OK, now spies in the books have their dead drops in cities, but our dead drops are always in a natural feature, like a fissure in the rock, or a cleft in a tree. To signal that there's a message, you just leave a mark that can be seen by a casual glance, so you don't have to check the dead drop itself, you just walk past and glance that way. There's an exposed rock face, in a little dip about 400 yards to the west of the gates of our compound and far enough away from the main buildings and the perimeter fence that pausing there won't arouse any suspicion if anyone happens to be watching. I need you to go and look for it later, OK?'

Karim nodded and wiped his eyes with the back of his hands.

'There's a crack about an inch wide at the base of the rock, where the winter frosts have penetrated it over the years,' continued Shepherd. 'It's a few inches deep, so anything you put in there won't be seen. Pretend you're getting a stone out of your sandal or something and you can squat down and you'll be hidden from sight. I've marked it with a chalk line on the rockface above it - when you've found it, rub out the chalk mark with your finger. Make a fresh mark when you want to alert me. A horizontal line will signal that there's a message in the dead drop, a vertical one is asking for a live drop - a meeting. If you - or I - ask for that, be at the place at sunset that night or on each subsequent night until the meet. I will check the dead drop when I'm taking my morning run, and you must do the same every day. He paused 'And Karim? Not a word about this to anyone else, OK?'

Karim nodded, face solemn. 'Thank you Spider. Don't worry, I won't let you down.'

'I know you won't. But listen, don't take any risks whatsoever around the Taliban. No amount of information about them is worth risking your life for. Now I want you to repeat everything I have just said to you so that I know you haven't forgotten anything.'

* * *

Major Gannon had talked to the American agents running the AID programme and discovered the date of the next convoy distributing US dollars to a series of villages and small towns, including Karim's home village. Shepherd put together his preferred four-man team - himself,

McIntyre, Mitchell and Harper - to piggyback on the convoy and then set up an OP overlooking the village.

'What's to stop them from just attacking the convoy?' Harper said.

'Nothing, except they know that if they do, they'll be killing the goose that's laying the golden eggs,' said Shepherd. 'If they keep ambushing the convoys, either they'll stop altogether or they'll be so heavily protected that it'll be a suicide mission for the Taliban. But if they wait for the Yanks to deliver the cash to the villages and then demand a share of it from the headmen, they'll get a lot more money with next to no risk.'

The following day they rode out of Bagram in an armoured truck, sharing it with six US soldiers and a pile of plastic-wrapped bundles of US dollar bills in different denominations stacked in the middle. 'You'd be tempted, wouldn't you?' Harper said, eyeing up the mound of money. 'I mean, I don't expect the villagers give receipts, since half of them can't write anyway.'

'Perhaps we can persuade the Taliban to give us their share,' McIntyre said with a grin.

American Humvees loaded with troops rode Point and Tail End Charlie ahead and behind the truck as they drove towards the mountains, while a Blackhawk armed with Hellfire missiles and 7.62mm machine guns flew top cover above them.

A few miles from the village the convoy passed through a dense stand of cedar and pine trees and it slowed to walking pace for a few seconds so that the SAS team could jump down, forward roll to absorb the impact of their fall and then disappear among the trees. They went to ground as the convoy accelerated again, rumbling on towards the village. An hour later, having distributed the cash, it returned the way it had come. By then, Shepherd had already led the others in to set up the OP on a steep hillside overlooking the village. The slopes were densely wooded but a landslide the previous winter had swept away part of the tree cover, giving them a clear sight of the whole village. They settled in and waited for the Taliban to arrive.

McIntyre lay back with his head on his bergen and closed his eyes. 'Unless anyone's got any objections, I'll take the second watch,' he said. 'I'm knackered and it'll be a long night because unless the Taliban are fucking psychic, they won't get word that the cash has arrived in time to get here before morning.' Within two minutes, they could hear his soft snores.

'Unbelievable,' Shepherd said. 'Is there anywhere that guy can't fall asleep?'

'Only when he's in your bed, shagging your wife,' Mitchell said, ducking as Shepherd launched a pine cone at his head.

They remained on watch, two awake and two resting, throughout the night, but as McIntyre had predicted there had been no sign of the Taliban by the time the first rays of the rising sun began to light the mountain peaks high above them. About ten that morning, however, a Toyota pick-up trailing a column of dust swept along the dirt-track road that ran down from the mountains guarding the Pakistan border. Through his spotter-scope, Shepherd watched a group of heavily armed "soldier monks" jump out in the middle of the village, their distinctive garb of black robes, red sashes and kohl-rimmed eyes marking them out as Taliban, even without the AK-47s and RPG launchers they carried.

Shepherd was on the net at once, calling up the Quick Reaction Force from Bagram, even before a nervous looking group of village elders had appeared to welcome the Taliban leader. 'Pity,' Shepherd said, studying the man through the scope, 'That's not Jabbaar, it's the Number Two, Hadir.'

'Then he'll have to do,' Mitchell said. Dozing a moment before, he was now on maximum alert. Shepherd had already zeroed his scope and rifle, and he kept it trained on Hadir, tracking his movements as he strutted across the village square. The Taliban group were 1,200 yards away from the OP, but that was comfortably within his range - kills with AI .50s had been recorded at distances of a mile and three quarters.

'Relax,' Mitchell said, sensing Shepherd's tension. 'The QRF'll be here inside ten minutes and then we'll get all of them. And if we get Hadir alive, we might even get good intel out of him.'

'Give me five minutes with him,' McIntyre growled, 'and I'll have him singing like a fucking canary. He'll-' He broke off as there was a sudden commotion in the village. The driver of the Toyota jumped out of it and ran to Hadir, and whatever he said to him was enough to galvanise the Taliban into action. Hadir and his men began running back to their pick-up.

'I don't get it,' Mitchell said. 'They couldn't have been more relaxed a minute ago, so what's stirred them up now? They haven't even collected their cash.'

'They've been tipped off,' said Shepherd.   'This op's been compromised like the rest. Someone's seen the QRF leave Bagram and got a warning to them.'

'How?' Mitchell said.

Shepherd shrugged. 'Who knows - cell phone, radio comms, or a fucking ouija board - what's it matter? They've been tipped off and they're getting away.'

He pressed the scope to his eye. There was no time for his usual meticulous preparation for the shot - Hadir had already reached the Toyota and was clambering into the passenger seat. As the pick-up began to move, Shepherd sighted and fired in one movement, taking up the first pressure on the trigger, breathing out and squeezing the trigger home in the space of less than a single second. He felt the recoil against his shoulder and simultaneously through his scope he saw the Taliban leader hurled back in his seat, arms flung outwards and a corona of blood spray around his head. It had been a lucky shot, Shepherd knew, but they all counted.

As the driver span the wheel and slewed the pick-up around, Hadir tumbled from the vehicle, sprawling in the dust. The exit wound had blown the back of his head off and he was stone dead as he hit the ground.

The pick-up slowed for a second but the Taliban made no attempt to retrieve the body. As the driver gunned the engine, the fighters fired bursts of automatic fire towards the site of the muzzle flash from Shepherd's rifle. One of the fighters fired an RPG round from his launcher but it was at extreme range and its automatic detonation after its four and a half second flight meant that it exploded short of the OP, though it was still close enough for Shepherd to feel the searing heat of its blast and hear shrapnel pinging off the rocks around them.

The remaining Taliban fighter had now jumped onto the pick-up and it roared off with the men still loosing off wild bursts of fire.

Shepherd fired twice more, but both shots missed their target as the Toyota bucked and bounced over the rutted road, heading back towards the border. Mitchell, McIntyre and Harper were at maximum range for their AK74s but also kept up a steady fire of short, targeted bursts, in the hope of at least delaying the Taliban until the heli-borne QRF arrived, but the pick-up accelerated away, and within a minute it was even out of range of Shepherd's AI .50. When the QRF eventually arrived, all that remained of the Taliban was the body of the dead Hadir.

At the debrief back at base later that day, there was much frustration and furious recriminations all round, but the source of the compromise remained unknown. Shepherd was still fuming when he went for his morning run the next day, so much so that he almost missed the vertical chalk mark scratched above the dead drop in the rockface, signalling that Karim wanted a meet.

When Shepherd told Mitchell about it, he insisted on riding shotgun on him for the meet. 'It'll be quite like old times,' Mitchell said. 'I did it for a couple of years in the Middle East, providing cover for MI6 guys working out of the embassies. If you're going to a dead drop you've got to have support because the chances of compromise are very high; it's how agents get knocked off all the time.'

'Bloody hell, Geordie,' Shepherd said. 'I'm going to see a kid. The meet's inside the base and he probably only wants to shake me down for some money because his tip-off proved right.'

'Just the same, you need someone watching your back. It's not just the direct threat. If anyone else is taking too much interest, you want to know about it, don't you?'

Shepherd knew better than to argue with his more experienced colleague. At six that night, he strolled out of the Special Forces compound and walked around the perimeter fence towards the meeting place. Mitchell had already been in position for an hour, in cover nearby, watching for anyone approaching the meeting place or observing it from a distance.

When Shepherd got to the edge of the dip where it was sited, he got a double click in his earpiece that told him the area was clear. He found Karim already there, sitting on a rock with his back to him.

'So Karim,' he said. 'Come to get some more money...' The words died on his lips as Karim turned to face him. The boy's face was ashen and his eyes were red from crying. 'What the hell's happened?'

'Jabbaar's men came back to our village to avenge the killing of Hadir,' said Karim, stumbling over the words. 'They took all the tribal elders away, and they took my father too.'

'Your father? What the hell was he doing there? He's an interpreter for the Americans, he must have known he'd be targeted.'

'My grandfather was dying. My father had gone to see him in secret, to say his last farewell, but someone must have seen him and betrayed him, because the Taliban knew he was there.'

'Then we'll set up an operation to rescue him,' Shepherd said. 'I'll get the lads on it right away. Don't worry, we'll sort this out, Karim, I promise.'

The boy shook his head. 'It's too late. Just before dawn, my grandfather's neighbour heard the noise of a vehicle stopping outside the house. He waited until it drove off, then went outside. My father's body had been thrown on the ground outside my grandfather's door. He had been tortured; his fingernails had been pulled off and his body was covered with burns and knife cuts. But there was worse...' He stopped, fighting for self-control. 'They had cut off his manhood and stuffed it in his mouth... the sign they use to mark informers.'

'Oh hell, Karim, I'm sorry. I'm so, so sorry.'

'He had bled to death. My only consolation is that my grandfather never saw his son like that, for he also died that night, in his sleep.' He paused and when he spoke again, his voice had a colder, steelier edge. 'It is now a blood feud for me. My father is dead, killed by Jabbaar.' He spat on the ground as he said the name. 'I was my father's only son, I live now only to avenge him. It is a matter of honour: either Jabbaar or I must die. Will you help me, Spider?'

Shepherd nodded. 'We'll find him, Karim, I promise you that.'

'And when we find him, he dies?'

'Yes Karim,' said Shepherd. 'We find him and he dies.'

Karim held his gaze. 'We don't have to find him, I already know where he is, or at least, where he will be in three days' time,' he said quietly.

Shepherd held up his hand. 'Don't tell me the rest until we're in a more secure area. You can come with us back to the compound. At least we don't have to worry about you being seen with me any more, because the Taliban will already have your card marked. If they've killed your father, they will come after you as well, the first chance they get.' He spoke into his throat-mic. 'Geordie, we're heading back now.'

'We?' Mitchell said.

'Yes, the boy's coming in with us.'

'Are you sure that's a good idea?'

'I've no choice. I'll explain later.'

'Are you sure you're not getting a little too personally involved with the boy, Spider?'

'The Taliban have killed his father.'

'That's very sad but you aren't responsible for that.'

'I'm not so sure about that, Geordie. Look, he's an orphan now. He's our responsibility.'

Mitchell came over to join them and they walked back to the compound together in silence. Shepherd vouched for the boy to the guard at the gates and then led him to his tent. 'Okay Karim,' he said, sitting down on his cot. 'Tell me why you think you know where Jabbaar will be.'

'I spied on two Afghan soldiers this morning and heard them talking,' the boy said. 'They wear the green uniform of the Afghan Army, but I know they are Taliban. I overheard one say they were going to Zadran on Saturday, to teach the thieves and whores there a lesson. That means there'll be whippings and thieves getting their hands cut off. It's the Taliban's version of sharia law, just like when they ruled the whole country and there were mutilations and executions almost every week. They even staged them in the football stadium in Kabul.'

'So, even assuming that's really what it is going to happen, why are you so sure that Jabbaar will be there?' asked Shepherd.

Mitchell sat down on another cot, watching Karim carefully.

'Because he takes pleasure from such things and Zadran is his home village,' said Karim. 'I told you his name means cruel and he lives up to it. He runs the opium trade there and has even forced some of the farmers to surrender their children to him to clear their debts.'

'What do you mean?'

'Zadran takes the children. He keeps the pretty ones and the others are taken across the border to be trained as suicide bombers.'

Shepherd looked over at Mitchell. 'Bastard,' Mitchell muttered under his breath.

Shepherd picked up a map and turned back to Karim. 'Where is Zadran exactly?'

'In the mountains about twenty miles east of Jalalabad.'

'Bandit country,' Mitchell said.

Shepherd studied the map. 'So what do you reckon?' he asked Mitchell.

Mitchell shrugged. 'Could be right. It's only a few miles from the tribal areas, so Jabbaar and his crew could easily slip across the border again. The only way we'll find out is to take a look, but we may struggle to convince the Boss on nothing more solid than the word of a twelve year old kid.' He paused, intercepting the boy's baleful look. 'No offence, Karim, I'm saying what the Boss will think, not what I think.'

'Karim was right before,' Shepherd said. 'And apart from any personal reasons, Jabbaar's a major target, Number One in the local Taliban hierarchy. Feathers in everyone's caps if we nail him.'

'Karim may well be right again, but there's another problem,' Mitchell said, studying the map. 'Zadran is in a valley that runs eastwards towards the Pakistan border. It's cut off from the rest of the country by a 3,000 metre range of mountains and the only way through them is by means of one of two passes, both of which cut through narrow defiles that are an ambusher's dream. Half a dozen well-armed men could hold off an army there. So we'll have to insert by helis and on previous form, as soon as we take off from Bagram, you can bet that the Taliban's spies and informers will be passing word that we're deploying.'

'Then we don't take off from Bagram,' Shepherd said.

Mitchell gave him a puzzled look. 'Meaning?'

'That for this op, we'll base ourselves away from Bagram. Fly it in two stages. Drop the helis in the middle of nowhere until we're ready for them.'

'But even if we do have their support, it'll be of limited use, because we can't bomb or rocket targets in the middle of a large, densely populated village, and even if Jabbaar is in Zadran, by the time we've fought our way past the Taliban pickets and into the market square, the chances are he'll be long gone.' Mitchell paused. 'That's if he's there at all. If he isn't, and we turn out to have been shooting up a village that's just going about its daily business, the Head Shed will have our guts for garters.'

'We'll do it covertly,' he said at last. 'I'll infiltrate the village and call the rest of you in when I've got a positive ID on Jabbaar and his crew.'

'And the boy?'

'Will come with me. He'll be my passport into Zadran. I'll be his long lost uncle and he can vouch for me to the locals.' He intercepted Mitchell's dubious look. 'He's got the right to be there; Jabbaar killed his father.'

'If you say so, but I'm guessing the Boss will take some convincing.'

'Then let's go persuade him.' He turned to the boy. 'Now if this is going to work, I'll need the right tribal dress, Karim, which is where you come in. I need a shalwar kameez.'

'I'll get you the best money can buy.'

'No, no, I want the opposite of that. It needs to be old, shabby and poor quality. I'm going to pose as a poor relative of yours, so I need to look the part. See what you can do, OK?' He handed him a few dollars. 'But Karim, you're not to leave Bagram yourself. Pay one of the other boys to go the bazaar for you, if you need to, but you stay on the base. At least we know the Taliban can't get at you here. You stick to us like camel shit on an army boot, okay?'

They walked with the boy up to the gates of the compound and then he hurried off. While they waited for him to return, Shepherd called a briefing for the team he wanted and outlined his plan to use Karim to get close to Jabbaar. Major Gannon heard him out in silence, but then shook his head emphatically. 'No can do, Spider. He's a twelve year old kid.'

'He's a twelve year old Afghan kid and that makes him twelve going on twenty-five in the West,' said Shepherd. 'He's seen and done things that the wildest street kid in the UK couldn't even imagine.'

'He's twelve, Spider. There's no getting away from that.'

'He's a twelve-year-old orphan whose father was butchered by the Taliban. And he wants revenge. And to be honest, boss, I think he's entitled. This isn't England, he can't go to the cops. He can't go to anyone. Except us. And if we don't help him, his father's murderer goes unpunished.'

'I'd be happier if you went and the kid stayed here.'

'But he's my ticket in, I can't get into Zadran without him.'

'But even setting aside the ethics of using the boy in an op at all, can you begin to imagine the international media shit-storm that would erupt if word of this ever got out? They'll be accusing us of using Afghan kids as human shields.'

'But word won't get out because there'll be nothing to say I'm British. It's the ultimate deniable op. If I'm killed - and you know I won't be captured, because I'll top myself before I'll let that happen - there'll be no traceable kit, no paper trail, nothing. I'll just be some dead foreigner, an Arab, an Uzbek, a Chechen or a Turkoman, meddling in an Afghan feud and paying the price for it. My death won't even rate a line in the Kabul newspapers, let alone the outside world.'

'But even if I agree to it, how do you propose to get into Zadran without being rumbled?'

Shepherd smiled as he realized that the Major was starting to come around. 'I'm going to pose as a shell-shocked local - thanks to the US bombing there's a lot of them about. I'm going to be Karim's uncle. He can speak for me if we're stopped and since I'm shell-shocked, I won't be speaking at all. And better yet, I'll be unarmed-'

'Are you off your head?' said Gannon. 'Have you looked in a mirror recently?'

'Just hear me out. In Afghanistan, every adult man carries a weapon. If you've no weapon, you can't be an adult and so you're treated as a semi-imbecile. There's no better way to disarm suspicion than to be someone who is beneath contempt, not worthy even of notice. And, of course, though I'll not appear to be carrying a weapon at all, I'll have a pistol, tucked away.'

'So that's you sorted then,' McIntyre said, after a pause. 'But how are the rest of us going to be inserting?'

Shepherd smiled. 'We send a couple of helis out into the desert, close enough to be able to get to me in minutes. When I need you I'll fire a flare.'

'You figure any spies won't know what you're up to?' asked the Major.

'We can muddy the water by using half a dozen Hughes 500 helis. Even though they're small, they pack a hell of a punch. They can be used as gunships – they're fitted with seven-shot rocket pods and 7.62 miniguns - or as troop carriers with one guy sitting next to the pilot and two, or even four more, at a pinch, strapped to the outside and standing on the skids. We can use six of them and stagger their departures from Bagram and no one will know they are meeting up.'

'So you call them in at the last moment?'

'They've got a range of a couple of hundred miles and a top speed of 160 miles an hour, and they're small and relatively quiet, so you can be less than two minutes flying time away from the target and be undetected by anyone there… which is just as well, because that's probably the maximum time I'll have before the Taliban start cutting my dick off and feeding it to me.'

'Okay,' the Boss said at last. 'You've just about convinced me. I'll get the paperwork sorted. We've got three days to prepare; let's make the most of them.'

'One more thing,' Shepherd said. 'It's a while since I've done any CQB training. I'll need a hand to build a Killing House I can practise in.'

'I'll go one better,' McIntyre said. 'Once we've built it, I'll train you up as well. You may be the dog's bollocks when it comes to sniping, but there's no one better than me when it comes to CQB.'

Shepherd and the team spent a few hours stacking sand-bags to form a Killing House about thirty feet square, where he could practise his shooting drills. McIntyre rigged up targets of various sizes at irregular intervals around it and Shepherd began his training, with McIntyre a hard taskmaster. 'You're best with a 9mm Glock,' he said. 'It's a little bigger than the Browning, but it's a beautiful weapon and it has no safety catch - and the split second that saves you might just be a life-saver too. If you've not used one before, you just have to remember that there's a hard pull on the trigger for the first shot, but after that it's just a short single pull to fire the rest of the magazine. You've got one in the spout and twelve in the mag, giving you thirteen shots, and you need to count the double taps as you fire them, so you've always got one shot left as you change magazines.

'You need to practise both shooting methods too. You already know the instinctive method, one-handed and effective up to ten or twelve metres range. If you can point you can shoot. But you also need to go a bit more old school and practise the Weaver method we used to use back in the day. It's a two-handed stance and it's more accurate at ranges from ten to twenty metres but slower than the instinctive method. Any further from Jabbaar than that and you might as well put your head between your legs and kiss your arse goodbye, because no matter how good a shot you are, you're only going to hit him by accident, not design. Ready? Right, let's get to it. You need to fire a couple of thousand rounds before I'm convinced you're ready... and that's supposing you manage to hit the target now and again. If you don't, it's going to be a long night.'

As Shepherd had admitted, it was some time since he'd practised his CQB skills, and he was rusty at first, slow to draw and change magazines, and with a couple of his shots just missing the killing zone: the triangle of head and upper body, where a double tap was certain to be fatal.

'That was shite,' McIntyre said, after his first session. 'You missed with two shots out of twenty-four. That might be good enough for the infantry, but you're not in the fucking infantry, you're in the SAS and we expect perfection - do it again.'

Shepherd did better on his second attempt and began to get back into the rhythm of CQB, drawing, firing a double-tap, rolling onto the ground and firing another double-tap, standing up and firing another, and then going to ground again, a constant rhythm of fire and movement, trying to ensure that he was never a static target, even when re-loading. Years of ops and practice in the Killing House at Hereford were meant to ensure that any SAS man could change magazines even while rolling across the ground, but Shepherd's focus on his sniping skills, and the continuous deployments on

CT ops, meant that he had practised his CQB skills much less often in recent years.

'Keep moving!' McIntyre bellowed as Shepherd paused for a split-second, fumbling with the magazine as he changed it. 'Do you think the fucking Taliban are going to politely stop firing and wait for you to change magazines before they shoot your arse full of holes?'

'You're lovely when you're angry,' Shepherd said, laughing, before he dived and rolled again. As he fired the double-taps, he counted the rounds religiously and changed the magazine still with one round in the chamber, so the pistol was never unloaded and he always had the means to take down an attacker. Not bad,' McIntyre said, as they took a breather after a couple of hours intensive practice and had a brew. Shepherd smiled to himself, it was as much praise as McIntyre could ever bring himself to give about anything.

'Shall I tell you something weird?' McIntyre said, as he stirred about half a pound of sugar into his brew. 'Did you know that British police can't fire double-taps because of a legal ruling that if you hit the target with the first shot, the second one constitutes excessive force.' He gave a bleak smile. 'Fucking ridiculous I know, but it's true. So if you shoot a bad guy, you have to hope he's dead, because if not, he gets a free shot at you before you can fire again.'

While Shepherd was practising his shooting drills, Karim had returned with a shalwar kameez for him. When he tried it on, Shepherd wrinkled his nose. 'Bloody hell, Karim, I know I said worn and patched, but I don't remember saying anything about it stinking.'

Karim grinned. 'But won't the smell just make it seem more authentic, Spider?'

'And was there any change from the dollars I gave you?'

Karim's smile grew even broader. 'Strangely enough, it was just the right amount.'

'Do you know, I had a funny feeling, it was going to be!' He paused. 'Now I've done my training, Karim, but there's one piece of kit, I need you

to use. When we're in Zadran and I give you the nod, you'll have to fire a
flare to alert McIntyre and Mitchell and the others that we need them to
come in all guns blazing. See this?' He showed him a pouch about the size
of two packs of cigarettes and then took out a metal tube three inches long,
fitted with a screw end and a small trigger. 'This a gun to fire mini-flares.
They were designed originally for people on yachts, but they're perfect for
our purpose too. These are the flares,' he said, pulling them out of the
pouch. 'See the green and red coloured bands on the ends? They show the
colour of the flare: a green flare signals "Go!" to our friends, a red one
warns of danger.' He winked at Karim. 'But you'll only need green ones.
Screw the flare on, press the trigger and it throws the flare up to 400 feet in
the air. My mates will be watching for the signal and as soon as they see it,
they'll come and join the party. But Karim, let's get one more thing clear. If
you're to come to Zadran with me, you have to do exactly as I say, when I
say it. And that means you fire the flare when I tell you, and then you drop
to the ground and stay flat, whatever happens, until I tell you it's safe.'

'You want me to be a coward?' Karim said, resentful.

'No, I want you to stay alive. The Taliban are no respecters of youth
and nor are the automatic weapons they fire. But don't worry, do as I say
and you'll have your revenge on Jabbaar, but I need to concentrate on my
own job without having to keep half an eye on you. OK?'

Karim nodded. 'Don't worry, I'll do as you say.'

Shepherd had a final briefing with the rest of the team the next day.
They would be inserting separately, with Shepherd and Karim making
directly for Zadran, aiming to lie up nearby overnight, and then enter the
village early the next morning, while the rest of the team left on the
helicopters.

Shepherd was dressed in his shalwar kameez, its odour only marginally
improved by a night in the open, hanging on the barbed wire fence.
Although it still appeared to be the typical Afghan clothing, Shepherd had
modified the long shirt. As he was right-handed, he had unpicked the seam

of the shirt all the way from the left shoulder down to the waist and then fixed Velcro strips to both sides of it, so that when closed, the shirt appeared untouched. He wore his Glock pistol in a holster so well-concealed that even someone searching him for weapons would be almost certain to miss it. Unlike a normal shoulder holster, this one fitted tight into the left armpit, and, even to a practised eye, left no outward sign that he was carrying a weapon at all, but when he needed to access it, he simply had to rip the Velcro open with his left hand and draw the pistol with his right. It took less than a second to draw and fire. To complete his disguise, he was wearing the usual Afghan knitted skullcap. He hadn't shaved for three days and his skin was nut brown from hours under the relentless Afghan sun.

An hour after sunset, Shepherd led Karim out to a waiting Blackhawk heli. It had landed within the SF compound itself, and while Taliban spies might still report it taking off, they could not see who or what it was carrying.

Karim was saucer-eyed as he clambered into the heli. 'Frightened?' Shepherd said, as he watched him looking around the interior.

The boy's eyes were shining as he met his gaze. 'No Spider, just excited.'

The heli took off and flew a diversionary route, flying west until out of sight of Bagram, before descending to low-level and switching onto its true course. The pilot was already wearing Passive Night Goggles. As well as his own, Shepherd had brought a pair for Karim and showed him how to use them. The boy was speechless for some time, gazing out into the darkness with a look of complete wonder on his face.

The Blackhawk put them down at an LZ twelve miles from Zadran and disappeared into the night, while they began a three hour walk through the darkness before finding a place to lie up close to Zadran.

Soon after dawn the next morning, Shepherd roused the boy and after drinking a few mouthfuls of water and eating some high energy snacks, they set off for Zadran. It was another clear and sunny morning and as they walked along the dirt-road towards the village, their feet scuffing in the dust, they were surrounded by clouds of butterflies, feeding on the nectar of the dog roses, juniper, thyme and lavender growing wild along the earth banks dividing the track from the surrounding fields. The peaks of the mountains of the Hindu Kush were visible to the north, permanently white-capped even in the heat of high summer, and standing out in stark relief against the azure blue of the sky.

'It's a beautiful country, Karim,' Shepherd said, as he looked around him. 'You'll have to show me it one day, when the Taliban have gone and people can live normal lives again.' At the sound of his voice, a shrike flew out of a thorn bush giving a rasping call to show its anger at being disturbed. Its prey, a small lizard, remained impaled on a thorn.

In contrast to the beauty of the country around Zadran, the village - large enough to qualify as a small town - was scarred and ugly, after decades of fighting. They passed through a wasteland of shelled and bombed mud-brick buildings, the facades of those still standing as scarred by bullet holes as the pock-marked faces of smallpox victims. Beyond them was a shanty town of rusting shipping containers where burqa-clad women and small children peered out at them from the dark interiors. 'We call this area Khair Khana,' Karim whispered. 'Container city.'

As the sun rose higher, a growing number of villagers were now in the streets. Shepherd attracted some curious or suspicious glances and there were a few muttered comments as they passed - strangers were always objects of suspicion in Afghanistan - but he was now well into his role, head bowed, mouth hanging open, and his eyes apparently unfocussed, staring at nothing, and none challenged them. Several people recognised Karim and called out greetings and queries about his companion, but he replied with grave respect, and they appeared to accept his explanations, while Shepherd's lack of a weapon and his vacant, unmanly demeanour, disarmed any remaining suspicions.

They reached the large open space that served as the market square and
sat among groups of men talking in the open fronted teahouse at one side of
the square. Karim ordered mint tea for them, paying with a few crumpled
Afghani notes. As they sipped their drinks, the smells of the market
assaulted their senses: the stench of animal dung and the stink of fumes
from the decrepit trucks and swarms of mopeds, battling with the fragrance
of sandalwood, cloves and spices from one stall. Most of the others were
only battered crates and cardboard boxes, and the stall holders squatted in
the dust alongside their meagre wares: used lightbulbs, sandals cut from old
tyres, empty cans and bottles, second-hand clothes, with bloodstains on
some suggesting their origins.

Alongside the staples of Afghan life - rice, green tea, sugar - the food
stalls sold radishes, cucumbers, tomatoes and grapes, but few could afford
the meat from the stall where the butcher flicked half-heartedly at the flies
swarming over his wares and a tethered goat awaited its turn under the
knife.

An ice-seller sat on a wooden cart drawn up in the shade of a mulberry
tree with a few fruits still clinging to the topmost branches. A trickle of
water ran from beneath the sackcloth shrouding the square blocks of ice that
were cut from the river in winter and stored in caves to preserve them from
the summer heat.

As Shepherd and Karim sipped their mint tea in silence, awaiting the
promised arrival of the Taliban, Mitchell's SAS group were twenty miles
away looking at the sky and waiting for the flare that would tell them that
they were needed at Zadran. The squad leaders, including Mitchell, were
sitting up front with the pilots, while the others stood on the skids and lashed
themselves to the side of the helis with air dispatch harnesses fastened with
a quick-release mechanism. The pilots fired up the engines, and then they
sat, engines idling and rotors turning slowly as the minutes ticked away and
the sun rose higher in the sky.

Shepherd and Karim had been sitting in the tea-house for over an hour when they heard the noise of engines and a commotion at the eastern side of the town. A few moments later a convoy of Taliban pick-ups came sweeping into the square. The fighters jumped down and began herding the population into the middle of the square. Four of them burst into the tea-house and drove out the customers, including Shepherd and Karim, with kicks and blows.

They were pushed towards a cordon of other Taliban who were searching every man. There was a shout as a fighter produced a Bollywood cassette tape he had found in one villager's pocket. Face ashen with fear, the man was dragged to one side and punched to the ground. Shepherd and Karim were now close to the front of the line and Shepherd was feeling uncomfortably aware of the Glock pistol in his armpit as a Taliban fighter stared at him, then shouted at him in Pushtu. Shepherd said nothing, letting his mouth hanging open and a dribble of spittle run from it, while Karim stammered an explanation. Suddenly there was the loud noise of a back-firing moped. At once, seizing his chance, Shepherd threw himself to the ground, covering his head with his arms and crying out in terror.

There was a burst of laughter from the Taliban fighters. One kicked him in the ribs and another spat on him, showing his contempt, but Shepherd's apparent terror had disarmed any suspicions they might have harboured about him. Karim helped him up and they moved on, unsearched and unchallenged, the mocking laughter of the Taliban fighters pursuing them, but Shepherd was also smiling to himself.

When the last of the villagers had been searched, another Taliban Toyota pick-up was driven into the market square, carrying two men and one woman in a burqa. It stopped in the middle of the square and the victims were pushed from the tailgate and allowed to fall to the ground. The woman's hands were tied behind her back and she fell heavily. As she was dragged back to her feet, Shepherd could see a spreading bloodstain on the cloth visor covering her face.

Shepherd had now spotted Jabbaar and began trying to work his way through the crowd towards him, but people were pressing forward, apparently eager for the spectacle to come and, afraid of losing touch with the boy, he had to bide his time. The villager who had been found with a cassette tape was the first to face Jabbaar's wrath. The man was dragged forward and Jabbaar confronted him, brandishing the cassette tape and shouting in his face, so close to him that the man's own face was flecked with spittle.

Some of the Taliban fighters were wearing lengths of electric cable wrapped around their waists like belts. They now untied them, took a couple of turns around their wrists and then began to use them as whips, lashing them down onto their helpless victim. The last few inches of frayed copper wire of the cables had been exposed, drawing blood as the lashes sliced angry weals across the man's back. Jabbaar himself used a thin, barbed branch torn from a thorn bush as a whip, flogging the victim until he lay still in a spreading pool of his own blood.

The second victim, accused of theft, was then dragged forward. Two soldiers held him, while another two gripped his right arm and he was forced to kneel in front of Jabbaar. He clicked his fingers and a man wearing a surgeon's mask, whether for hygiene or to conceal his identity, stepped out of the crowd. He placed a scuffed brown leather case on the ground, took out a hypodermic and injected the man's arm, then tied a tourniquet around his forearm with a strip of thin leather. There was a murmur of anticipation from the crowd as the surgeon then produced a scalpel from his bag. Playing to the crowd, he held it above his head for a moment, so it gleamed in the sunlight.

The victim still stared straight ahead, only the set of his jaw and a pulsing vein in his temple betraying his emotion as the surgeon began to cut through the flesh around his wrist. As blood spurted out, he cut the tendons and then broke the wrist with a sound like the snap of a breaking stick that echoed around the hushed square.

As the surgeon held the severed hand aloft, there were shouts of 'Allahu akbar' from the Taliban fighters and some of the crowd. Shepherd suppressed a shudder; the ritual seemed even more barbaric when carried out by a man using the trappings of modern medicine, than it would have if done by some Taliban warlord, hacking off the hand with a sword or an axe.

A third man was then dragged forward, accused and convicted by Taliban decree of killing a farmer's son in an argument over a piece of disputed land. The father of the murdered boy was led forward and Jabbaar said something to him.

'He's asking if the man can find it in his heart to have mercy,' Karim whispered.

The old man gave an emphatic shake of his head. 'My heart, my honour, demand revenge.'

His words were greeted with a roar from the crowd. Jabbaar then handed the old man an AK47. As one of the fighters moved to cover the victim's eyes with a scarf, Jabbaar stopped him. He gestured impatiently to the old man, who raised the rifle and fired, but his hand shook and the shot struck the victim in the shoulder rather than the heart, the impact sending him sprawling. There were screams from a woman in the crowd, who had also collapsed, clutching at her thigh. The round had passed clean through the victim and struck the woman as well, knocking her on her back. Her burqa had ridden up, exposing her legs to the knee. One of the Taliban rushed to her, pulled it down again and then turned his back, concerned only about the indecency, not the wound she had suffered.

Jabbaar scowled and dragged the old man forward until he was standing directly over the victim and gestured to him to finish the job. The wounded man lay staring up at him, making no sound, as the man held the barrel to his head and pressed the trigger a second time. As a mess of blood and brains splashed into the dust of the square, there was another roar from the crowd. The Taliban fighters dragged the body away and threw it into the back of the pick-up.

Another pick-up was then driven into the square, its back loaded with a heap of stones. Realisation dawned on Shepherd as he saw the last victim, the woman, being dragged towards a wooden post set in the ground. There was a buzz of excitement from the crowd and men and young boys ran to the Toyota and began loading themselves with as many stones as they could carry.

Jabbaar pronounced sentence: the woman was guilty of adultery, the penalty death by stoning. Shepherd felt sick at the thought, but as the crowd of men jostled for position, waiting for the signal to start, he saw his chance. Jabbaar was now standing slightly off to one side and his attention and that of his men and the crowd was focussed solely on the woman. As Jabbaar raised his hand, ready to signal the start of the stoning, Shepherd nudged Karim, who dragged his gaze away from the horrific spectacle.

'In three,' Shepherd murmured 'From... Now!'

As Jabbaar lowered his arm and the first stones began to fly, striking the woman's body with dull thuds like axe strokes on wood, Shepherd sprinted out of the crowd, elbowing a woman aside and bowling over a man who stood in his way. There was a loud whoosh as Karim launched the flare. It tore upwards and burst in a green flash overhead. All eyes were drawn to it, except Shepherd's. He ripped open the velcro on his shirt with his left hand and drew his pistol in one movement with his right.

A Taliban fighter swung to face him, but Shepherd double-tapped him, dived to the ground, firing another double-tap as he rolled over, to take down another fighter, and firing again as he sprang upright. A third Taliban fighter dropped as the burst from his own weapon passed harmlessly over Shepherd's head.

Shepherd had already dived and rolled once more and came up within five metres of Jabbaar. The stoning had stopped and the crowd was in uproar, most of them unable to comprehend what was happening, so fast was Shepherd's fire and movement. Jabbaar was scrabbling to pull his AK47 from his shoulder and bring it to bear, but he was too slow. Shepherd double-tapped him, two shots to the chest, just above the heart. Jabbaar crashed to the ground and his rifle skittered away across the square.

Shepherd was already diving to the ground again, rolling sideways, firing another double-tap as he went, still counting his shots: ten fired, two left before a magazine change. He sprang up again and fired another double-tap towards the Taliban fighters by the pick-up. They were too far away for a kill to be guaranteed but he hoped the incoming fire would disturb their own aim. He now had just one shot left and flung himself to the ground again, whipping out the magazine and inserting a new one even as he rolled across the square, dust matting his clothes and hair.

Many of the villagers had now fled in panic, but one man, braver than the rest, tried to lash out at Shepherd with his foot. He dodged the kick, sprang up to pistol-whip the man to the ground, and then moved again as a burst of automatic fire tore the air apart in the place where he had just been standing.

As he dived and rolled again, he heard the clatter of rotors and the rattle of mini-guns as the helis flashed overhead.

The Taliban fighters swung to face this new threat, but they were now outgunned and outnumbered. Two attack helis kept up a withering fire, the mini-guns' incessant rattle punctuated by the whoosh of rockets flashing from their pods and torching the Taliban pick-ups.

The other four helis landed at the edge of the square in a whirlwind of dust and debris. McIntyre, Mitchell and the others jumped off the helis and joined the fight, pouring in a torrent of rounds that cut the Taliban apart.

The sound of double-taps echoed through the square as the SAS killed the Taliban fighters with ruthless efficiency, flattening any villager who stood in their way. They kicked their legs from under them or punched them to the ground and while the SAS assault teams kept up their withering fire, others secured the villagers' wrists with plastic ties. When the battle was over, they would be searched and identified and any Taliban who'd thrown away their weapons and tried to hide among them would receive short shrift.

The sound of gunshots and double-taps slowed and then stopped altogether as the last fighter was cut down. Every local had fled and the square was now completely deserted, but for the dead and wounded and the SAS troopers patrolling the perimeter, still watchful and alert. Mitchell moved among the wounded, treating two SAS men who had non-fatal gunshot wounds.

Mitchell had spotted Shepherd and ran over to him as he dusted himself down and looked around for Karim. 'All right, Spider?'

'I'm fine, not a scratch on me,' he said. 'But see what you can do for her.' He gestured to where the burqa-clad woman slumped against the wooden post that held her. Mitchell ran over to her and after checking her over gave Shepherd a thumbs up. 'She's badly bruised and has a couple of broken bones, but she'll live,' he said.

Shepherd pointed at the woman who had been shot. She was curled up in a ball, sobbing. 'She took a round in the thigh, can we patch her up before we go?' asked Shepherd. 'If not we can take her with us.'

'I'm on it,' said Mitchell.

Shepherd looked around again and shouted for Karim again. The boy suddenly appeared from behind one of the market stalls, grinning from ear to ear and holding a fistful of dollar bills in one hand. 'The stall-holder doesn't seem to want these any more,' he said, as he ran over to Shepherd, 'so I thought we might as well have them.'

Shepherd smiled. 'We? You nicked it, you keep it.' He put a hand on the boy's shoulder. 'It's time to go,' he said. 'We're finished here.'

'I have one thing to do,' said Karim, reaching into his bag and pulling out a curved knife. 'I have to do to Jabbaar what he did to my father.'

'He's dead, Karim. That's enough.'

Karim's eyes blazed. 'I will cut off his dick and put it in his mouth. And I will tell everyone that I did it to avenge my father, Qaseem.'

Shepherd put a hand on the boy's shoulder. 'Do that, and you'll be no better than him,' he said. 'You need to remember your father as the good man he was. He wanted the best for you, he wouldn't want you to be ruled by revenge. Jabbaar is dead. It's over.'

Karim looked as if he wanted to argue, but eventually he nodded and put away the knife. One of the helicopters lifted off and flew away. 'Thank you, Spider,' said Karim.

'It was a pleasure,' said Shepherd. 'I liked your father. I hope I can be as good a dad to my boy as he was to you.' A second helicopter lifted off and Shepherd clapped Karim on the shoulder. 'Come on or we'll miss our lift home.'

KILL ZONE

AFGHANISTAN

October 2002.

Spider Shepherd squatted on his heels outside his tent, drinking his first brew of the day from a battered mug as he watched the wind stirring dust devils from the dirt floor of the compound. The dust covered every surface, leaving everything as brown and drab as the wintry Afghan hills that surrounded him. Unshaven and wearing a tee-shirt and fatigues worn and sun-faded from long use, Shepherd drank the last of his brew and tossed the dregs into the dirt. 'Why does a brew never taste right out here?' he asked.

Sitting next to him with his legs outstretched was Geordie Mitchell, an SAS medic who was a couple of years older than Shepherd. 'That'd be one of those rhetorical questions, would it?' said Geordie. He had a floppy hat pulled low over his head. His hair was thinning and his scalp was always the first area to burn under the hot Afghan sun.

Shepherd stood up and stretched. 'It just never tastes right, that's all.'

'It's because we use bottled water, plus the altitude we're at affects the boiling point of the water, plus the milk is crap. Plus the sand gets everywhere.' Geordie stood up and looked at his watch, a rugged Rolex Submariner. 'Soon be time for morning prayers,' he said.

The two men strolled across the compound, their AK47s hanging on slings on their backs. They heard raised voices at the entrance to the compound and headed in that direction.

They found a young SAS officer, Captain Todd, in the middle of a furious altercation with the guard at the gates. Like all the Regiment's officers, Harry Todd had been seconded to the SAS from his own regiment for a three-year tour of duty, and was on his first trip with them. He'd only been in Afghanistan for two months and he was finding it tough going. As if his Oxford, Sandhurst and The Guards background was not already enough to raise hackles among the men he nominally led, Todd's blond hair flopped over his eyes like a poor man's Hugh Grant and, despite his youth, his nervous habit of clearing his throat made him sound like some ancient brigadier harrumphing over the Daily Telegraph in the Army & Navy Club.

Shepherd had managed to avoid the Captain so far, which suited him just fine. The Major had realised that Todd was going to be an awkward fit and soon after he'd arrived he had detached him from the Squadron to the Intelligence Clearing Centre, largely with the aim of keeping him from getting under everybody's feet. The Clearing Centre was where all the intelligence received was collated and evaluated. It came from a variety of sources; satellite and drone surveillance imagery, communication intercepts from GCHQ, and humint – human intelligence – in all its varied forms, from "eyes on" information from SAS observation posts right down to tip-offs of often dubious value from assorted spies, grasses and ordinary Afghans with grudges against their neighbours. Todd's job was to sift the intelligence as it came in and then brief the OC - the Boss - at the morning prayers held at 0800 every day. Like documents passing across some bureaucrat's desk, the intelligence was divided into three categories: "For Immediate Action" that might be acted on within hours or even minutes; "Pending", for events that might be coming up in the near future; and "File For Future Use". Documents in the latter category often disappeared into the back of a filing cabinet and never saw the light of day again. Much of his work was humdrum and routine, but Todd had clearly been looking for an opportunity to show his worth and by the look of it, he had decided that today was the day.

Todd was standing next to an Afghan in a black dishdasha, with an AK 74 slung across his back. Initially Shepherd was more interested in the weapon than the Afghan - its orange plastic furniture and magazine made it easy to identify as the updated and improved version of the ubiquitous AK47, and it was an unusual weapon for an Afghan to be carrying.

As Shepherd and Geordie walked over, the Afghan turned to look at them. He had the hook-nosed profile, sun and wind-burned skin, and dark beard and hair of a typical Afghan, but he had a distinguishing feature that Shepherd noticed at once - though his right eye was hazel, the pupil of his left one was a strange, milky white, almost opalescent colour.

Todd was haranguing two armed guards at the entrance who appeared to be refusing to allow the Captain and the Afghan into the compound. 'I'll have you on a charge for this, I'm warning you!' said Todd.

'What's the problem, Captain?' Geordie said.

'This guard is refusing to let us into the compound,' Todd said, flicking his hair from his eyes.

Geordie grinned. 'That's probably because you've got an armed and unknown Afghan with you,' he said. He didn't call the officer 'sir.' That was the SAS way. No saluting and no honorifics, though the Major was always referred to as 'Boss'.

'This man is Ahmad Khan, a Surrendered Enemy Personnel,' said the Captain.

'Well, that doesn't carry too much weight in these parts,' said Geordie. 'I can tell you from my own experience that SEPs are like junkies - they're only with you long enough to get their next fix: cash, weapons, whatever, and then they're gone again. With respect, Captain, no experienced guy would trust an SEP as far as he could throw him.'

Todd glared at the medic. 'This man has vital intelligence I need to put before the Boss and I am not going to exclude him from the compound just because of your prejudice against SEPs and perhaps Afghans in general.'

Shepherd could see that Geordie was close to giving the officer a piece of his mind, and while he preferred not to get involved, he figured that he should at least try to defuse the situation. 'It's not about prejudice,' he said, choosing his words carefully. 'It's based on bitter experience. We've had more than our fair share of green on blue attacks out here.' He pointed at the Afghan's rifle. 'One: He's carrying a loaded AK74. Only the top guys in the Taliban carry them. So he's not some tribesman picking up a few extra dollars for fighting the faranji invaders, he's one of their leaders. Two: This is a secure compound. Not even a Brit would get in here without being vetted or vouched for, and yet you're trying to bring an armed Taliban fighter in here.'

Geordie pointed a finger at the officer. 'The thing is, Captain, you're not only jeopardising the safety of everyone here, but you'd better watch your own back, because I'd take odds that he'd rub you out if he thought he could get away with it.'

'Your comments are noted,' Todd said, barely keeping the fury from his voice. 'Now step aside, the OC needs to hear what he has to say.'

The two guards – both paratroopers – stood their ground, their weapons in the ready position.

'With the greatest of respect, Captain, they're not going to let you in while your SEP has a loaded weapon,' said Shepherd. 'But if he unloads his weapon and leaves the magazine and his ammunition belt with the guards, he can probably be allowed into the compound. He can pick them up again on his way out.'

Ahmad Khan looked to Todd for guidance, then shrugged and began unloading his AK 74, but he glared at Shepherd, clearly unhappy.

'Do you speak English?' Geordie asked the Afghan.

'Enough,' said the man, handing his ammunition belt and magazine to one of the paratroopers.

'What's your name?'

'Ahmad Khan.'

'Well, Ahmad Khan, you'd better be on your best behaviour while you're here because we'll be watching you.'

The Afghan smiled. 'Do I scare you, soldier? Is that it?' He nodded slowly. 'Yes, I can see the fear in your eyes.' He chuckled.

'You don't scare me, mate,' said Geordie. 'I've slotted more than my fair share of guys like you.'

The Afghan gave a mirthless smile. 'Tread carefully, my friend. We Afghans are a proud people. We don't give in to threats, nor tolerate insults to our honour.'

'Leave it, Geordie,' said Shepherd, putting a hand on the medic's shoulder. 'He can't hurt anyone now.' He nodded at the Captain. 'Morning prayers are about to start,' he said.

Shepherd and Geordie walked away from the entrance as the two paratroopers stepped aside to allow the Captain and the Afghan to enter. They caught up with Jim 'Jimbo' Shortt, an SAS trooper who had been on selection with Shepherd four years earlier.

'What's up with Goldilocks?' asked Jimbo as Shepherd and Geordie fell into step with him. 'Porridge too cold?'

'He's come in with an SEP,' Shepherd said. 'And because the guy speaks English, Todd thinks he's some sort of Deep Throat in a dishdasha.'

Jimbo gave a weary shake of his head. 'Typical fucking Rupert,' he said. 'They always think locals who can speak English must be trustworthy.'

They walked up to the HQ - a grandiose name for the mud-brick building shielded by berms and banks of sandbags, that served as camp office, briefing room, and sleeping quarters for the officers. They filed through the doorway and along a corridor with a series of small, dark rooms opening off it, lit only by narrow windows high up in the walls. There was no furniture in the rooms, just mattresses on the floor with personal belongings kept in plastic bags hanging from nails hammered into the walls. At the far end was a larger space, the office and briefing room, with two trestle tables pushed together in the centre of the room and the walls and every available surface covered with maps, documents and surveillance photographs.

There were already half a dozen troopers there and the three men flopped down into empty chairs. Major Allan Gannon appeared and took his place at the head of the table. He was a big man with wide shoulders and a nose that had been broken at least twice. The Major looked at his watch just as Captain Todd appeared. The Captain nodded at the Major. 'Sorry, Boss,' he said.

'No problem,' said The Major.

The Captain led the morning prayers, giving his intelligence briefing including outlining possible targets on satellite surveillance photographs. When he'd finished, he folded his arms and looked at the Major. 'I have some very interesting human intel that I want to take advantage of,' he said to the Major. 'I have access to an SEP who has just defected. He's on the compound as we speak. But Ahmad Khan has not only defected himself, he has persuaded the rest of his group of twenty Taliban fighters to surrender as well. I need an escort. All his fighters want is five hundred US dollars each and the guarantee of safe conduct that your presence will provide.'

The Major raised his eyebrows. 'Where has this come from?'

'He walked up to an Afghan Army patrol and gave himself up. He said he wanted to speak to the Brits.'

'And not the Yanks?' said The Major.

'He says he doesn't trust the Americans.'

'Is that so? And what is he exactly? A Taliban fighter?'

'He was a sniper, but he's been trained in explosives and IEDs.'

'Has he now?'

'Boss, this stinks to high Heaven,' said Geordie. 'If this was genuine then his men would have come in with him.'

'He thinks there is a risk to their safety if they come in on their own. His men fear that the Afghans might be trigger-happy. They want an escort to bring them in.'

'Boss, I wouldn't trust this raghead as far as I can throw him,' said Geordie. 'I certainly won't be taking a trip up the road with him.'

'That sort of language is unacceptable,' said the Captain.

'What sort of language?' asked Geordie.

'You know what I'm talking about,' said the Captain. He looked over at the Major, obviously hoping for his support.

'I think we do need to tread carefully,' said the Major.

'Talk about into the lion's den,' said Jimbo. 'For all we know, he could be setting up an ambush.'

'I've spoken to the man, I can vouch for him,' said Todd.

'Then you can go and bring in his men,' said Geordie.

'You can't trust these guys,' said Jock McIntyre, his voice a Glaswegian growl. Jock was a twelve-year veteran of the SAS and had been a Para for eight years before that. In all he had five times as much experience as the Captain, and both men knew it. 'If they switch sides once, they'll do it again. And I wouldn't want them in the compound with guns in their hands.'

Captain Todd was faced with a row of nodding heads and his lips tightened into a thin white line. Although he outranked them, Todd had already discovered that in the SAS, respect was given only to skill and battlefield experience, not to stripes on the sleeve or pips on the shoulder.

'And I'm certainly not going to be volunteering to ride off into the middle of nowhere with this Ahmad Kahn,' said Jock. 'No matter who vouches for him.'

The Captain glanced at the Major for support again. 'Ahmad Khan has already proved his worth by identifying a previously unknown Taliban commander,' said Todd. 'B Squadron are dealing with him.'

'If he's previously unknown, we've only the SEP's word that the guy really is a Taliban commander,' said Jock. 'He could just be some local warlord or the leader of a rival faction that he wants to get rid of. And even if the SEP's men seriously do want to switch sides, why would we take the risk of providing them with an escort, when they could just come in themselves?'

'Because they're afraid that they'll be walking into an ambush,' Todd said.

Jock shrugged. 'The same fear that we'd have about going to an RV in the mountains with them, then. I've not heard anything to change my mind.' There was a rumble of agreement from the other SAS men. Jock was one of the most experienced men in the Squadron and one of the most highly-regarded.

Todd looked over at the Major but Gannon just shrugged. It wasn't the sort of mission that he could force on his men. 'Right,' Todd said, after a lengthy pause. 'I'll see if the members of the Para Support Group are less mule-headed.'

Todd strode out of the room.

'Tosser,' said one of the troopers.

'Bloody Rupert,' said another.

'Give the guy a break, lads,' said the Major. 'He's still wet behind the ears.'

'I know he's keen, Boss, but this has all the makings of a trap,' said Shepherd. 'We've seen this guy and something doesn't smell right.'

'Yeah, and it's not just the fact that he hasn't showered for a month,' said Geordie.

'No one's forcing any of you to go,' said the Major.

'Someone needs to tell him he's playing with fire,' said Shepherd.

'Let's see how it plays out,' said the Major. 'If he's right then it could be an intel coup for us. He could ID a lot of local bad guys for us.'

Shepherd wasn't convinced but knew better than to press his luck with the Major. He walked out of the HQ with Geordie. Shepherd saw Lex Harper running around the perimeter of the compound with a large rucksack on his back. The young Para had already watched Shepherd's back while serving as his spotter on a couple of previous ops and Shepherd realised he had the chance to return the favour.

'He's keen,' said Geordie.

'He's a good lad,' said Shepherd. 'He's wasted in the Paras. I'm going to suggest he puts himself for Selection when he gets back to the UK.' He waved over at Lex and the Para sprinted over to them. He'd clearly been running for a while and he leaned forward, hands on his knees, his chest heaving and sweat dripping from his brow into the dust.

'Sure you're cut out for this line of work?' Shepherd said with a grin. 'Special Forces never sweat.'

'Is that right?' Lex said, grinning back. 'They talk a lot of shite, though. So what's up?'

'Todd's looking for volunteers for a job,' Shepherd said. 'Make sure you're not one of them.'

Lex gave him a curious look. 'Any particular reason why?'

Shepherd shrugged. 'We've just got a bad feeling about it.'

Geordie hawked and spat. 'He's wanting the Paras to take his new Taliban boyfriend up country,' he growled. 'And on a good day, they'll be bringing back another twenty SEPs, Pied Piper style.'

'And on a bad day?'

'On a bad day it could all turn to shit,' said Shepherd. 'So no volunteering, okay?'

Lex nodded. 'Okay, got it,' he said. 'Thanks. I owe you one.'

'What's in the rucksack?' asked Geordie.

Lex grinned and shrugged the rucksack off his back. It hit the ground with a thud. 'Just some gear. Dirty laundry, mainly.'

Geordie laughed. 'Bricks, mate. That's what you need. Bricks wrapped in newspapers.'

'That's a wind-up, right?' said Lex, looking at Shepherd.

Shepherd grinned. 'Nah, it's Gospel,' he said. 'Geordie got me into it years ago. You need something heavy, really heavy. That's what builds muscle and stamina. The harder you train, the easier it is when it's for real.' He pointed down at Lex's dust-covered Nikes. 'And lose the training shoes. You want to run in boots.'

'Bloody hell, you want to make it difficult for yourself, don't you?' said the Para.

'That's the point,' said Shepherd. 'Train hard, fight easy. The times in your life when you'll need to run like the devil are probably the times when you're not wearing your Nikes.'

Lex nodded. 'Thanks,' he said.

'And remember – no volunteering.'

* * *

An hour later, Shepherd and Geordie saw a Landrover pull out of the compound. Two Paras sat in front, with another one alongside Ahmad Khan in the back. There was a Gimpy - a General Purpose Machine Gun - mounted on the bonnet and the three Paras all carried M16s. The Afghan had his AK74 cradled in his lap.

'I see Captain Dickhead isn't with them,' said Geordie.

'No back up, either,' said Shepherd. 'I tell you, this is going to go tits-up.'

'You're preaching to the converted, mate.'

Jock walked over, carrying two green ammo boxes. Shepherd gestured at the disappearing Landrover. 'No back-up? What's the story?'

'Todd reckons the RV with the Taliban fighters is in an area that had been pacified and was largely peaceful, at least by day. Says one vehicle is all they need.'

'Bollocks,' said Jimbo. 'There are Taliban insurgents everywhere, staging hit and run raids, extorting money and supplies, or assassinating village elders suspected of collaborating with the British and Americans. Where does he come up with "pacified?" The man's a bloody idiot and he's going to get people killed.'

'Are you volunteering to go with them?" asked Jock.

'It's too late anyway,' said Shepherd. The Landrover had just disappeared around a bend in the road.

* * *

According to Jock, it should have taken the Landrover just over ninety minutes to reach the RV. Assuming it would take half an hour to muster the Taliban fighters, and a maximum of two hours to get them back to the compound, they should have returned by two o'clock in the afternoon at the latest.

At one o'clock Shepherd wandered over to the entrance of the compound. Half an hour later he was joined by Lex. 'No sign?' asked the Para.

'We don't know what transport the Taliban guys have,' said Shepherd.

'I don't suppose they'll be walking.'

'Anything on comms?' asked Shepherd.

'They said they were approaching the RV but nothing since,' said Lex. 'That's not good, is it?'

'No, mate. Not good at all.'

The two men paced up and down under the hot Afghan sun. 'You married, Spider?' asked the Para.

'Yeah, why do you ask?'

'One of the guys was saying you had a wife and kid. But you don't wear a ring.'

'Never been a big fan of jewellery,' said Shepherd. 'But yeah, I've been married for going on five years. And my boy's four. You?'

'Nah, had a girlfriend but that went south when I signed up.'

'Yeah, it's not easy being involved with a soldier. My wife's forever nagging me to hand in my papers.'

'Serious?'

'Dead serious. She reckons that it's too dangerous.'

'Bless her,' said Lex, and the two men laughed.

'She's got a point, though,' said Shepherd. 'It was different when I was based in Hereford and could get home most nights. I could help around the house and be a dad for Liam. I've missed two of his last birthdays and it's looking like we're going to be here over Christmas.'

'That goes with the job, though,' said Lex.

'She's a Hereford girl so she understands that. But when she married me she had no way of knowing how crazy the world was going to get.'

'And will you do it? Hand in your papers?'

'And do what?' said Shepherd. 'I'm a soldier, that's what I do. I can't go back and work in an office.' He shrugged. 'I've told her to wait and see how this works out. I can see us being here for ever.'

'I'm not sure about this,' said Lex. 'It's a right mess here. The Russians couldn't control this country and I don't see that we'll do a better job. And I don't know about you but I'm getting a bad feeling about Iraq.'

'In what way?'

'I think the Yanks want to invade. And if they go in Blair will have us in on Uncle Sam's coat tails.'

Shepherd smiled ruefully. 'I hope Sue doesn't start thinking that way,' he said.

'I'm serious, Spider. Since 9-11 the Yanks have been on a mission.'

Shepherd nodded. 'You might be right.'

Geordie jogged over, his round face bathed in sweat. 'Boss wants you in the briefing room,' he said.

'Problem?'

'He reckons they've been gone long enough. And there's been nothing on comms for a while.'

'Can I come?' asked Lex.

'Don't see why not,' said Shepherd. The three men hurried over to the briefing room where the Major was huddled over a map with Jimbo, Jock and two other SAS troopers. There was no sign of Captain Todd.

The Major looked up. 'I'm getting a bad feeling about this,' he said. 'I'm asking Jock to put together a Quick Reaction Force, a small group with a big punch if it's needed.' He nodded at Jock. 'Don't take a heap of men with you though, but you'll need a Forward Air Controller and a Royal Engineer Search Team, in case of mines or booby traps. And take a couple of Laser Target Markers. I'll make sure there are fast jets with Paveways in the air and in the area the whole time that you're on the ground.'

'Okay Boss,' Jock said. 'We might be best with B-52s out of Diego Garcia. You know what the Bagram jet jockeys are like, they hate being too close to the ground because it puts them within range of the muj SAM-7s. If they're flying low and one of them is launched, they've got to go on the tail and race the missile up to 15,000 feet, hoping it'll run out of fuel before it blows their arseholes out through their nostrils. The B 52s'll just cruise out of sight, well above the SAM-7's height ceiling, and if we get an LTM on a target, they can just drop the iron bomb and let the laser detector on the Paveway's nose and the fins on its tail do the rest.'

'Okay,' the Boss said. 'And I want you to take Todd with you. He caused this fuck-up. Make sure that he sees the consequences of his pig-headedness and learns from it'. He looked at his watch. 'Let's get moving.'

The SAS troopers headed out of the briefing room. 'Spider, can I tag along?' asked Lex.

'Is that okay with you, Jock?' asked Shepherd.

'Better than okay,' growled Jock. 'In fact he can bring half a dozen or so of his mates. I'll get a one-tonner sorted.'

'Off you go, mate,' said Shepherd. 'We'll clear it with your boss. As much firepower as you can carry.'

Lex nodded and ran off.

'Right Spider, we've got work to do,' said Jock, patting him on the back.

* * *

With sunset less than three hours away, Jock led a convoy of three SAS Landrovers and a one-tonner full of Paras and Engineers out of the compound to search for the missing men, though only the most optimistic of them expected to find the three Paras alive. They were armed with Gimpies, assault rifles and grenade launchers.

Shepherd sat next to Jock and Captain Todd sat in the back. The officer didn't speak during the drive over the rough and shell-cratered road towards the mountains.

The place where Ahmad Khan had taken the Paras to RV with his Taliban fighters was a dead-end valley with steep-sided hills surrounding it. Jock called the convoy to a halt near the valley entrance, where the road narrowed to little more than a dirt track running alongside the bed of a dried up river. He ordered four of the Paras to set up a perimeter around the vehicles then gathered the SAS and the rest of the Paras around him. 'Right,' he said. 'It's been the same old story in Afghan warfare since Adam was a lad: whoever controls the high ground controls the battle. So, two groups of four - Jimbo, you take one, Geordie the other - one either side of the valley, picketing the high ground. Spider, you stay with me. Each group, carry an LTM. We've no mortars, unfortunately - too heavy for this job - but we've got all the air support we need, so if there are muj heavy weapons or concentrations of fighters up there, get an LTM on them and we'll call in the cavalry. We'll give you thirty minutes to get into position and then we'll begin moving up the valley floor at 1520.'

The two groups formed and moved off, Jimbo and Geordie leading the way, Geordie's short steps contrasting with Jimbo's rangy, ground-eating stride, but both men covered the ground equally fast, moving up the sides of the valley as smoothly as if they were on an escalator.

The rest of the men waited on the valley floor with Jock and Shepherd. Shepherd walked over to the Forward Air Controller. 'Keep the jets high,' Shepherd said. 'Out of sight and sound. We don't want to spoil the surprise for any muj who might be here, now do we?'

Todd appeared at his elbow. 'The REs look jumpy,' he said.

Shepherd looked across at the engineers, huddled in a group near the back of the one-tonner. They looked painfully young, white-faced and twitchy with nerves. 'Not surprising, is it?' he said. 'They're the poor saps who have to find the devices before the Bomb Disposal guys can deal with them. Wherever they're serving, none of them last more than a couple of tours. Once they realise the risks, they leave the Army PDQ, or at least those of them who are still alive do. Worst job in the army, pretty much.'

He glanced at his watch and spoke into his throat mic. 'In position?' There was a double click in his ear-piece, followed a moment later by another as Jimbo and Geordie acknowledged.

'They're ready, Jock,' said Shepherd. Jock nodded and signalled to the others to move out and began to lead the advance along the road, his gaze never still, raking the road ahead and the ground to either side. Todd followed a couple of paces behind Shepherd. They had been moving forward slowly but steadily for some twenty minutes when they cleared a low rise and saw the Landrover some way ahead of them, nose down in a ditch at the side of the road. Two figures were visible, still in their seats, though both sprawled at odd angles. Another lay in the dirt a yard or so away. Shepherd felt a surge of anger and wanted to lash out at once at the officer who had sent them to their deaths, but there was no time for recriminations - they were all in danger until the job was done. He tried to put the cold focus of his anger on the enemy, not the man behind him.

When he saw the Landrover, Todd let out a sound that was somewhere between a gasp and a cry and began to stumble towards it. 'Freeze!' Shepherd barked. Todd stopped dead, his gaze still fixed on the Landrover. 'There may be an IED or a booby-trap,' Shepherd said. 'We wait while the REs clear the area.' He nodded to the engineers and they fanned out into a line and began inching their way forward, some sweeping mine detectors in arcs over the ground ahead of them, while others probed with thin steel prodders.

'They're not probing for mines are they?' Todd said, nervously. 'If they hit a mine with one of those rods, they'll blow themselves to pieces.'

'They're looking for command wires,' said Shepherd. 'Our AWACs and Nimrods can suppress the wireless initiation of devices but the Taliban usually prefer the old-fashioned methods.' They watched in silence as the REs continued the search, moving steadily away from them and towards the Landrover. Suddenly there was a "Pop" sound in the distance.

Shepherd recognised the sound immediately. 'Mortar!' he shouted.

'Take cover,' Todd yelled, throwing himself flat and worming towards the ditch at the side of the road. Up ahead the REs searching for command wires had also flattened themselves to the ground.

Shepherd smiled despite the seriousness of the situation. 'No rush,' he said, strolling over to the ditch and squatting down alongside Todd. 'Time of flight for a mortar is a good thirty seconds and after that all you can do is hope for the best.'

The seconds ticked by with agonising slowness. There was no way of predicting where the mortar shell would fall nor, if it landed close by, any way of avoiding its murderous shrapnel. The jagged fragments of steel, white hot from the furnace of the explosion, would blast outwards with devastating force and if it landed on top you it was game over. After half a minute of stomach churning tension, there was a loud "crump!" sound that

Shepherd felt in the pit of his stomach as dirt and smoke erupted into the air. The mortar round had exploded about fifty feet away from the engineers. 'They're not after us,' Shepherd said. 'They're after the Search Team.'

A cloud of smoke and dust dispersed slowly on the breeze and the REs got to their feet, unhurt, and resumed their slow, methodical search.

Shepherd spoke into his throat mic. 'Pickets, keep your eyes peeled for that mortar crew.'

Again there was the double-click of acknowledgement from Jimbo and Geordie. Shepherd glanced up towards the ridgelines on either side, and saw a faint movement as the pickets moved further up the valley, hunting for a position from which they could spot the hidden mortar crew.

At random intervals a handful of mortar rounds dropped into the valley, bracketing the search team as they moved towards the Landrover.

'Any sign of them?' called Jock.

'They're well hidden,' said Shepherd.

'Why can't the pickets spot them?' Todd asked.

'Because the Taliban are being very cautious,' Shepherd said. 'Weapons are ten a penny but good mortar crews are precious. Takes a long time to train a crew so they make sure they're protected.'

There was another popping sound off in the distance and half a minute later another mortar round exploded. This time it was much closer to the Search Team and one of the REs, lying prone in the dirt, was picked up and flung sideways by the blast. He lay on the ground screaming in pain and fear as a Paratrooper medic ran to him. The medic crouched over him and pressed a trauma pad onto a wound on his thigh.

'This is a bloody nightmare,' said Todd.

'He's probably all right,' Shepherd said. 'Geordie always reckons that if they're making that much noise, they're going to be okay. It's the ones who make no sound at all who have serious trauma.' Shepherd didn't feel half as calm as he sounded. The mortar strikes were ranging in on the Search

Team, and though that round might not have been fatal, the next one might well be.

A moment later, Geordie's voice crackled in Shepherd's earpiece. 'Spotted them - three muj with a mortar.'

'Bingo,' Shepherd said. 'Mark them with the LTD.'

'Laying LTD now.'

Once Geordie had aimed his laser at the mortar crew the bombers would be able to take it out with pinpoint accuracy.

'LTD laid,' said Geordie. An instant later, Shepherd heard the Forward Air Controller on the net to the AWACs, calling in an airstrike.

'How will we know when it's going to happen?' asked Todd.

Shepherd shrugged. 'We won't. The first news we'll get is "Bang!" You ever seen a five hundred pound bomb go off? It's quite a show. The LTD doesn't have to be anywhere near the target; as long as it's in line of sight with it, that's enough. We'll not see or hear the jet. The pilot doesn't even aim, he just drops it blind and the detector in the nose cone homes in along the laser light track emitted from the LTD, and steers itself onto the target with the fins on its tail.'

'Sounds like a video game,' said Todd.

'It pretty much is,' said Shepherd. 'Except you only get the one life.'

The minutes ticked by in a silence broken only by the now muted cries of the wounded RE when suddenly there was vivid flash from the ridge to the north-east. Red-orange flame and oily black smoke boiled upwards while fragments that might have been rock, metal - or body parts - were flung out, black against the sky. A moment later the sound of the blast rolled over them like a clap of thunder, and the shock wave swept through in a storm of fine dust and debris. As Shepherd dusted himself down he heard Geordie's laconic voice in his earpiece: 'Target neutralised'.

The REs showed less signs of nerves as they resumed their work and five minutes later there was an excited shout as one of them reached down into the dirt and held up a length of a command wire. 'Got it!' he shouted.

He used a pair of wire cutters to sever the wire before moving towards the Landrover with the rest of the REs. Lex and a group of Paras tracked the wire in the other direction, weapons at the ready. The wire extended to a clump of wind-stunted acacia trees that had provided cover for the bombers, but they had already fled and the Paras returned empty-handed.

The REs had followed the command wire to a device buried by the wrecked Landrover. It contained enough explosive to blow up the Landrover and anyone near it.

'It's safe!' shouted one of the Res.

Shepherd, Jock and Todd walked over to the Landrover. Jock checked the bodies for life signs one by one, even though there was no doubt that they were all stone dead.

They had all been shot at close range with a semi-automatic weapon. None of their weapons had been fired. Two of the men were still in their seats. The one who had been sitting behind the driver had a bullet hole above his left ear and a much larger exit wound on the other side of his head. The front-seat passenger had been shot in the back of the head; his blood and brains covered the windscreen. The driver had had time to jump from his seat, but had then been cut down by a burst of fire in the back before he had gone a yard. There was no sign of Ahmad Khan and no blood on the seat he had been occupying, but the floor around it was littered with ejected 5.45 cases.

The Captain stared at the cases.

'That's right, they're from an AK74,' said Shepherd.

'Khan shot them, is that what you're saying?'

'What do you think, Captain? Seriously?'

Todd put a hand up to his face, covering his eyes. 'I had no idea.'

'We warned you,' said Jock. 'You can't trust these ragheads.'

Todd's face had gone white. He began to shake and then he threw up over the offside front wheel. Jock shook his head in disgust.

Shepherd waved over at the Paras and they came over and began to load the bodies of their dead comrades into the truck.

Todd walked away from the Landrover and stood staring at the ground, cradling his carbine.

'Part of me wants to give him a piece of my mind, part of me wants to tell him that we all make mistakes,' Shepherd said to Jock.

'Yeah, but not all mistakes end up with three dead Paras,' said Jock. He cursed under his breath. 'I should've stopped them going. I knew it was a mistake. I should have told the Boss to stop them.'

'Could have, would have, should have,' said Shepherd.

'I'm just saying, this is partly my fault.'

'Don't be a prick, Jock. You told them it was a bad idea and you were overruled by a Captain and a Major.'

'Ours not to reason why, eh?'

'Something like that.' Shepherd spat at the ground. 'We do our best, it's just sometimes our best isn't good enough.' He nodded over at the Captain. 'He knows what he did was wrong and he'll never make that mistake again. What we need to do is find the murdering bastard and sort him out.'

Jock nodded. 'Amen to that.'

* * *

The body bags containing the dead Paras were heli-ed out later that day, beginning the long journey home that would end, not with a silent procession through the streets of the Para Support Group's base at St Asaph, but in near-anonymous funerals attended only by their family and close friends. In common with other Special Forces deaths, the casualties would be acknowledged but the regimental affiliations of the dead men would be concealed to preserve the secrecy of SAS operations.

Anyone who bothered to study the small print of combat deaths would have been surprised at how many men from the Royal Anglian Regiment had apparently lost their lives in Afghanistan. It had become so noticeable that in recent months the Mercian and Yorkshire Regiments had also been used as cover for the deaths of Special Forces soldiers.

Todd kept a very low profile over the next few days, but though he was censured, he was allowed to remain with the SAS Squadron, to Jock's undisguised disgust. 'If we'd pulled that kind of fuck up, we'd have been RTU'd toot sweet,' he said in his trademark Glaswegian growl. 'But as it's a Rupert, they just put it down to the learning curve and let him carry on.'

Shepherd nodded. 'I know, but look, he knows how badly he fucked up and to be honest when we were young and keen most of us caused cock-ups that could have been just as disastrous. I don't know about you, but I certainly thought I knew it all when I passed Selection.'

'You've got that right,' Jock said. 'I've never seen such a cocky bugger.'

Shepherd grinned. 'I had my moments, didn't I? Anyway, we're stuck with Todd for now, and however hard we are on him about it, I'm sure he'll be a hell of a sight harder on himself, so let's give him a break, okay?'

You're too soft sometimes, you know that?'

'Yeah, so I've been told.'

* * *

For the next week Spider was engaged on routine surveillance, intelligence gathering and their trademark hearts and minds work, with Geordie dispensing drugs and dressings and carrying out minor operations on the local villagers. It was work that had won the SAS local allies in every campaign in which they'd fought but it was hard going in Afghanistan as Geordie ruefully remarked as they made their way back to the FOB after another long, tiring day in the field. 'Hearts and Minds is fine when we're operating on our own. But it only takes the Yanks to fire one Hellfire missile into the middle of an Afghan wedding party to fuck up six months of patient work.'

Shepherd enjoyed meeting the local Afghans and he got some satisfaction from actually being able to help. Antibiotics were in short supply and infections often went untreated. It was amazing to see the difference that a few tablets could make.

After seven days in the field, they were recalled to the main base at Bagram. As the heli landed on the sprawling base, shared with U.S. forces and awash with American personnel, vehicles and kit, they could see that the mountains of military equipment were still being added to, as forklift trucks shuttled between giant C5 transports on the concrete hard standing and the supply dumps ringing the base. It was clear that the Americans were in Afghanistan to stay – for the foreseeable future at least.

As the heli came to a stand and the rotors wound down, Shepherd jumped down and glanced around. 'Do you know what?' he said. 'After a few weeks in that fly-blown dust-bowl we laughingly call an FOB, even Bagram is beginning to look quite civilised.'

'Don't get too excited,' Jock said. 'The Boss has set up a briefing for seventeen hundred hours today. So we may not be here for long.'

The briefing room was a windowless, air-conditioned room, set below ground in a building shielded by concrete blast walls and berms bulldozed out of the sandy Afghan soil. As Shepherd, Jock, Jimbo and Geordie and the other members of the Squadron filed into the briefing room, they found Todd already there, adjusting a laptop projector and spreading a series of maps and documents on the table. He waited until they had all seated themselves before speaking. 'Before we get the briefing under way, I have something I need to say.' He took a deep breath, then turned to face Shepherd and Jock directly. 'I owe you all an apology. I screwed up badly over Ahmad Khan. I was an idiot and three men paid the ultimate price for my stupidity. I know nothing can bring those men back, but I want to make what amends I can, and to do so I'm claiming "Droit de Seigneur". I want to be in at the kill.'

Shepherds eyebrows shot skywards and he could see several of the troopers frowning in confusion.

'Twat what?' said Jimbo, and Spider threw him a withering look.

'How do you know about that?' Shepherd said.

There was a tradition within the Regiment that the murderer of any SAS guy killed in cold blood would be hunted until he was found and killed. Any man claiming Droit de Seigneur because of his personal involvement with the original incident or friendship with the dead man, had the right to be involved in any operation to kill the murderer.

The Captain saw that several of the men were confused so he struggled to explain himself. Droit de Seigneur goes back to the Middle Ages, when feudal lords claimed the right to deflower the local virgins. In the Regiment it refers to the right for revenge. One of the "old and bold" SAS guys told me about it. He said he'd claimed the right in Oman, after his best mate was killed, but it had also happened as far back as Borneo in the 1960s, when a captured SAS man was tortured and murdered by an Indonesian Army Sergeant. The Squadron offered blood money to the local highland tribes to kill the man responsible and it was paid after the tribesmen produced the head of the Indonesian sergeant as proof that he had been killed.'

Jock raised a hand. 'You're confusing me, now. This is about Ahmad Khan?'

Todd flicked his fringe away from his eyes. 'Very much so.'

'You know where he is?'

'That's the purpose of this briefing. Yes.' He looked over at the Major who was sitting at the back of the room, his arms folded across his chest. The Major nodded, letting Todd know that he should get on with it.

'Right,' said Todd, his confidence returning. 'We've received very credible intelligence that a mud brick building in the tribal areas across the Pakistan border is a money clearing house, where some of the proceeds of the Taliban's opium trafficking, protection rackets, etc, etc, are being paid out to the local fighters to keep them loyal. We believe there are around a dozen Taliban there. I've spent a lot of Intelligence funds tracking Khan, and a fair bit of my own money too. Like I said, I screwed up and I'm doing my best to put it right. Anyway, I have good humint, that's been assessed by the Boss as well as by me, that Khan is at the clearing house.'

'Right enough,' Jock said. 'Spend enough money, you can always get humint.' Jimbo murmured in agreement.

Todd took a deep breath. He was clearly uneasy about speaking in public. 'According to the reports, one of the Taliban there has a curious eye defect - one brown pupil, one milky-white one. The source got close enough to see a group of men in Afghan dress outside the building. Most were holding AK47s, but one had an AK74 slung over his shoulder. I'm ninety per cent sure that we have identified Ahmad Khan.' He shook his head. 'Correction, I'm one hundred per cent sure. It's him. And we need to take him out.' He nodded at the Major, who had his chin on his chest and seemed to be staring at his boots. 'I've asked the Boss for the chance to lead the group to do the job.' He paused again, staring unseeing at the wall at the far end of the room. 'As you all know, I have a personal debt to repay, but if you're willing to be part of the team, I'd like you men alongside me when we do the job.' He looked directly at Shepherd and Jock.

Shepherd nodded immediately. Jock flashed him a sideways look. 'Seriously?' he whispered.

'Why not?' said Shepherd.

Jimbo held up his hand. 'Count me in,' he said.

Jock sighed and slowly raised his hands. 'In for a penny,' he said.

'Just like the three musketeers,' said Jimbo.

'Make that four,' said Geordie.

'We're all in,' said Shepherd, and the Captain smiled gratefully.

The Major stood up. 'Five should be enough,' he said. 'We'll leave you to it. Considering this is over the border, the less we know the better.'

The Major left the room, followed by the rest of the SAS troopers. The Captain walked over to a table that was overflowing with maps, surveillance imagery and intelligence data. Jock, Spider, Jimbo and Geordie joined him.

'What's the plan ?' Jock asked Todd.

'We take out anyone in the building and destroy any money that's there,' said the Captain. 'That alone will make the mission worthwhile. But there are some very heavy hitters going in and out of that building and every one of them is a viable target. But what I want is the chance to take out Ahmad Kahn. That's the mission, but obviously you guys have the experience so I'm going to be relying on your know-how.'

As the most experienced man there, Jock took the lead but standard practice was for every man to chip in if he had any suggestions or reservations. 'Usual rules,' Jock said. 'If you've anything to say about the plan we're putting together, say it now. If it all goes tits up, and you've said nothing at the planning stage, you don't get to whine about it afterwards.' All the men nodded, including the Captain.

'Okay,' continued Jock, studying the map and frowning. 'Insertion will be by Chinook and, given the distance to the target and the time we're going to need there, it's going to be close to maximum range even with an extra fuel tank in the cargo bay. So we're going to have to strip out everything inessential from the heli and make our own kit and equipment as light as possible. It's going to be a long and not particularly comfortable flight, because the only place left for us and our kit is going to be the tailgate, so we'll either have to stand or lie on the floor. I think six is the maximum we can take which means we can take one more.'

'Who do you suggest ?' asked the Captain.

'I'll grab Billy Armstrong,' said Jock. He's around somewhere.

'It's a long flight, Jock,' said Shepherd. 'To save weight we could cut back on the crew.'

Jock nodded. The Chinook would normally be crewed by four men - two pilots and two crewmen, with the second pilot acting as navigator. 'We can take three pilots and use one of them as a navigator. But Spider's right, with all the fuel and equipment we'll need, it's going to be a heavy flight.' He looked across at Captain Todd. 'You've not been on one of these super-heavy flights before, have you? Just so you know, when it's fully loaded - and on this flight it'll probably be overloaded - the Chinook pilots achieve take off by rolling along the runway until they've built up enough momentum and sufficient lift to get airborne. It can be a bit scary if you're not expecting it.'

'What about the landing zone?' asked the Captain.

'The best type of LZ is a dome-shaped feature because then the wind will usually dissipate the sound of the heli, making it very difficult for Taliban spotters or sentries to pinpoint where it is,' said Geordie. 'We've often found that it's impossible to even detect whether a heli is there at all until you can get visual on it, and since we'll be night-flying without navigation lights, the Taliban will probably have to be sitting on the same hilltop to spot us.'

'It also gives us a further advantage,' Shepherd said, 'because with a feature that's accessible from all directions, even if we're observed landing, it's impossible for anyone to predict in what direction we're going to move away from there.'

The Captain nodded. It was clear from his expression that this was all very new to him.

They began pouring over a large-scale map of the area around the target. 'For us to be absolutely certain that the Chinook won't be detected by anyone at or near the target, the LZ needs to be a minimum of ten kilometres away,' said Jock. 'Let's say twelve clicks for safety.'

'Which might make this,' Todd said, tapping the map at a point where the contour lines indicated a roughly round-topped hill with steep, but usable slopes on all sides, 'a very plausible LZ.'

Shepherd glanced at it. 'Looks good to me,' he said. 'What about getting to the site? We're going on foot?'

Jock shook his head. 'With the extra fuel tank filling the load space, we don't have the room or the weight allowance to use quad bikes. And because it's a cross-border op, all our kit and particularly anything we're leaving behind, needs to be non-attributable. I'm thinking 50cc mopeds.'

Geordie laughed out loud. 'You're taking the piss, right?'

'I'm serious, mate,' said Jock. 'They're small, quiet and relatively light, and they're similar to the ones the Taliban use. That'll be a big plus if we get spotted by the muj. The heli will land on the Afghan side of the border and we'll cross on the bikes.'

'It's not a great distance,' Todd said. 'As you'd expect, the clearing house is very close to the border.' He rubbed his chin thoughtfully. 'It works for me.'

Jock nodded. 'Now, Comms. Because weight is an absolute premium we will not be taking any comms kit other than our Personal Locator Beacons. Once activated, the PLBs send out a pulse signal which will be picked up on a pre-determined frequency by a Nimrod or AWACs aircraft. Activating a single PLB at the selected time will indicate that everything is OK. If more than one PLB is activated at any other time, it will be an emergency signal and the Nimrod will send the Chinook back to the area. It will do a linear approach along the route we are exiting for an immediate pick up. All we have to do is hit a valley and go along it and the Chinook will find us. For short range comms to the Chinook there is a voice capability to talk the heli in to the LZ.'

Todd cleared his throat. 'Yes, Captain?' Shepherd said.

'I understand that weight is at a premium, but I'm wondering why we're leaving ourselves so light on comms equipment and yet taking half a dozen mopeds for what is only a relatively short distance. We could walk in to the target in a couple of hours.'

'True,' Jock said. 'We could, but when we detonate those charges, every muj within fifty miles is going to come running. So we need to be in like Flynn, do the job and get out again. Okay?' He waited for a nod from Todd before continuing.

'Right, I'm thinking all we need is six, four to form a defensive cordon around the building and stop our one-eyed friend, or anyone else for that matter, from escaping, and a two-man assault group. Geordie will be the team medic for emergencies.' He looked across at the Captain. 'Spider's got explosives experience, so I suggest that he and you form the assault group. That gives you the chance to be in at the kill.'

'That's fine by me,' said Todd.

Jock looked at Shepherd. 'Sure,' said Shepherd.

'All good,' said Jock. 'Now, arms. All of us will carry AKS 74s, the ones with the folding butts, that can be slung across the chest ready for immediate use. We're using them because weight restrictions are going to be very tight and the 5.45 cal ammo the AK 74 uses is very light, so we can carry a lot of it. Each man will also carry a three foot length of a sectional ladder, for the assault on our friends' hide-out.' He glanced at Todd. 'Don't worry, we often use them. They're standard kit for Counter-Terrorist teams, short enough to carry in vehicles - or on mopeds - and obtainable from most heavy lift aircraft. In theory you can make a ladder as long as you want it, but, judging from the description of the target, we'll not need more than eighteen feet. It's a three-storey building and like all assaults we'll be doing it top down, because it's impossible to clear a building by going up the stairs. Even a kid with a catapult can be enough to stop a highly-trained team of experts.' He nodded at Shepherd. 'Explosives?'

'I'm thinking of using shaped charges of standard issue, PE4 to effect entry by blowing holes through the walls.' Shepherd paused. 'Have you done any demolitions, Captain?' Captain Todd shook his head. 'Well, the shaped charges are PE4 plastic explosives held in triangular-shaped sections of plastic material. Because the charge is shaped, it will go through any material: metal, brick, concrete, whatever, without a lot of collateral damage. Provided you protect your ears, you can stand quite near to it, even as close as one or two yards if you're feeling really lucky, although you're a lot safer if you're around a corner when it goes off. Obviously it requires an initiation set to get it to explode and we'll be using a Number 33 electric detonator - a length of cable and an initiator, either battery or exploder.'

Todd frowned. 'There may be twelve or even more Taliban fighters inside the building. Are you confident that an assault team of two will be enough? And, apart from the AK74s, what weapons we'll be using to clear the rooms inside the building of the Taliban?'

'A dustpan and brush would be handy,' Jock said, provoking a burst of laughter from the others.

'There won't be any Taliban to deal with because anyone inside that building will be dead,' explained Shepherd. 'What kills anyone inside a room when a shaped charge detonates is not the debris blown in by the explosion but the sudden increase in air pressure. It's known as "overpressure" and it instantly destroys most of the organs in the human body.' He showed Todd a well-thumbed booklet full of columns of figures. 'Normally SAS demolitions work with a precise amount of PE4, calculated using these tables in response to the thickness and materials of the walls to be breached and the estimated size of the rooms beyond. You then fill the plastic form that holds the shaped charge with just the right amount of PE4 to breach the walls.'

'So what form will we be using for this?' Jimbo asked.

Shepherd shrugged. 'Well, we've got what are probably double-skinned mud-brick walls, and rooms of around two hundred square feet, but knowing that a rat's nest of Taliban are going to be hiding inside those walls, including the bastard who killed three of our guys, I'm not too worried about precision, so screw them, let's just go for P for Plenty and pack in enough PE4 to destroy a reinforced concrete wall, never mind a mud-brick one. Any objections?' No voices were raised in protest. Jock patted him on the back.

'Lastly, RVs,' Jock said. 'First RV here.' His finger jabbed at a point on the map. 'Emergency RV here,' he pointed to another, 'open until daybreak. The war RV is here,' he said, moving his finger to another point further from the target. 'That'll be good until midnight the following night. After that, anyone separated from the main group will have to make their own E and E. Okay, that's it. Sunset's at sixteen-fifty hours local time today. Final briefing at fifteen hundred hours, take-off at sixteen hundred.'

The briefing over, the men filed out of the room. Jock and Shepherd stayed behind until they were alone with the Captain.

Todd looked at Jock. It was clear that the trooper had something on his mind.

'Permission to speak frankly,' said Jock.

'Of course,' said Todd, frowning.

Jock nodded. 'We all fuck up somewhere along the way, Captain, and it takes balls to admit it when we do. But only a total twat fucks up twice. With that proviso, we're with you all the way, but if we are going to work together on this job, there is one other thing we also need to get clear. As you may already have noticed, this isn't the green army; when we're at work, experience counts more than rank. If I or Spider or Geordie or Jimbo or any of the others tell you to do something, we don't expect to have a fucking discussion about it. If one of us tells you to fire, all we ever want to hear from you is "Bang!" Got it?'

Todd nodded. 'Understood.'

Jock smiled. 'Then we're good to go,' he said. 'Let's go get that bastard and give him the good news.'

As they left the room, Lex hurried over to Shepherd. 'What's the story?' he asked.

'What have you heard?' asked Shepherd. Jock walked away but Shepherd called him back.

'Nothing much,' said Lex. 'Just that there's something up.'

'It's Ahmad Khan. We think we know where he is.'

'And you're going after him?'

'That's the plan,' said Shepherd.

'Spider, I want to come.' He put a hand on Shepherd's shoulder. 'I need to be on this mission.'

'It's SAS only,' said Jock. 'Sorry, mate.'

'Guys, please. It could have been me in that Landrover. If you hadn't had a word, I'd have volunteered. So one of those guys died in my place.'

Shepherd nodded at Jock. 'He's got a point.'

'So he's claiming Singing Twat like the Captain?'

'Droit de Seigneur,' said Shepherd. 'Look, a bird in the hand, right? We're not even sure where Billy is. Lex is here and ready to go.'

'What the hell are you talking about?' asked Lex, totally confused.

Jock ignored him and continued to stare at Shepherd. 'If he comes with us, he's your responsibility,' he said.

'Not a problem.'

'Okay. I'll tell the Captain.'

'I can go?' asked Lex.

'Get your kit,' said Shepherd. 'No overnight gear. Grab an AK74. And lots of ammo. All you can carry.'

* * *

Just before four that afternoon, the six-man team jogged over to the concrete hard standing where a Chinook waited, its twin rotors already turning idly. The cargo area of the massive helicopter, normally big enough to house two Land Rovers, was almost entirely filled by a huge additional fuel tank. It gave the Chinook the range and the time in or near the target area to complete the mission and make the long return flight back to Bagram. Six mopeds were already lashed to the tailgate and the SAS men clambered up with Lex, each with an AK74 carried on a sling around his neck with the folding butt closed. Their pockets were jammed with spare clips for their weapon and their bergens were loaded with more ammunition.

As the Chinook's crew completed their final checks before take-off, the SAS settled themselves, sitting or lying on the tailgate among the mopeds. Lex sat down next to Shepherd. He grinned and nodded at Shepherd but there was no disguising the apprehension in his eyes. Shepherd winked at him.

The din of the rotors increased to a nerve-jangling roar and the Chinook shook and rattled as it began to move, almost invisible inside the fog of dust and dirt stirred up by the groundwash. As Jock had predicted at the briefing, the heli did not rise vertically into the air but began to rumble down the runway like a fixed wing aircraft, so heavily laden that its only means of getting airborne was to build enough forward momentum to generate the necessary lift.

With the engines screaming and the whole airframe vibrating and rattling like a boiler about to explode, the Chinook finally lumbered into the air, its dispensers punching out clouds of chaff and flares to deflect any missiles that might be launched at them. Even above the most fortified and heavily protected military base in the country, the threat of terrorist attacks was never underestimated.

The Chinook rose high into the sky as it cleared the immediate area surrounding the base, and set a course heading due west. Once safe from the prying eyes of the Taliban spies - who watched all air traffic in and out of the base and reported the heading of any troop carrying helicopters - the Chinook descended to low-level and swung round on to its true course, making for the tribal areas.

The first part of the flight was in the low sun of the remaining minutes of daylight. To the north, Shepherd could see the aquamarine ice fields and glaciers high on the slopes of the mountains of the Hindu Kush, with spindrifts of snow spilling from the ridges in the ferocious winds at those heights. He tapped Lex on the shoulder and pointed at the beautiful but forbidding snow-capped peaks as they caught the last rays of the setting sun, turning gold and then deep blood-red as it sank to the western horizon. 'Wow,' mouthed Lex. 'That's awesome.'

The Chinook flew on, so close to the ground that the wash of the rotors shook the trees. Its course twisted and turned as the pilots skirted every town and village and used every natural feature to screen their flight from view. It almost doubled the distance to the target but was the best way of ensuring that they would reach it undetected. The Chinook skimmed a ridge and flew up a narrow valley, following the course of the braided river channels, the turquoise green meltwater from the glaciers in the mountains constantly finding fresh ways through the moraines of rock and gravel washed down by the ferocious spring floods.

Night had fallen and the soldiers put on their Passive Night Goggles. The heli was in total darkness with the pilots also using PNGs to steer and navigate. Through his own goggles, Shepherd could see the starlight reflecting from the surface of the river below them, tracing its course as clearly as if it were floodlit. The wash of the rotors stirred blizzards of dead leaves from the scrub willows and the poplars along the banks, and in the yellow-tinged world view through the goggles, the leaves shone like flakes of gold, circling in eddies around the bare trunks before the river carried them away.

He glanced around him and saw that, true to form, indifferent to the beauty of the natural world over which they were passing, Jock and Geordie were cat-napping. Not for the first time, Shepherd marvelled at their ability to fall asleep anywhere, even on their way to a job that might see them killed, riding in a bucketing Chinook with the thunder of the rotors so loud it was rattling their teeth.

They had been flying for over five hours, when he heard the pilot's voice in his earpiece. 'LZ in fifteen minutes.'

Jock and Geordie were instantly as awake and watchful as the others, their weapons at the ready in case the LZ was compromised. A quarter of an hour later, the Chinook cleared a low ridge, dropped to the floor of a plateau and then rose again, following the steep slopes of the round-topped hill they had identified from the map. The heli came to a hover and landed as the groundwash stirred up a storm of dust and debris.

Jock, Geordie, Jimbo and Lex jumped down and went into positions of all-round defence while Shepherd and the Captain unloaded the mopeds. They remained crouched and watchful as the Chinook took off, rolling forward and plummeting off the hill-top, building speed to generate additional lift. It crawled into the sky, then wheeled away to fly a circuitous holding pattern twenty or thirty miles away, far enough away to avoid any risk of compromise to the operation but near enough to make a fast return when a signal on the tactical beacon called it back to the LZ to extract the team once their job was done.

The team took a few more minutes to watch and listen, allowing their hearing to become attuned to the quietness of the night after the din of the heli. They scanned the surrounding countryside for any movement or sign that might suggest they had been spotted. All was dark and quiet, and eventually Jock signalled to them to move out. He led the column of mopeds down the hill before looping around to make their way to the target.

Jock and Shepherd rode at the head of the column, with Lex, Todd and Jimbo behind them and Geordie as "Tail-end Charlie" at the rear of the line. They rode without lights, their Passive Night Goggles allowing them enough vision to avoid potholes and obstacles in the path. They passed through fields of opium poppies. Milked of their sap, the remaining seed heads had withered and dried brown and hard under the fierce Afghan sun and as the mopeds passed between them, they made a rattling sound that Shepherd could hear above the sound of the moped engine.

Jock led the way up a ridge, following the ghostly line of an animal track and passing the skeleton of a long dead goat. Stripped by vultures of its flesh, patches of skin still clung to the bleached bones, mummified by the sun and the dry cold wind that was constantly blowing through the mountains.

The night was icy, the wind stinging their faces as they cleared the top of the ridge. Jock checked his GPS, signalled to the rest of the team, silenced his engine and freewheeled down the slope, towards the dark, indistinct shape of a tall building set into a fold of the hills.

They hid the mopeds in a clump of trees a hundred yards from the target and moved forward on foot, carrying the sections of ladder and the prepared charges, and leaving a faint trail of their boot-prints on the frost-covered ground. Shepherd caught a whiff of woodsmoke on the breeze as they approached from downwind, and a moment later, the tall shape of the target building loomed out of the surrounding darkness, the wall facing them glowing an eerie yellow through the goggles as it caught and reflected the moonlight filtering through the clouds.

There was a straggle of huts and outbuildings surrounding it and a pile of rubble that might once have been another house. While the others kept watch on the main building, Jimbo and Geordie made sure that all the outbuildings were deserted.

They dug in and watched the main building. In the early hours of the night, two small groups of men arrived and left again. Another hour passed and then a solitary figure, shrouded by a black cloak, emerged from the door and disappeared into the darkness. After that, there was no more traffic, and the faint glow of a lantern inside the building was extinguished well before midnight.

Eventually the area was in darkness, the cloud cover masked the starlight. They waited another full hour before assembling the ladder. Shepherd and Todd crept silently towards the building while the others set up a cordon and covered them. Even if any of the Taliban managed to escape before the charges were detonated, they would not avoid the deadly crossfire from the waiting soldiers.

Shepherd and the Captain placed the ladder against the wall and, after listening for any sound from within the building, Shepherd climbed up and began to place shaped charges against the wall on each floor. He allowed the cables of the initiators to trail over his shoulder as he moved up. When he'd finished, he slid back down the ladder without using the rungs, slowing his descent by using his hands and feet on the outside of the uprights as brakes. He glanced at Todd and mimed protecting his ears.

Todd slipped round the corner and Shepherd followed him, pressing his fingers into his ears to protect them from the shock wave as he triggered the charges. The blasts of the three shaped charges came so close together that they could have been a single explosion.

Within seconds of the detonation, Shepherd was on the move, rushing up the ladder with Todd hard on his heels. The two men stormed through the gaping hole that had been blown in the top floor wall. A thick fog of dust and debris still hung in the air as they swung around their AK74s. Four Taliban lay on the floor, killed as they lay sleeping, their internal organs pulverised by the devastating concussive force of the blast wave. They moved slowly through the building, clearing the rooms one at a time.

The top two floors were sleeping areas, littered with Taliban dead, but the ground floor was where the cash was stored and disbursed. As they blew in the walls, the shaped charges had created a blizzard of hundred dollar bills. The cash was all in US dollars, traded for drugs in Pakistan, extorted from businesses in the areas they controlled, or plundered from the avalanches of cash that the Americans had been pouring into the country in their attempts to buy the loyalty of warlords and tribal elders. Stacked on the floor were crates of ammunition, a few rocket-propelled grenades and a rack of AK 47s.

They turned over the last bodies, three men killed as they slept around the fire on the ground floor. Their faces were contorted in their death agony, but none of them had the distinctive milky white eye of Ahmad Khan. 'He's not here,' Shepherd said. 'We missed him. Bastard.' He looked over at the Captain. 'No point in leaving what's left of the cash and weapons and ammo for any Taliban who turn up later,' he said. 'Flip your goggles up or turn your back while I get a nice fire going for them. The flare in your goggles will blind you for ten minutes if you don't.'

He dragged a few bits of bedding, rags and broken chairs and tables together in the centre of the room, kicked the embers of the fire across the floor and then stacked boxes of the Taliban's ammunition next to the pile. He surveyed his handiwork for a moment, then scooped up a stray $100 bill and set fire to it. He dropped it onto the pile of debris and waited until it was well alight before murmuring into his throat mic, 'Coming out'.

Todd climbed out through the hole in the wall first. As Shepherd moved to follow him, he heard the whiplash crack of an assault rifle and saw Todd fall backwards. There was a second crack as the Captain dropped to the ground, gouts of blood pumping from his throat. Shepherd had seen no muzzle flash but heard answering fire from the SAS cordon and swung up his own weapon, loosing off a burst, firing blind just to keep the muj heads down before he slid down the ladder and ran over to Todd and crouched next to him.

Todd lay sprawled in the dirt, blood still spouting from his throat. The first round had struck his head, close to the left ear, gouging out a chunk of skull. The second had torn out Todd's larynx. Either wound might have been fatal, the two together guaranteed it. Shepherd cursed under his breath, took a syrette of morphine and injected him, squeezing the body of the syrette to push out the drug like toothpaste from a tube. He began fixing a trauma dressing over the wounds, even though he knew he was merely going through the motions, because nothing could save the Captain now. Death was seconds away, a minute or so at the most.

Once the dressings were in place he cradled Todd's head against his chest, listening to the wet, sucking sound of the air bubbling through his shattered larynx as blood soaked his shirt.

The Captain grabbed at his arm as his body began to shudder. There were more bursts of fire off to Shepherd's left. Todd was staring at

Shepherd, his eyes fearful. 'You did good, Captain,' Shepherd said. 'You did good.'

A fresh spasm shook Todd, his eyes rolled up into his head and he slumped sideways to the ground.

As Shepherd looked up, he saw a movement in the shadows by a pile of rubble at the edge of the compound. A dark shape resolved itself into a crouching figure and Shepherd saw a milky-white eye staring at him, though, seen through his goggles, it glowed an eerie yellow. Shepherd grabbed his weapon and swung it up but in the same instant he saw a double muzzle flash. The first round tugged at his sleeve, but the next smashed into his shoulder, a sledgehammer blow knocking him flat on his back, leaving the burst of fire from his own weapon arcing harmlessly into the sky.

A further burst of fire chewed the ground around him, and his face was needled by cuts from rock splinters, though they were no more than gnat bites compared with the searing pain in his shoulder. From the corner of his eye, Shepherd saw Jock swivelling to face the danger and loosing off a controlled burst of double taps, but Ahmad Khan had already ducked into cover behind the rubble.

Shepherd looked down at his shoulder. There was a spreading pool of blood on his jacket, glistening like wet tar in the flickering light of the muzzle flashes as his team kept up a barrage of suppressing fire.

Jimbo ran over, pulling a field dressing from his jacket. 'Stay down,' he shouted and slapped the dressing over the bullet wound. Shepherd took slow, deep breaths and fought to stay calm. 'Geordie, get over here !' shouted Jimbo. 'Spider's hit!'

Geordie sprinted over, bent double. He looked at Todd but could see without checking that the Captain was already dead. He hurried over to Shepherd. 'You okay?' he asked.

Shepherd shook his head. He was far from okay. He opened his mouth to speak but the words were lost as he coughed and choked and his mouth filled with blood. Helpless, he saw the dark shape of the Taliban killer move away, inching around the rubble heap and then disappearing into the darkness beyond. He tried to point at the escaping Afghan but all the strength had drained from his arms.

'I'm on it,' said Jimbo, standing up and firing a burst in the direction of the escaping Afghan.

Spider tried to sit up but Geordie's big, powerful hand pressed him flat again. 'Keep still and let me work on you,' he growled. Geordie clamped the trauma pad over the wound, compressed it and bound it as tight as he could. 'Oboe! Oboe! All stations minimize,' said Geordie into his mic, SAS-speak ordering all unnecessary traffic off the radios. Geordie looked down at Shepherd and slapped him gently across the face. 'Stay with me Spider.'

Shepherd nodded. 'I'm all right,' he said, though each word was a strain.

Geordie spoke into his mic again. 'Oboe! Oboe! We have casualties: Alpha 1, Alpha 5. One KIA, one serious trauma of the right shoulder and chest. He needs fluids fast and we've no plasma or saline because of weight limits. We have to get him out of here. Request immediate casevac. Repeat: one serious trauma of chest and shoulder, request immediate casevac.'

Geordie was leaning over Shepherd again. 'I can't give you morphine yet, Spider, we need you alert for this. We're going to have to take you out Red Indian style.'

Jock rushed over with a section of the ladder that Shepherd had used to gain access to the building. Jock and Geordie lifted Shepherd onto the ladder and tied him to it with a nylon tac line.

Jock nodded over at the body of the Captain. 'We're taking him with us,' he said.

Geordie nodded. Todd was dead but the SAS made a point of not leaving its people behind, no matter what the circumstances.

Covered by fire from Jimbo and Lex, they ran with their makeshift stretcher to the first RV point where they'd left the mopeds. Geordie began lashing the end of the ladder to the back of one of them, leaving the other end and Shepherd's feet trailing in the dirt. Jock ran to get another section of ladder and lashed Todd to it before dragging it back to the mopeds.

Shepherd heard a voice in his earpiece. 'Speed it up. They're round us like flies on shit.' He couldn't tell if it was Jimbo or Lex.

Drawn by the noise of firing and explosions, tribesmen and Taliban fighters were pouring from their scattered huts and houses and racing over the fields towards the burning building. They fired from the hip as they ran so their bullets went wide. Jimbo and Lex fired methodically, taking out more than a dozen of the Taliban fighters with carefully-placed shots.

Geordie fired a short bust at the wheels of Shepherd and Todd's mopeds, disabling them so that the Taliban couldn't use them to give chase. Jock attached the ladder with Todd's body to the back of Geordie's moped, then checked it was secure. 'Let's get out of here!' he shouted.

Jock climbed on to the moped attached to Shepherd's makeshift stretcher. 'This is going to hurt, Spider, but we've got to get you out of here.'

Shepherd nodded, using his hand to keep the pressure on the dressing. Jock kicked the engine into life.

As Jimbo and Lex continued to give covering fire, Jock and Geordie sped away. Shepherd gritted his teeth as the improvised stretcher bumped and jolted over the rough terrain. Jimbo and Lex fired final bursts, climbed onto their mopeds and sped after Jock and Geordie.

Behind them, they heard a barrage of explosions and saw the sky light up with tracer as the fire in the burning building reached the Taliban's ammunition store.

Every bump and jolt caused Shepherd agonising pain but he clamped his jaw to stop himself from crying out and tried to focus on the column of flame shrinking behind them as they sped towards the heli landing site. They had covered only half the distance when Shepherd heard Geordie's voice in his earpiece, 'We'll have to stop. The jolting's loosened his trauma pads, he's bleeding like a stuck pig.'

'Roger that,' said Jock, applying his brakes. 'Alpha 3 and 7 drop back and set up an Immediate Ambush. Buy us a little time.'

The bikes slewed to a halt as Jimbo and Lex peeled off and circled back before jumping off their bikes and diving into cover.

Jock stayed on his moped as Geordie hurried over to Shepherd.

Shepherd felt the fierce pressure on his chest as Geordie slapped on a fresh trauma pack and tightened the bindings with a savage jerk.

'Are you okay, mate?' asked the medic.

Shepherd nodded and grunted. He could feel blood still oozing from the wound and it hurt like hell, but he didn't feel weak and he wasn't going numb so he figured that the injury was survivable, so long as they got him back to base without delay.

A moment later the agonised bumping and jolting began again as the moped sped on towards the LZ. Behind them there was the chatter of firing as Lex and Jimbo let rip with their AK74s, cutting down three of their pursuers and sending the rest diving for cover. Moments later the SAS men were mobile again, gunning their mopeds as they sped over the dusty terrain towards the hill where the Chinook was already landing, its rotors thundering in the night air.

Lex and Jimbo took up defensive positions while Jock and Geordie manhandled Shepherd's improvised stretcher onto the tailgate. The helicopter's six-barrelled M134 Minigun, operated by the co-pilot from the side window, unleashed a further torrent of fire at the Taliban pursuers as they closed on the hill.

Geordie checked Shepherd's dressing while Jock ran back for the Captain. He threw the body over his shoulder and ran back to the Chinook. Lex and Jimbo fired final bursts at the Taliban fighters and then threw themselves into the belly of the helicopter.

There was a shout of 'Go! Go! Go!' and the Chinook's still-bellowing engines wound up another octave and the airframe juddered and shuddered as the heli lumbered forward.

Shepherd felt a sudden drop in the pit of his stomach as, engines screaming, the Chinook plunged off the hilltop and dropped. The whirling rotors fought to generate lift and then the helicopter started to climb. It climbed higher, swinging away from the pursuit, the tinny rattle of a few last rounds against its armoured fuselage fading as it climbed higher and set a course for the distant base at Bagram.

Shepherd felt the stab of a morphine syrette in his arm. At once his agony began to fade into a hazy blur and he heard Geordie's voice as if it was coming to him from the bottom of a well. 'I need to get the bullet out and tie off some of these bleeders.'

Jock shouted over the roar of the engines. 'We're airborne. Geordie, do what you need to do.'

Geordie loomed over Shepherd. 'Spider, I'm going to have to take the bullet out now so I can stem the bleeding.'

'Just do it,' said Shepherd, and he gritted his teeth.

Shepherd saw the glint of steel and felt the bite as the scalpel opened the wound further and Geordie began probing for the bullet.

Shepherd grunted and turned to the side to see Lex looking at him, clearly concerned. Shepherd forced a smile. 'There's one good thing to come out of this,' he said.

'Yeah?' said Lex. 'What's that?'

'At least I'll be back with my family for Christmas.' He closed his eyes and grunted as Geordie dug deep for the bullet.

* * *

Spider Shepherd left the SAS at the end of 2002 and joined an elite police undercover unit. You can read the first of his undercover adventures in Hard Landing, where he goes undercover in a high security prison to unmask a drugs dealer who is killing off witnesses to his crimes. The Spider Shepherd series continues with Soft Target, Cold Kill, Hot Blood, Dead Men, Live Fire, Rough Justice, Fair Game, False Friends, True Colours and White Lies.